44

Becoming Self

Ania K

Purchased Dec 15 2021

About This Book

I still remember, as if it was yesterday… the pen in my hand… and the blank page in front of me.

Deep inside me was something urging me to write a book.

I asked that "thing" that was talking to me, "What should the story be?"

And the Voice answered: ***OF YOUR LIFE…***

Then a quote by Ernest Hemingway came to my mind:

"Any man's life, told truly, is a novel."

Indeed. He was right.

It took me a long time-six years, to be exact-to be right here. Though joys and pains, doubts and hopes, I have persevered. And now, when you hold my debut novel in your hands, that's all that truly matters: I have finished it.

I am releasing it in times of major uncertainty and isolation. The world has finally slowed down so the humanity can wake up to the Truth and experience one of the biggest shifts in history.

Where will we go from here…? Who knows…

But what I know for sure is that I will keep on writing!

Thank you for allowing me to tell you my story.

Ania K

Table of Contents

CHAPTER 1

Birth

"Moje Kochanie, my sweet little child. Again, you have asked me for this experience on the other side… This pleases me immensely, that you acknowledge Who-You-Really-Are, The Magnificent Creator and The Extension of Us."

She looked around the forest; in this ancient grove stood these sequoia trees, unshakable and strong, holding onto the secrets of every soul that has entered this realm… The earth, the fern flowers, the moist soil… everything her inchoate eyes were able to perceive held one vibration: of Love.

"You've existed before, in thousands of lives…

"You've lived as a triumphant ruler and warrior, admired and dignified… You've been poor and enslaved, cruelly abused and unfairly judged, and all of those journeys set forth strong intents for this very day to come.

"What now you remember… soon, you will forget… Therefore, before you go there, listen carefully to every word I say."

"Yes, Master, I'm listening," she said looking at Him… but all of a sudden she got overwhelmed with… His Encompassing Aura of Eternal Wisdom-illuminating and blinding her eyes… with His Mysterious Genius and Vibrant Presence-Unlimited and Undefined… with His Potential of Creation-mastered by Deliberate Intent…

Her… Angel and this old woodland forest were all connected into One Universe.

"As it was before, so it will be now, you will be equipped with an extraordinary sense of an Inner Guidance helping you to overcome any challenges ahead. And yes, there will be many that will cause you to stumble and lose true sight of Who-You-Really–Are…

"You will find your passion and fulfill your intent only if you won't let the storm and stress of humans' existence to diminish your pure Self.

"Remember, never give up on what-You feel is right!

"And, when you get lost or feel despair, reach deep into your own heart; there lays the Endless Field of Love. Withdraw from its reservoir and you will be recharged… again."

The steady cadence of his voice was pulsing in her veins as she intuited every syllable of these profound words.

Her mind was expanding, and her brain soaked in these messages she knew so well…

"You are forever loved… Look into yourself to find everything you need.

"It's always there. Nothing is ever missing, although you'll never be complete, for there is no ending in this co-creation of eternal expansion for ALL THAT IS."

He closed His eyes.

"You are an extension of Source. You can Be, Do, or Have anything you want. Keep your vibration high. Direct it. And then, allow it to flow.

"WE will be co-creating with you, together, as we have always done, eternally, with no end, becoming more beyond space and time.

"Listen, Kochanie… do you hear that sound?"

Music has drifted in, filling the crystal air with sublime sounds of harps. Their melodies plucked by the Divine Hand started to play softly joined by Angels' harmonious prayer… there she was safe, standing beneath this primordial branch; her tiny feet were feeling the eons-old stable ground.

The smells of moist pine trees were so familiar to her; so were the birds' songs…

And as they sang out, welcoming another of her returns, Chopin's rubato hit the melancholic notes, calling her forth into a Polish land…

The Angel smiled and the glorious light glowed softly from his aura and simultaneously from the Golden Sun.

"Are you ready, Beloved?"

She drew in the beauty of this unconditional love into her newborn Being and answered:

"Tak!"

"Good," Angel said.

"This is a call from your heart and that means: My Child, your time is about to come…

"You'll hear my Voice speaking inside you even when you don't see me.

"For a while, you may think you are alone but you will never be.

"I am always there with you… omnipresent… aware of your path…

"I'll be in the ocean and in the sky, in the smile of a baby and in the dogs' warm eyes…

"I will sing to you with the powerful winds and love you dearly with other people's hearts…

"It is all connected, there's no separation, only in humans' minds.

"The name you receive there will be Ania. To humans, it means "grace." Carry it with dignity, pride, and unashamed confidence.

"When you find your purpose we shall meet again, in another forest, in 44 years…

"Are you ready, Beloved?"

"I am," she answered, pulsing with life.

"Then close your eyes.

"Pass through the veil… and…

"GO…!

"NOW…!"

CHAPTER 2

Their Place

44

A gold number 11 shines from the top of the green door to this three-bedroom apartment. That's where They live, on the second floor, in an old bricked house, where two streets come together to make a T-sign.

The walls of this house had been signed by the hand of the second war's last bullets' shot before its end. Now, deeply engraved in a dark grey façade, these holes are forever reminders of when Germans lost their harbor town.

Four floors, white windows, and a reddish-brown roof are visible from the top of a hill, and located there are schools. From those schools, rivers of students flood down the street every day to the nearby tramway's stop. Painted in the color of blood, heavy wagons scream each time they come out of the loop's curve, and then, shake each house they pass.

That noise is so disturbing that it could wake up a dead man in his grave… Somehow Their Family got used to living with that.

Not much peace is in this household… yet not many will know this fact… for those are the secrets very well hidden behind a green door inside…

But on the surface, to a stranger, everything looks just fine… a married couple, a grandmother and this four-year-old child…

She stands there shaking… the fear has completely taken over her… Her tiny arms are pulled behind her, folded up behind her little back…

Her little fingers are in a fist, nervously grasped, and she's playing with them as if is trying to save herself some time.

"Go and apologize!" the Mother has said, and then has pushed her toward His room… to this door by which now she stands.

Still, she doesn't understand. What's made Him so upset…? What has she done to the Father that he had to raise his voice at her…?

That voice of his is so strong that when He starts to shout, everyone in Their Family in an instant, just stops.

"Go in, because if you don't, he won't talk to you and will blame me for how I raised you. Say "I am sorry" and all will be good!"

She hears these words flying over her small, confused head but cannot make any move forward… is… too afraid…

Somewhere, inside her being, something says:

YOU HAVE DONE NOTHING WRONG!

How can it be that even though He never hits her, this silent punishment hurts much more…?

Each time, when He's upset, He doesn't speak at all, ignoring her so completely as if she's not of his own.

Her heartbeat is rising, she doesn't want to go inside, but the Mother is opening His door and that means there's no escape from this trap.

She looks down… puts her head through the crack… and takes the first step…

A cold sweat takes over her innocent skin… Fear paralyzes her again.

"Someone is here to see you!" Mother's words are jumping over her blonde ponytails.

A hand from behind gives her back one more push… she swallows her breath… and looks straight ahead…

There… He sits by his desk… as if He's already dead.

He was seven years old when September 1st came and Hitler invaded Poland; he still remembers those years…

Everything after that has changed for him… his father started to drink and… that mine had exploded on a playground's field…

He was just playing with a toolbox when it had happened, and then all he remembered was the blood… he saw it… everywhere. Four fingers were gone from his left, shredded palm… his pinky, was the only one left… but he had survived.

It took a long time for his hand to heal, but as with everything else, life had moved on… and so he became one of the best students Polytechnic School has ever had, and later on that engineer who gave Junak bike to the world. Motorcycles and cars were his driving force and if not for that suppressing communism… he knew he would have accomplished much more…

These dreams, never fulfilled… went into this child, a girl born out the marriage that lacked true love. Popular at school, he could have any girl; it was his charisma, not height that was so charming to them. But he had chosen the one his mother has never made peace with, a woman from a poor village, not the doctor she desired her daughter-in-law to be.

"Tatusiu… I am here… I want to apologize…" She says from a doorstep, wanting it all to end, somehow.

Her sweet voice must have woken his frozen body up. It turns around,

"Come over here." He says pointing at the spot.

Obediently, her small feet step forward… and stop right at his face.

It seems to be much calmer now… is no longer red.

"Don't ever do it again, Ania. That made me very upset." This voice of His… it always makes her heart beat faster in her little chest.

"No, I won't… I am so sorry…", she whispers and puts her face down. If He could only tell her what the mistake was, she would do her best to straighten her act…

His brown eyes land on her, filled with the sadness which cannot hide. And then… all of a sudden… his arms open up wide… and as they wrap around her existence, and she disappears in his hug, knows how to behave, only in a way He wants her to, they know They all will be fine.

Her small body walks back to The Mother who awaits with a big smile. She must be a good girl since she has apologized?

It doesn't matter. It's over. From both of them, she wants to escape, and be around the only person who understands her in there.

At the end of the corridor, a white door seems to be closed. She comes closer and as was told to, places on it two gentle knocks.

"Yes?" the voice that always means well asks from the other side.

"Babciu, can I come in, please…?"

"Of course you can, my little child!"

A round handle makes a twist under her tiny hand, all of her strength is used to release the door from being stuck in the wooden frame.

Finally, it gives up the fight and opens up to her favorite room that always welcomes her inside. She loves everything that's in here… this sewing machine by which the Grandma spends most of her days…, this wooden cabinet filled up with black-and-white picture taken from Babcia's young colorful years, these Burda catalogs with hundreds of fashionable forms that all are being used for the fabrics to be cut out from.

Oh, and there's one more thing that she likes so much, she can't stop staring at it… That chair is so magical, as if some king must have owned it once upon a time… When she looks at it long enough, she can almost see his face in those times of indecisions as he used to sit on its royal velvet to contemplate. And then, once the answers started coming forth he was leaning in between these two lions' heads. Their mouths are still open to protect whoever comes in possession of this powerful chair.

"Please close the door behind you, my dear. Take a seat and relax. And don't worry about what happened there. You're a good girl, I know that you are."

Grandma's words settle her down on the top of the big bed. Now, when she is close to Babcia, all is well, again.

The pedal of the sewing machine moves under her old foot; the soft fabric falls over sore knees and lands on the floor of the room.

"What is it, Babciu? What are you making?" She moves closer to see. Her big eyes grow even more when she gets curious like this.

The Grandma stops sewing and turns to her with a smile… this joy in these old eyes always comes through heavy glasses seated on the crooked nose's mark.

"Is it another apron that you like to wear?"

"No, Wnusiu…" Long wrinkled fingers lift up fallen silk.

"This time it will be a summer dress."

Babcia's hand reaches toward the balcony's French door. As soon as it opens, it invites a humid blow.

"Can't you feel it, Wnusiu, how hot it is outside?"

Now, with coming in heat, she can hear those trains at the railway station where the Grandpa used to work when he was still alive…

Although she never met him, she was told that he was the one who has moved Their Family to Szczecin, to occupy a new Polish town.

Babcia went through so much with him since he had always lived on the edge.

When Russians threw him into Stalin's jail, all of their money was spent on getting him out of there.

He had fought as hard as he had drunk… Babcia's done everything to keep peace in their house… Those two wars which came over were enough to build her strength… after those, she could survive anything…

Even the death of her three-year-old girl… or a mine's explosion smashing her boy's hand…

And then, when the alcohol finally won and took her husband away, all the love that was left in her she gave to her only son…

Now, he has his daughter; she may not care for his wife, but she knows that this child is special and can one day become someone they never had a chance to be in their uncertain lives.

"Dinner is ready!" suddenly Mother's voice comes from behind the white door-she must have been there for a while, with an ear stuck to it listening to them talk…

"I'm coming. Five more minutes," she responds politely, not even hungry… But another fight? Oh no, no… she cannot handle that…

"Babciu, I will be back, once I'm done over there. Then… would you read the cards for me, please? Today is Friday! It's the right day!"

"Yes, Wnusiu. I will."

Grandma smiles; this girl remembers everything, her memory is so sharp. The little mind knows that only on Fridays cards tell the truth, if read on Sundays it's bad luck, and on Wednesday the message may not come true.

The smell of a fish calls her to the kitchen. Here, Mother already awaits with a plate. Today, since it's a fast day, it is salmon, mashed potatoes, and sauerkraut, which Their Family makes. To drink is a strawberry compote, served in a highball glass, painted with yellow lemons and held by this metal thing that shakes each time it's lifted up.

"Sit down and eat before it gets cold." Mother says while passing her a small silver fork. Slowly she digs in to the fish's skin to separate it from the fishbones, once she had almost choked because of them, that's how she learned that they could kill. Soft flesh melts in her mouth- that means it's okay to swallow it up.

"Is it good, Anusiu?" Mother asks.

"Yes, very good," she answers, smacks her thong, and turns the blonde head away. Now, she does not want to talk but only look out the window at those departing trains…

There, on the other side, the sky is so blue, the sugar clouds swim around, and to those who stayed on the platforms chimney say: "Farewell."

There, the Odra river, after all ships have been docked, becomes so calm… maybe it's because they've made it before the weekend so the workers could go home?

The water splashes under Mother's hands.

She turns back and looks at her shiny black hair.

It's always made into a tall bun that sticks up from the top of her head; not many would ever know how long and beautiful it is.

Her glasses, in thick frames, are intentionally big, to hide all of those tears that nobody should ever be able to see. Her hands are constantly busy and clean all the time to the point that her skin gets very used and even bleeds sometimes.

But that's how she was raised in the countryside where she came from, told that to be a good wife she must work hard and sacrifice everything she wants. It was six of them together taking care of their little farm… all they ever had were those chickens, one horse, and two cows…

What their present was like was exactly what the future would bring… but she wanted a different life, in a big city, with her job and a small family.

And so she has found a town to live in and a man to fall in love with, but little did she know then how cruel he could be… When they met he held a promise of a happy life…

That she wasn't welcome the mother in law had made very clear from the first day she moved into their flat. Still, she was holding on to hope that maybe with time things will change…?

But they have not… If anything they only got worse…

And now it's too late to leave him… how she will make it on her own, a single mother with a child? At least He provides them a home…

"Mamusiu, is everything all right?" She asks, seeing a tear dropping down on Mother's smooth face.

"Yes… yes, Anusiu… everything is fine… have you finished already? If so you can go and play."

Mother's hand wipes off the tear and dives right back inside the sink. Another wet plate is pulled out so a white cotton cloth can circulate it several times.

“Don’t cry, Mamusiu, don’t worry, I went there… I’ve apologized…” Her little hands come from behind Mother’s knees to grab them in the smallest hug.

“Look, I’ve eaten it all…!” An empty plate is places in the front of her teary eyes.

“Oh, Anusiu… I’m so glad…” A soft kiss bounces off her tiny cheek, leaving behind a wet mark.

Maybe she should just leave…? Maybe it’s her talking that causes more tears to come…?

“Thank you, Mamusiu.” She turns around and reminds herself to ask the cards what her life is going to be like…

CHAPTER 3

Winter

"Are we going to have a replay from the previous year and another brutal winter?"

She has overheard on the radio while exiting the flat. Now, standing by the front door of her school, she can understand why that reporter said it-for this excruciating cold is unlike any other she's experienced before.

It cuts through the skin. Goes straight to the bones, and has no mercy for those who don't hide inside their homes.

Even these wool-gloves that Mother has woven by hand cannot warm up her tiny palms.

But how could they, when it's -10 degrees Celsius?

Once more she pushes on the door's handle, still without any success.

"Hmm... very strange..." She ponders, "Usually this place is packed at 8 a.m..."

Her nose sticks to a glass door, but it doesn't matter how much closer it gets, there's not a sign of a single soul... nobody is in there...

Not even that nice lady who always sits on the top of the stairs and greets every passing her pupil by name when they are passing her by... How that janitor knows all of their names by heart none knows...

"Wanda"- is hers, that's what a nametag says, worn over a green nylon uniform.

"Maybe I should check from behind the building...?"

She decides and carefully takes down the stairs since no broom has touched them this morning and the snow has completely taken over. His white signature rug spreads out to the back. It is here, in this schoolyard, where the sport's games are being played.

But not today, for none of the athletes, decided to show up... not even to build a snowman not even to fight...

"Enough of it, I should go back home, otherwise I will catch a cold."

"Babciu! Nobody was at the school today! Do you know what's going on?"

Hot air wraps around her as soon as she is in Their flat.

"Oh, Wnusiu... The Parents haven't told you...?"

The Grandma's head sticks out from the kitchen, where she is often to be found around 9 am.

"My God… I can't believe it… poor thing you could get sick… take off your jacket and come over here. I will make you something warm to drink."

Babcia opens an old stove and pulls out a small pot. The white one, that's all beat up, perhaps it still remembers the war? Then, Babcia turns toward the fridge, where she finds fresh milk that was left at the front door this morning; a farmer has delivered it.

The white liquid is slowly poured inside the beat up pot. Babcia grabs a single match and turns the gas on. Then, two full spoons of brown powder make a short journey from a metal can.

"Wnusiu, all schools have been closed."

The Grandma says while stirring a spoon, so the powder can blend with the milk.

"Oh, really, Babciu…? For… how… long?"

"We don't know, Wnusiu, we are at martial war… no one knows those things."

The Grandma keeps looking down at the boiling pot.

"A war, Babciu…?! Oh no…"

"Well…," The Grandma exhales. "…we are living in times in which the history books will be writing about.

"Our constitution has been broken, and the political system is going to change. The Russian Army stationed their tanks on our borders, just in case Solidarnosc decides to fight. And that means the war, my little girl…"

"I see, Babciu… is that why yesterday everyone was crying at the mass?"

"Yes, but it was also from the gas which soldiers had purposefully sprayed inside."

"Why would they do that, Babciu…?"

"To weaken a human's spirit, which always gets strengthened from being at church. You see, when we pray, we unite. This country was suppressed for so long… people finally had enough of that.

“Poland has always been like this, when life is simple and easy, we only complain, but when we are faced with the same enemy, somehow we come together. Something which I will never understand…

“Those communists know it too… oh, yes, they do… they are cruel but also very intelligent. They had to be to wash peoples’ brains.”

Hot chocolate fills up the mug.

“But you’re too young to worry about this stuff. Now drink; it will warm you up.”

She takes a sip, slowly, not to burn herself. No matter the circumstances, the chocolate always tastes excellent.

“Thank you, Babciu.”

She picks up the mug with both hands and carefully takes it into Father’s room since he still decided to go to work.

Perhaps, when he comes back home, he can explain to her how long this war will go on?

Because he understands politics, he watches TV a lot…

And then he always comments on what those talking heads say…

Also, inside his bar, under the lock, he keeps the longest cigarettes. It’s one roll without a filter, stored inside a clear plastic bag. Once, she opened it, allowing the tobacco’s smell to spread all around his room. “Put it back!” He yelled as if it was the holy grail.

After she did, he explained to her that the prices on those things will soon increase.

She moves closer to the window; that frost has used it for its canvas and painted white-silver damask over it. Her pointy finger touches a cold glass and stays there until the art starts to meltdown.

DON'T WORRY… YOU ARE SAFE…

The Voice says from inside.

CHAPTER 4

The Race

She ties up her laces. The race is about to start. Wearing these sprinter shoes for the very first time.

The coach has explained to her that the bolts underneath will make her run much faster than she normally could.

There are 600 meters ahead… and ten of them to compete…

It has been a year already since she started to train for this race.

"You should know that she is a great runner."

The coach has said to Father once. "She knows how to divide her strength and stretch it out to the finish line. Marathons are what I see for her, but for now, I'd like her to try the race that will take place in six months. Are you up for it? What you think?"

"Yes, of course, we should apply. Put her name on the list." Father has said back.

Now he's in the audience, ready to watch her run. He did prepare her for it, ten times around the stadium, no excuses, every day.

So she better make it… otherwise it would be such a shame …

"Who are you chasing, Wnusiu?" Babcia has asked her… but she couldn't answer that.

Still, Grandma's question has soaked deep inside her mind and made her wonder why she works so hard instead of being more, like other teenagers who are having fun?

Dead silence covers the stadium. All runners step on a chalk line. The breaths become shallow.

"What if we fail…?" Thoughts almost make a sound.

"Ready!" The gun is lifted and every muscle gets tense. Lean legs are well-positioned.

"Steady!" The backs bend like those of cats.

"Go!" Shoots high in the sky and sets the bodies free!

She knows now is not the time to think but to keep moving her feet!

Last in the pack… it doesn't matter… still, she's not too far away from the rest…

The first corner, she comes out on a straight… and then suddenly something says deep inside her says:

YOU CAN GO FASTER! YOU CAN DO IT! JUST GO! JUST RUN!

She hears The Voice inside and the new energy is taking over her flesh!

Some kind of electric power is entering her veins… Her legs are speeding up their moves and the purpose of those bolts is being served…

As they're bouncing off the ground and lift her high into the air she's catching up with the last runner and in a few seconds with the next!

A man stands up in the audience: "Incredible!" …his shout stays far behind…

"Go! Go! Go! Number eight," the tribunes are screaming out loud.

They must be cheering for her… she comes to realize… because that's what her jersey has said when she was putting it on before the race had begun…

Feeling of love is flooding down from the audience…

She's passing another girl…

Father gets up from his seat.

"One more round!" the megaphone shouts right above her head.

But her feet can go on like this forever… so this love… will never end… There is no pain in her body but only pure joy pouring out from each cell…

"And just a few more meters!" the speaker confirms.

Last straight. She doesn't give up… for there is no limit to this zone she's in…

"Yes, Ania! Yes!" The coach's voice comes from the right side.

"Oh… dear audience…! What a race! This is the finish line!"

The commentator sounds as excited as is everyone else: "Bravo…! Bravo…! Bravo…! Bravo to number eight!"

The coach points at her name highlighted on the results board.

"You've made it, Ania! You've made it! You came as the fourth!"

She looks up at the yellow neon flashing above strangers' smiles…

It wasn't me, but that energy... she says to herself, seeing tears in Father's eyes…

CHAPTER 5

Sweden

The bus drives out from the harbor."Swinoujscie" sign stays behind. Big wheels hit an empty road, which cuts the wide forest in half.

Oak trees in their early gold glory welcome her back to her homeland, and as the morning sun touches her face through the window, she reflects on how her Swedish trip went…

Not everything has turned out as good as she was expecting it then… two years before, when she had answered a call from Izabela, her best friend:

"My mom knows someone in Sweden who can help you to get a job. Would you be interested in it?"

"Of course I would!" she answered at the speed of light.

How would she not take a chance to fulfill one of her biggest dreams to live in a foreign country where everyone said "Hello" on the streets? There, where people smile one to another and stores sell beautiful things, not like here… complaining grumpy faces and jealousy when others succeed.

"Okay, so what is that job, Iza?" The offer intrigued her.

"Sweden…" she pondered for a moment,

"Is it the country where I'm supposed to live…?"

"My mom will call you tomorrow and tell you what it is about. That's so exciting, Ania. You're going to move abroad, I have no doubt!"

A few weeks later, at Their apartment, Father was shaking Thomas's hand.

"You promise to take care of my daughter? Will you?"

She's never seen such a look on his face. Tense and uncertain, it was showing how concerned he was.

"Yes, sir, I will. I promise." Thomas responded. "You have my word."

Tall, skinny with disproportional long limbs and the weirdest smile over his anorexic face, he was sending out mixed impressions… something was off about him… that look in his eyes… that cocky attitude he had…

If a body's language could be translated, his would say: "Do not trust!"

But she didn't care, ahead was an awaiting adventure, and, with a current exchange rate, a great job.

The next morning, their ferry arrived in Malmo, and Thomas's car drove out on Swedish land.

"We have about two hours to get to Tibro. It's a small town; only five thousand people live there."

He looked at her in a rear mirror. Politely, she smiled back.

Outside the window, the small houses were dominating the view and, like in a moving kaleidoscope, kept changing from white into blue and into white again.

April's grass dropped fresh green at perfect front yards, everything seemed much cleaner … simpler… more organized.

"So that is Scandinavian scenery…" she was thinking when finally they've reached his two-story house.

The living room and the guest room were downstairs, the office, supposedly on the second floor.

"This one will be yours." He pointed at a door next to the kitchen.

"It was my daughter's… before my wife and I got divorced a year ago."

She walked in, looked around… a small bed was covered with white cotton sheets, nearby stood a four-drawer cabinet, a single dark wood chair, right next to it. In a corner, a silver floor lamp was topped with a beige linen shade, probably purchased at IKEA because she saw a similar one when she was there.

In a far-left end was a window with no curtains but a view of neighbors' homes. They all looked the same way.

"Make yourself comfortable. I will go to do some grocery shopping now. Oh…"

He turned around,

"If you wish, you're welcome to go outside. The weather is perfect today.

Towel and blankets are in the kitchen, in the last cabinet."

She heard the loud sound of the front door being shut by his skinny hand.

Then, grabbed a beach towel and put her favorite bikini on… the long trip was taking its toll… the warm sun was quickly taking her mind away…

Suddenly, his voice came from above her and a big shadow covered the bright sunny light.

"Wow, look at you! With a body like this, have you ever thought about modeling?"

She stood up as if hit by an electric shock.

"No, I have not."

"Well, maybe you should…"

"Not for me. But thanks."

Again… that weird smile appeared… and those eyes… she felt… as if they wanted to touch her everywhere.

"Don't go, I may join you…"

"I'm hungry."

She picked up the blanket and walked away.

Two weeks have passed by, and still, there was no job, he said that those people who promised it before were working on it; he's just waiting to hear back from them.

By that time, she already knew he was a liar, but calling her parents for help was not an option, they would blame her for why she went with a strange man…

I must go to town… A thought has crossed her mind.

I have to find the job myself…

The day for fulfilling her plan was ideal. Thomas left the house early and was supposed to come back very late. Tibro was a small town, which was helpful because most of the businesses were located just on a few blocks. Once that railway track is crossed, and a train station is left behind… she'll already be in town, and she could start knocking on doors…

The sky was cloudless… the streets were quiet… there was no noise that could distract her from her goal…

And then suddenly, that strange feeling came over her… as if there was some kind of presence aware of her… soft and gentle… comforting her with those words:

DON'T WORRY… EVERYTHING WILL BE ALL RIGHT…

The Voice has spoken from inside:

GO TO THAT GREY BUILDING ON THE LEFT...

She looked across the square… there stood a three-story house.

Short stairs brought her up to the front door. She knocked. No one responded. She knocked again.

Finally, the vacuum answered.

A door's bell followed her step.

It was a restaurant… all the tables were empty and had chairs resting on their tops.

"Hi there… Can I help you?"

A tall, dark-skinned young man was holding on to the vacuum's pipe.

Their eyes met, and in a split of a second, his hazelnut browns hit her greens like a stroke of light.

"Good morning. Are you the boss here?" she smiled under his scanning of her gaze.

He turned off the vacuum.

"No, he's away but during his absence, I'm in charge of the place. You're not from here, are you? I don't think I've seen you before."

She blushed.

"No, I am not. I'm from Poland. Just visiting… a friend…"

"From Poland… I see… How can I help you?"

"I am looking for a job…," her lips spit out with desperation.

"…Anything… whatever you have."

He looked at her closely.

"Okay, let's talk."

He flipped two chairs. She mirrored his face.

"Well… the only job I can give you without papers, which I don't think you have, is a dishwasher position not so sure if that is something you would be interested in. It looks to me like you're not the kind of person who deals with dirty stuff everyday…"

If he only knew my situation...

"A misconception, I will take it! It's great!"

His mouth opened wide and the brightest white smile highlighted his caramel face.

"Oh really…? You will? Happy to hear that! Just to let you know, it doesn't pay much… but, it will always be cash.

"That's perfect! When can I start?"

He looked down at his watch.

"Hmm… how about, tomorrow at 10 am? That's when we are preparing for lunch. Does that sound good?"

"Of course it does! Thank you so much…"

She felt the softness of his skin.

"What's your name? I'm Hammed."

"Ania."

"Then Ania, I will see you tomorrow at 10 am."

Her neck felt his eyes as she flew outside.

That night, unlike any other, she fell asleep right away… until that moment when she overheard a conversation taking place in a living room between two drunk men.

Thomas was back and talking in Swedish to someone whose voice she couldn't recognize…

They were smoking and drinking… opening beer bottles… several toasts have been made…

She turned her face on the other side of the pillow, trying to ignore their noise…

… and then… there was a knock on her door… the door opened up…

Thomas walked in… cigarette smoke followed… joined by a strong smell of alcohol… like a stinky cloud, it hung around him, and then he asked,"

"Ania… are you up?"

She couldn't believe that he was doing that…

"No, I am sleeping…," she answered from her pillow.

"Can I… come in?"

What is he doing?

"I just want to ask you something…"

"My friend and I were wondering if you could do something for us… I told him about you… how beautiful you are… and that you have an amazing body he would enjoy looking at…"

What…?!

"And so, he said that he will pay you 1500 KR if you would dance for him tonight. It's just one dance, Ania, that's all he's asking. So, will you do it? It's easy money. Remember, you wanted me to get you a job?"

Cold sweat went over her body… What shall she do now? Runaway…? But where…? But how…?

He stood there, over a doorstep, with a cigarette in his hand… the light was coming in from behind him.

She felt her breath get deeper… and deeper and… then … suddenly something has shifted inside… as if within her was a force fully aware of her.

"No! I will not! Can you hear me?! I won't do it! Leave me alone! Go away!"

She shouted out with that powerful energy which was completely taking over.

Unafraid and uncompromised, it was bringing the courage she needed to protect herself.

"So is "THIS" what you had promised my Father when you shook his hand?!

"I can't believe it! How would you feel if your daughter were treated like a slut by someone?! Go ahead and tell him he can stick that money in his ass!"

Motionless, he stood there… until his eyes slowly went down. Then he turned around, walked toward the door, and closed it behind him.

Was it because I mentioned his daughter...?

Still shaking, she wondered this while the stench of alcohol evaporated in the air.

The tears could not be held any longer…

"*I just want to be safe, God... I just want to be safe...*"

How she felt asleep after that… she could not remember…

A week later, Linda, a waitress she met at the restaurant, asked her to move into her place.

She left Thomas' house early in the morning, and had never saw him again.

The old Saab in faded yellow with scratches all over the place, in spite of its ancient age, was still able to take her to Hammed's place. Linda never had any problem with lending it to her as long as she brought it back to Tibro before kids were ready for school at 9 am.

There were three kids, each one of them came from a different father and that was enough to get social support. Many women have lived in that way in Sweden, as it was also Linda's choice.

She watched and learned very quickly, Hammed played a big part… anyone who's been around them at the restaurant knew that for those two to date, it was just a matter of time.

Naturally, without playing games, things between them started to unfold and then… one day she realized it had already been month since their romance had begun…

The only challenge to keep it going was the distance between their towns; Tibro was an hour away by bus from Skovde, that's when the old Saab came to her rescue and cut the commute time in half.

Skovdè had a larger population, more businesses, and nightclubs, which on weekends were always packed. There was a big shopping mall where the youngsters hung out daily, also a much bigger chance to find a better job.

It seemed as if the stars were aligned for her because Hammed's uncle owned a pizzeria in town, supposedly one of the best in Skovde, which by then to her it was not a bit of a surprise.

A well-known fact was that Swedish men were mostly bankers or lawyers, not restaurant owners like those Middle-Eastern immigrants, who came to Sweden with nothing, worked hard, and popped up their business all over the town.

Such was the case with Omar, who just like Hammed, had moved from Cairo in Egypt, following many relatives and friends. They all supported one another; it was a brotherhood unlike she ever thought a man could have.

Sometimes she even wondered if they would kill someone who tried to harm one of them… Becoming Hammed's girlfriend, she also became a part of their tribe, that meant being protected by them.

Day after day she washed dirty dishes and wiped the filthy floor. The food was free, money was better and, once in a while, clients left tips for her, like that guy, David, who always showed up for lunch and sat at the same table by the front door.

It didn't take a long time for them to become friends.

He was so proud of his Assyrian heritage.

"It was a mecca of the world. Everything has started there," he used to say.

His heart was as golden as his necklace with a pendent of Babylonian God.

David was always there when she needed some help or a piece of great advice.

He explained Assyrian culture to her and how their families were came to agreements upon their children's best match.

Occasionally, some rebels broke away from old rules as he did himself. He had chosen Layla to be his bride but then, shortly after the wedding, he found out the painful truth about how much influence her mother had on their lives…

Diamonds, gold, and, money, plus how much of it he could provide, was all his wife and mother- in-law were after. Their marriage ended after two years. It took him another two to recover from that.

Hammed was getting jealous of how much time she was spending with her new friend. It has sat their relationship on the rocks. But in truth, they both knew from the very beginning it was never going to last anyway…

She remembered when she saw him for the first time and how his confidence dressed him more than his clothes.

"Johnson. Brother of my ex." David's introduction was short.

"Finally I have a chance to meet you, Ania! David talks about you non-stop!"

"Johnson? Hmm… like Magic Johnson?" She laughed at her joke.

"That's right!" His smile was charming. His hair was extremely curly. His palms were beyond soft.

"Are you a musician?" she asked him.

"Yes… how… can you tell?"

"Your fingers are very long."

"I play the keyboard… and compose… after work…"

"Johnson takes care of their whole clan."

"David, that is not true."

"Where do you work?"

"In Volvo's factory, at the production line…"

"He's the best, I'm telling you. I don't know how it's even possible that Leyla shares the same blood with this man. Of course, he works his ass off so they can buy more of that gold shit!"

"David, I think you are too much…"

"Well, it is a fact!"

She felt a sudden urge to end their uncomfortable chat.

"Okay guys, what's the plan for tonight?"

"You're right, enough of it; how about dinner and maybe a drink?"

She looked at her newly met companion.

"I will call you Magic."

"Sure, I like it… no one else calls me this…"

Time was passing by in between her fingers like those lakes between the vast Swedish land. And, to those lakes, David, Magic and her went often, as well as to the gym, or the nightclub, every other Saturday.

"The best recording studios are in Sweden; even Michael Jackson records in Stockholm." Magic used to say.

But to her, what was more surprising was the way the Swedish people enjoyed themselves. The prohibition made beer the number one choice to get drunk with at the clubs. There was a system to that strange lifestyle: first, a guy picks up a girl, then, steps away from a dance floor to prove on the streets how tough he is to her. If she likes it, they call it a night, and if not, he moves onto the next.

Vikings' blood was alive and showing off in the fights on the streets.

Just like it had that night when she needed to catch some fresh air…

"Can I join you?" Magic asked her… and they walked until the club's noise disappeared.

"He's into you," David told her, again and again, but she deliberately kept ignoring the prophecy of his words.

They've reached a corner… and suddenly Magic's hand went around hers…

Somehow she knew that something was coming, still was not prepared for that …

"Do you know that I like you…?" She heard his statement, feeling her confidence go away…

His long fingers took ownership of hers.

"I like you, Ania… a lot…"

Her eyes went into his and then… dropped on the ground…

His body moved closer…

Her shyness got ignored…

He was all smiles when she looked up again…

Without permission, his lips landed on hers, sending an electric stream through her legs…

His arms pulled her in… and in them, she relaxed… hit by an instant love… fully embraced…

Magic's family was not as enthusiastic about his new girl. That too was predicted by David: "His brothers will like you. His mother and Leyla-will hate you."

Yet Magic's response was unwavering: "It's my life and I can live it on my terms!"

Still, she could not get over the way his mother's eyes were scanned her when she visited his flat… That look was so vicious and so unfriendly, as if it wanted to cause her some kind of pain… There was an aura around that woman… heavy… dark… thick… a knife could cut through it in the air…

"She's evil; be careful," David advised after she shared how she felt.

More and more, she was coming to understand, why David's marriage had to end.

But her love for Magic was growing stronger with each passing day. She adored his mind, his charisma… and the way they were made love to Mariah Carey's songs playing in the background…

He was the only one she had eyes for. Every other guy became irrelevant.

And then it came, the very last week before she would return home.

There they were again, like on that Saturday night… his long fingers wrapped around her hand.

"Will you come back?" His voice was shaking for the very first time.

If he only knew how much she wanted to stay with him in Sweden, he would never have to question it…

"Of course… Magic… I'll do everything I can…"

The last kiss introduced a bitter taste of her tears.

He turned around, and all she had left was his back saying "Goodbye."

She knew that he too was crying and trying to hide falling in love…

"Two jobs should take care of it…" It was her strategy on how to finance her comeback.

No days off, different shifts, which have included the nights, and absolutely zero complaints.

Committed, disciplined, and focused, she followed the plan, working at Radisson Hotel as a phone operator, and in a perfume store, as a sales associate.

Christmas came and brought Mariah Carey's new record, as well as those memories of when Magic was close…

But six months without having any contact made her start to doubt if their closeness was something he still wanted…

And then… one day… unexpectedly… that letter arrived… It was from David:

"Hi, Ania, how are you? I hope you are doing great!

Me, and Magic, (you know I can tell even when he doesn't say a thing!), we miss you a lot…

It's not the same here without you but we still believe that you'll be back.

In the meantime, I've decided to look at business opportunities in Poland since we may be opening the pizzeria there, with Sanjay, my Indian friend.

Yes, this means we are coming to Szczecin! The three of us! Guess who is joining us as well?! I hope this message makes you happy.

We'll see you within the next few months. I will call you very soon to discuss everything. Till then,

Love you, as always,

David,

Your friend"

She put the letter aside and couldn't stop wondering how could it be that her reunion with Magic was manifesting in such an unpredictable way?

And so they arrived, in February, not the best month for visiting Poland, when it's still gray, cold, miserable, and the snow isn't ready to meltdown.

Regardless of that freezing weather, she welcomed them with warm, open arms.

As had The Parents who put their Polish hospitality on display; the table was covered with the dishes The Mother prepared for dinners at Their flat.

They stayed for two weeks, in the hotel, near Old Town. She introduced them to all of her close friends.

Magic was more caring than she would have expected, and even admitted that he too had fallen in love with her.

"One more month, Magic, I should be ready to return in March."

They left with clarity for the business venture not to be persuaded, but to her, the most important thing was the fact that Magic wanted her to be back.

Time flew, and the bus took her to Gothenburg's main square, where Magic was supposed to wait.

When she got there he was absent. Patiently, she sat, for an hour trying to understand why he wasn't waiting for her?

Finally, he arrived.

In an instant, she knew something was wrong…

It seemed as if he wasn't too happy to see her again.

"Is everything okay?" she asked him.

"Yes. Everything is fine," he murmured… but couldn't hide the frustration; his face was showing more than his words.

"Maybe he's just tired, he works very hard…"

She soothed herself in a train to Skovde where Julian, Magic's friend, provided her shelter, a studio, in which she stayed for a month… sleeping on a floor with not much money. She didn't see Magic often… but when one is in love, one overlooks those facts…

"Soon," he said, "things will improve."

Rina and George were his cousins and lived in a much bigger house.

They too, just like David, never trusted Magic's mom…

Indeed things were improving… at least she thought so while she was moving into their two-story house.

It was a safe, cozy, place, with a small garden on the back. There, their two little children were running around; boy's name was-Lenny, girl's name was-Linette.

Rina was an attractive woman, confident, very smart, always well dressed, always with full makeup on, always committed to her fitness rituals. It was a promise she made to herself that unlike most of the Assyrian women she won't use her kids as an excuse to stay out of shape.

George was a loving and supportive husband, that kind of man who always puts his family first. His well-paid job at Volvo allowed Rina to stay home.

That move has helped… at least in the beginning. Magic was again acting like himself but then George got the promotion, which required them to move to Gothenburg.

In the meantime, Magic applied for a flat. The answer was supposed to come back on any given day.

Their plan was: once he's approved she moves in to live with him.

There was that thing in Sweden called: "Sambo" which allowed couples to live together for two years and to have the right to legally work.

And, he did get an apartment in Skovde when she was already living in Gothenburg.

It was a small studio, but big enough for the two of them.

She came back from visiting him so happy, so ready to pack her stuff! Finally, on the horizon, things were looking great.

They were… until that Sunday morning… she was in the kitchen, and the phone rang.

Rina went to pick it up.

"It's for you, Ania. Magic."

"Hi!" she answered all in smiles.

"Hi." A cold voice on the other side made her question if it was him… or someone else… perhaps?

"Are you sitting down now?"

"No… Magic, I'm not…"

"Okay, I want you to sit down."

She thought he was joking around.

"Okay. I am on the ground."

For a few seconds, a dead silence was in charge.

"Hello… Magic…? Are you there?"

"I don't want you to come back to Skovde."

She felt her heart speeding up its beat… and her chest losing breath…

"It's not going to work for me. Tomorrow I am proposing to another girl.

"I know that you may hate me for this, but honestly I don't care. We always knew that there was no future for us. I'm sure you'll find a much better man."

The world began spinning around her…

Those questions were bombarding her mind like the bullet shots:

Was it… my fault? Was I… too needy? Did I love him too much…?

"What are you saying… Magic… Who is the girl…?"

"It doesn't matter who she is. I want you to go back. Poland is a beautiful country. You will be fine. Do not contact me again. Take care, Ania. Goodbye."

She heard him hang up the phone.

Her body went numb.

The phone fell out from her hand, and as it hit the floor, made an uncomfortable sound.

Her face turned white and very thin, like a sheet of paper…

Her eyes kept staring ahead at blank point as she relived the last two years of her life… invested in the future…

Rina appeared by her knees.

"My sweetheart… what happened? Are you all right?"

Her ears heard a question but her lips were unable to move.

Rina persevered: "What did he say to you?"

Somehow she found some strength to respond through an avalanche of tears.

"He said… that he wants me to go back to Poland because tomorrow he is proposing to another girl…"

"Another girl…? Proposing…? What is he talking about!?"

Rina was getting furious. She had never seen her act like that.

"It's that witch; it's his mother! It must be her job! Oh, she will get it back one day… oh yes, God, she will… big time! I know you are hurting, sweetheart… I'm so sorry… I'm so sorry girl…"

Her body was wrapped in Rina's arms, but she felt nothing…

The following week, something else breathed life into her…

Whatever that thing was, it was turning Monday into Wednesday and Thursday into Saturday… How she survived those days she couldn't remember; all that she could recall was buried deep inside her pain…

That pain was not allowed to come out until she was inside the bus on the way back.

On the ferry, she shared a cabin with an older lady who slept on the upper bed.

In the middle of a night, she woke up from excruciating pain… and started vomiting a yellow liquid… for the hours on and on…

That lady got very concerned, called for the doctor. He came in, checked her pulse, and injected a shot.

"We may need to call a helicopter if it gets worse…" Barely conscious, she overheard his words.

"Please, keep your eyes on her, ma'am."

"Am I dying…?"She asked as soon as he left.

"You will be okay sweetheart… you will be okay…" The stranger's words were putting her to sleep, or perhaps it was that shot he injected her with.

The next morning she woke up to a woman's face.

"Oh... my dear... Thank God... I was praying all night..."

The ferry was no longer moving. The doctor returned.

"It's a miracle. You've made it. What else can I say... this woman has saved your life..."

The bus drives out of the harbor. "Swinoujscie" sign stays behind. Big wheels hit an empty road which cuts the wide forest in half. The trees in their early gold glory, welcome her back to her homeland, and as the morning sun touches her face through the window she is reflecting on how her Swedish trip went...

CHAPTER 6

Oasis

"Here, take a look at the new jobs." The newspaper swishes in Mother's hand.

"You will feel much better being occupied and you may even make some new friends."

"Perhaps you're right, Mom, it's already been three months since I have returned..."

The paper goes under her eyes:

"A front desk receptionist needed, please contact Julia for more details."

The free-standing building has five floors. Her new employer occupies two of them.

The location of her new job is perfect, about 20 minutes away from Their flat.

She has heard of the company's owner who has succeeded at a young age in becoming the richest man in the city. He's tall, charismatic, handsome, and he has black hair and three little kids from a gorgeous wife, plus countless "invisible" girlfriends entertaining him on the side.

But none of that is her business. The front desk is like a confessional at church. She sees a lot but zips her mouth and stays focused on memorizing all those individuals' names instead:

"George"- he is a partner in the business who lives in the United States. He doesn't visit the office very often, once or twice per year. He owns two spa-retreats, one in Poland, near the Baltic Coast, another one in Woodstock, a two-hour drive from the city of New York.

"Armand"- he is the owner's school mate, although his not-too-close buddy, somehow he has managed to get a vice president position, something she can't understand since he doesn't do much except walk incredibly fast. Perhaps that is his intention-to be perceived as if he is a busy guy.

"Alicia"- she is the owner's older sister, her office is on the fifth floor. There is a rumor going around that she's having an affair with George. Even though George's wife, Ilona, of twenty-five years, is aware of that. So is Christof, Alicia's husband, who works at the office downstairs.

“Beata”- Alicia’s assistant is probably the most normal among them all. She is an energetic, easy-going woman with a great sense of humor that lights up everybody’s day.

Then, there is “Darek”- a director of sales who always introduces himself over the phone:

“It writes as it rains.”, because that is fact; his last name in Polish means “rain.”

“John”- is the owner’s bodyguard and also his closest friend. Not an intellectual type, but it was his muscles, not his brain, that got him the job in the first place.

“Ewa” and “Mariusz”- are another couple but not romantically involved; they work as a team in the PR department with those clients who demand the most.

This role is perfect for Ewa who uses the charm of her long, blonde hair, seductively throwing it aside while negotiating with those powerful businessmen. Her outfits, always by the top designers’ are expensive to impress; supposedly it helps to close those important deals (also to date wealthy and successful men).

Then, last but not least, there is “Julia,”- a personal assistant to the boss, who is the most responsible and professional employee and always keeps her word. No matter what’s going around the office, Julia stays on top of things, unwilling to participate in silly games…

There are only a few invoices left to send out and she can call it a day.

The bell rings. She presses the button.

The front door opens up… first to a loud laughter… then to the sky-blue eyes…

They keep on approaching, joined by a movie-star smile. Behind this blond, handsome stranger is another man, not even half as interesting as the leading one…

“Hi. I’m John. I came to see my father. Do you know if he’s in there?”

Must be George’s son…

She comes to a quick conclusion. Yesterday Julia mentioned that George arrived from the United States.

"Yes. He's at the president's office, all the way…"

"I know where to go!" he cuts her off.

Good looking… but what a jerk!

"Oh… you do…? That's great, there you go!" she responds, and in an instant, reminds herself to calm down her nerves, that it is her job. Otherwise she would tell him what she thinks of rich, rude men.

In ten minutes, or less, his white cotton shirt leans over her desk.

"Hello again, I want to apologize for not being nice. Are you new here?"

What a shift…? Unfortunately, I have to respond.

"Yes, I am."

"I thought so… I'm John by the way."

"I ALREADY know your name."

"Oh… that's right… that's right… I've said it before when I was being such a jerk."

His laughter is quite charming. She has to admit.

"And yours? What is your name…?"

Her poker face meets a Hollywood smile on his.

"Ania."

"Your eyes…"

"What about them?"

"I've never seen such beautiful eyes…"

"I'm sure I'm not the first one hearing it at this desk."

"Oh, you don't believe me? That's fine. By the way, what are you doing there?"

His body moves closer to the fax machine, and the sky blue eyes dominate everything she sees.

"Faxing invoices to clients so they can pay us on time."

"It seems to me that only Julia and you are working here; everyone else just hangs around."

"You think so? Hmm… there is some truth to that. It is a kind of telenovela, what else can I say…?"

"You're funny!"

She likes his laughter, a lot.

"So, Ania, what are your plans for this Saturday?"

One is gone, another one comes…

"May I invite you for a drink?"

Just in the perfect moment, the fax machine makes a loud sound.

"I will pick you up from wherever you live."

Her eyes look directly into his.

"You always do it, don't you?"

"Do what?"

"Hit on the front desk girls. This is your specialty."

"Not really. Besides, there haven't been many who had your eyes."

If he only knew what I have just gone through...

An image of Magic flashes through her mind...

GO FOR IT... YOU NEED TO HAVE FUN... IT WILL HELP YOU TO FORGET...

The Voice says from within.

"Still no answer? Honestly, am I this bad?"

BESIDES, HE LIVES FAR AWAY...

The Voice convinces from inside.

She puts nine digits on a piece of paper.

"Here you go, John. We'll see if you call me."

"Oh, again you don't trust? Watch out and you may be very surprised. I'll call you on Friday. Really, I cannot wait to hang out with you this Saturday!"

"Ilona." She hears the name and as soon as their hands come to a touch, the clearest message is transmuted, she's already been disapproved by George's wife.

Barely a few minutes have passed from the moment John has introduced her to his mom, and even though, before this visit, he's spoken highly about his new girlfriend, still, there is a thick wall made of ice.

This ice, no matter how hard her attempt, is never going to meltdown, at least not in her presence; she can tell by looking at the fakest smile.

"Nice to meet you."

The fakeness continues, leaving no confusion about how unsatisfied Ilona is with her son's choice.

"Thank you for allowing me to stay in this beautiful place."

John's hand supports her from the back… but it can't help with the inner battle of the emotions, which are giving her dizziness, thoughts…

I'm not enough…

A thought rises to the surface… she pushes it down…

I'm not rich like them…

Another one emerges.

I don't live in a mansion… I don't drive a luxurious car…

If it weren't for him she would already go back but that's not polite; he has invited her here, and she knows that he genuinely wants her to enjoy these two short days…

When at work, she has mentioned that she'll be spending a weekend at George's retreat; those coworkers who've already been here had told her how magical the place is…:

"There is a spa and a tennis court, and you only need to cross the road to stand on Baltic's sands…"

"Okay. Let's go!" John's hand pulls her out of the mental trance.

Ilona, her face frozen, walks them away until they reach another house.

The guests stay here. This is where she belongs.

"I don't think she likes me."

"So what, do you think I care? Trust me both of my parents are quite messed up." John seems undisturbed.

"Give her some time, she's an artist and that's how artists act."

"Moody, you mean?"

"Exactly, stop worrying so much, all right?" His lips touch her cheek before the front door opens to the wooden stairs… and then all her eyes can perceive is every existing shade of beige.

They must love it a lot since it seems to be everywhere… it covers the walls, rests on the sofas, and sits on the burlap lounge chairs. The bright sun adds even more warmth to it as it highlights the entire space with its afternoon's spark that comes in through those framed by the large, heavy oak windows and unrushed bounce-off from mosaic shades of the table lamps. Once set free, it then lands on the walls, turning into a colorful spider net that creates a form of art that cannot ever be replicated again.

"What a beautiful place…"

"I'm glad you like, your room is upstairs."

His hand reaching into a pocket of his cargo pants.

A single key unlocks the door… and here they step into more beige…

And then, all of her attention is taken by the patchwork covering a king-size bed…

For sure it has to been made by someone's very talented hand, also very patient because it must have taken hours or perhaps even days to put those squares of silk, cotton, and velvet together into one perfect throw…

"This is so lovely… where does it come from?"

"Oh… this thing…? My mom made it."

His mom… who would have ever thought…?

Suddenly Ice Queen Ilona becomes humanized, for one who lacks feelings or soul would never be able to create anything like that.

"She did? Please tell her that I love her work."

"I will. I'm sure she will appreciate hearing it.

Okay. Come over here…"

His hand locks the door… but before they lay down, she makes sure that this beautiful patchwork is safe and set aside, without any crease, on the nearest chair…

"Thanks. We'll be there shortly."

John hangs up the phone.

One hour of napping made a huge difference; her mind emptied of those low self-esteem thoughts.

"They've said that dinner is ready."

"Can I change?"

"Of course you can… I'll leave the front door open. You will find us upstairs."

Quick shower and time to pick up the right outfit… that actually may help a lot…

Nothing crazy, although she loves fashion, this is not the place to show her free-flowing Spice Girls' style… Conservative, all black, just like they dress in New York… It won't create any drama or add another reason to be judged…

Although she remembers precisely that boring dress Ilona had on…

Not my house and not my place to give my opinion...

So let it be black, from head to toe... cashmere v-neck sweater... slick cigarette pants, just like those Audrey Hepburn wore…

As John said, so it is, the front door is left open…

She walks inside…

Right away, the look of a hallway takes her back to that winter trip on which her Parents took her when she was nine…

There, in Karpaty Mountains, the highlanders' homes were also made from a timber wood and smelled like the pine trees after the rain, except here, this smell comes from candles and vegan food.

Let's see if this vegan stuff has any taste...

She begins the climb. Those many steps ahead of her can be used to prepare her feelings inside.

Thoughts - only positive...

Nerves - calm...

Emotion - under control...

She repeats the mantra... and the higher she gets the more music blends with voices of Alicia and George…

Oh this could be interesting... the telenovela goes on...

"Good evening, everyone."

She enters the large room with a big smile.

George's head pops up from behind the kitchen's cabinet door.

"Oh… Ania, you've made it! How do you like it so far?"

With him, she's never had any problem, perhaps because they have not seen each other much. Still, from those short interactions, she's learned that he is a straightforward kind of guy who always says what he means and never wastes people's precious time.

"Breathtaking… and, I don't mean the stairs!" Her joke makes her laugh. It helps, it releases the tension.

She looks around the space…

Beige- it shows up again but it doesn't dominate like it does in the other house.

The lighting seems more settled, perhaps because of those linen shades covering floor lamps?

There is no spider net on the walls, instead of some metal sculptures in strange, abstract shapes…

A huge cream sofa that centers the room has several wool blankets thrown over its edge…

The two big matching armchairs keep a perfect symmetry at the front of a fireplace…

One of them is occupied by Ilona… with a book in her hand.

Whatever it is, the story must be so captivating that she is oblivious to saying "Good evening" in response to her.

"You're funny!" John giggles while throwing more briquettes into the fireplace.

Ilona's serious façade is highlighted by the golden glow.

Is there a glimpse of a smile? No way…

She catches a sudden change of face.

"Oh, I didn't know you were coming. If I'd known, I could have given you a ride." Alicia suddenly acts like her best friend.

A black mini skirt barely covers her butt, showing a great set of legs that everyone at the office knows by heart; those are Alicia's strongest assets to get a rich man.

"Well, it was the whole point that she comes with me, don't you think?"

"Oh, really, Johnny, is it so…?" Long legs are stretching out as Alicia's body leans over the bar's chair…

She's flirting with him in my presence…? Are you serious?!

She tries to exhale the tension, otherwise she knows it will build up fast.

Emotions under control, calm nerves…

"Would you like some wine, Ania?" John turns into a bartender.

"Yes, please. Make it a full glass."

At this point, she could not care less about what they think of her.

John was right… they're all messed up…

A decent sip helps not to give a rip.

A deep corner of the sofa helps to bring stability back.

"Have you ever been in the United States, Ania?"

"No, Alicia, I have not. Have you?"

"Yes, of course! Last year, George had invited us to his Florida house. Oh, we had such a great time..."

"I'm sure you did." She empties the glass.

Ilona chuckles; she must have heard it even though her armchair stands far away.

"Johnny, honey, could you bring me some water, please?"

"Of course, Mom."

His mommy's boy... the way he speaks to her...

"John could send you an invitation to apply for a visa, in Warsaw Consulate. And then you could visit us."

Us...? Who is "Us"? She's not George's wife... how awkward for Ilona to be hearing these words...

"We'll see... it's not a country I'm obsessed with like most people are."

"Oh, what country is it then?"

"Australia, I've always wanted to visit it, since I was a child."

"Australia sounds great, but why can't the US be first? Alicia is right. Come to New York, you must see it, there is no other place like it in the world!" John's arm lands on her shoulder- so do Alicia's eyes.

"Would you invite me?"

"Of course I would. Consider it done!"

His hand tightens its grasp.

"We'll see how things go... maybe next year in summertime..."

"In summer we always come here." Suddenly Ilona gets a voice.

"So then before or after, we'll figure it out, Mom."

"And what do you think Magda would say?"

"Mom, I don't care..."

"John... who is Magda?"

"The ex-girlfriend he wanted to get back before the two of you met." Ilona speaks back.

"They have been dating for a very long time."

"I... did not... know that..."

"My dear, there are many things you don't know about. Magda was his fiancé. You see, she's at law school-so beautiful, so smart. Soon will be an attorney… comes from a great family…"

John's arm is removed, his body gets tense.

"Mom, that wasn't nice. I don't appreciate the way you speak to my guest. And, that you get everyone involved with my personal life. This is not the place for that."

"Honey, it's all good, calm down, my son…"

"You know what? It's Friday, something's got to be open. We will eat in town."

Suddenly, his hand pulls her so wherever he goes, she does as well.

"Let's go, Ania."

"John, you better behave!"

"I'm not staying, Dad. You all can enjoy this vegan food. Anyway, it tastes like shit!"

The same stairs which she has just conquered take them downstairs. Except now instead of her inner mantra, she is accompanied by George's angry voice:

"John! Come back here right now!"

Do I want to be like them...?

As John's hand slams the front door behind their backs, she welcomes a thought…

Goodbyes are hard on her… they can make her sad …

She wonders why when you start to like someone, the moment to part ways always comes so quickly, always much too fast, and always makes you realize that it could be the last encounter both of you will have ever have…

And so she prolongs it, deliberately, trying to stretch out the time, but his arms don't mind staying wrapped around her tiny body and warming it up.

Because it's cold, as usual, it is late December, also, as usual, by 5 pm already dark.

Her cheek touches his blond hair… Like it was yesterday when his white shirt leaned over the office's desk with a Hollywood smile… giving him her phone number is something she will never regret…

"I'll call you once we get home. You'll come to visit me, right?"

"Yes… of course… I will do whatever it takes…"

Her eyes move aside.

He shouldn't see any tears, for they could expose what's in her heart… but that's life, cannot be planned…

"Try to get to know Alicia; she's not as bad as you think. Spend some time with her at the New Year Eve's party. I'm sure she would appreciate your help a lot.

And, you can stay in my room. I'm cool with that."

"Okay, John… I will…"

I will miss you so much... No... no... I shouldn't say it... Magda... he will probably get back with his ex…

"So… goodbye, Ania."

"Bye, John, have a safe flight…"

Last kiss… his sport's car takes off… and her face turns around pretending everything is okay.

These old bricked walls have seen the real tears cried in much harder times… but those were for freedom… for a bit of hope… not like hers for those men that always leave her when she falls in love…

CHAPTER 7

Florence

"PIAZZA ADUA"-states a stone plate hanging over an ancient house.

She reads the sign while stretching out her legs; no wonder they were getting numb; those last fifteen hours spent on the bus have made it the longest trip she's ever had, but when she was going through the discomfort she kept reminding herself of what those friends who've been to Italy have said:

"You'll fall in love with those narrow streets… those Cyprus trees on top of the hills… those flea markets selling the best leather stuff… and those beautiful people who all seem to be in love."

"All roads lead to Rome." People say…

Florence in my case…

She ponders taking John's advice and giving Alicia a chance. Because if she doesn't help at the New Year's Eve party she would not meet Petra, her new Italian friend…

There!

She sees a white Corolla and already familiar, waist-length brown hair.

"Hi, Petra, I am so glad that you came."

"Of course, I've told you that I'd pick you up! How was your trip? I bet very long?"

"Yes, but so worth it, I mean, look at this place…"

Just as they turn around the two young boys begin their chase behind the highest stilettos any human could bear, "Que Bella! Amore! Ti amo ragazza!" Their screams follow a sexy woman's back.

"We're very expressive here."

Petra says while throwing the suitcase inside the car's trunk.

"How's John doing by the way?"

"Well, I don't know… it's been eight months since we lost touch…"

"Men, tell me about it, all the same crap."

The Toyota takes off escorted by the honks.

"Watch out for those scooters; very often, the one that sits on the back pulls handbags off women's hands."

"Thanks for the advice."

After a few narrow streets and a few rough turns the scooters are gone.

The car stops in a narrow street with not much light.

"Here we are, it's a prominent area, only doctors, politicians, and lawyers are allowed to live in this house."

The Italian hand points at the large widows where thick lace tries to hide perhaps an enormous wealth away from a mediocre eye.

"Our apartment is on the third floor. There's no elevator. Grab your bag."

Order must be obeyed... she thinks and proceeds to the massive stone stairs.

As they reflect the soles of her shoes, a stinky air is getting glued to her skin, becoming thicker and thicker until she walks inside and in an instant starts wondering if the place projects such a dead vibe...? Or these walls painted in miserable grey...? Or is it the dust that's been cumulating probably over many months?

"Prominent"? Hmm, it doesn't look like it to me...

"The bathroom is to the right." Petra points at a white door.

"Oh, one more thing, I've almost forgotten to mention it, we'll be staying here one night. Tomorrow early morning we'll go to Viareggio, to our summer house."

She freezes right in between miserable grey walls and a cloud of stinky dust.

"I thought we'd be staying in Florence for a week?"

"Yeah, I know, but I've changed my mind. We have a villa by the sea. My grandma, Nona is already there, expecting us. No worries, you'll share the room with me. Anyway, locals never stay here during the summertime. Too many tourists; pain in the ass."

But I am one of them... I have come from so far...

"Besides, I need to study very hard. In two weeks we'll have a huge exam. Law school is not a joke. Trust me, one day in Florence is enough. Now go and refresh yourself, after we go out to eat in town."

She turns around to hide disappointment, because no matter how hard she tries, her face always shows what's going on inside her mind.

The plan was to explore the city and to look at the art...

To walk those narrow streets and have late dinners on those ancient squares under moonlight...

The bathroom gives some privacy and a chance to take a few deep breaths. At least a mirror delivers the good news that somehow, in spite of those fifteen hours on the bus, she still looks great.

The parmesan cheese is being shredded over, and over again.

Nona holds a thick brick in an old wrinkled hand making a yellow rain that comes down over a white bowl that is steaming with ravioli served at another dinner at another 6 o'clock.

There are four of them by the table: her, Petra, Nona and Nona's brother Luigi who always pours red wine into everyone's glass, and while he's doing it he keeps mentioning that he's made it himself at his house on the countryside.

It's amazing how fast time flies and how much in those last five days she has come to like this small town by the Tyrrhenian Sea with its weather, its reaching the sky palm- trees and its crowd that gathers every night to dance...

Here, where Ferraris park next to Lancias, and Lamborghinis next to Fiats, one thing that matters more than anyone's income is the desire to enjoy life!

"Thank you. It was beyond delicious." She finishes her plate.

"Would you like some more?"

"Oh, no, Petra... literally I have no more space."

"Mangia Ania! Mangia!" Nona's look disapproves.

"My grandmother thinks that you're too skinny and you should eat to get some curves."

"Does she? Well, you can tell her that I'm not Italian like you."

The phone rings in another room.

Oh, how grateful she is that it does. Otherwise, she would tell them how rude it is to comment on people's weight; she never says a word when a person is fat.

"Scuzii tutti, let me get it." Petra walks away from the steaming bowl.

"Certo, amore mio." Luigi keeps on pouring the very wine he has made at his home.

"Hello? Si, questo Petra…"

She knows this is a perfect time to step outside.

"Grazie molto Donna Francesca."

"Oh… non ce di que, Ania…"

She finds a metal chair and pulls underneath the oak's branch.

She loves this garden… with this gentle wind softly whistling above her head and sent from a nearby sea…

She loves those pink roses that are getting ready to reach their fullest blooms… and those lemon trees that are preparing to soon give out their juiciest fruits…

Dolce vita... It must be it...

Gratitude fills her heart…

"Hi, there, can we talk?" Petra's voice opens up her eyes.

There, on Italian face, is not a sign of bliss but, instead, a sarcastic smile she has not yet had a chance to see.

"Sure, Petra, is everything okay?"

"Well, it depends on how you look at it."

Something moves inside her heart… and replaces the gratitude with the fear…

"Listen, my friends are coming here and we're going to study together, remember, I told you about the exam? Unfortunately, there's not enough room for all of us, that's why I want you to be out of the house."

Silence stops the time. Time freezes every form… and she feels trapped inside a room without an exit door…

"And to go back to Poland, did you hear what I've just said? Hello, are you listening to me?!"

The room's walls are crashing down.

"Yes, Petra… I am…"

The world that a minute ago was at peace is now is ripped apart…

"But…"

"There is no "but." I am dead serious. You have to go."

"You know that August is the busiest month… I booked the last tickets in March…"

"I'm sure we'll find something or if not you will take a train.

"Anyway, stop dramatizing and start to pack. They'll be here on Monday. I want you out of the house-this is my last word!"

The last word disappears behind the villa's old walls, the beauty of which she was admiring ten minutes ago… Now it seems to no longer be there… and there is no comfort on a metal chair…

Confused… alone… rejected… she remains under the oak's branch…

For months she was saving the money to visit Italy…

How is it possible for things to change so rapidly?

How is it possible for the same host to kick out the same guest who was invited in?

One more week is left before I am supposed to go back...

And Florence, I have not seen much of it...

What to do... what to do...?

The worries turn into clouds… oh, she knows them very well… and that when they're allowed to hang around for too long can completely paralyze her from any future act…

There must be a solution... and a safe way out...

That her mind has no bottom she was not aware of…

The more she dwells on finding the answer, the deeper she dives into a black hole…

Suddenly something moves within her and she hears the Voice:

BREATHE, ANIA... BREATHE...

PLEASE DO NOT WORRY... EVERYTHING WILL BE ALL RIGHT...

As directed, she takes in a deep breath. It continues to speak up:

TONIGHT, GO TO TOWN JUST BY YOURSELF...

Alone…?

YES... ALONE... THERE IS A REASON FOR THAT...

In a split of a second, the Voice is gone, leaving her with a new vibration that keeps swimming through her thoughts.

It was the answer to my question...!

Awareness hits her like a clap of thunder!

Her carry-on is in Petra's room… Somehow she knew that black mini dress and these patent leather shoes, gifted to her by the Mother, were supposed to be packed…

How did she know that these two-inch heels will be perfect for a walk she's about to take?

It is too early to leave…? putting red lipstick on, she asks herself.

No, it is not. It's better to be waiting outside the club than to hang out here where I'm no longer allowed.

The Mother's shoes are clicking… step by step by step…

How weird is it that no one has even noticed that she has left the house…?

She can hear the noise coming from those drivers that are passing the good-looking girls. That was the behavior she noticed in those last few nights when Petra was still kind enough to be taking her out to dance.

Indeed, as soon as the corner is reached, the main street becomes a fact.

The crowd is already present and it covers the street's sides.

Loud music is calling inside the clubs so are the flashing neon lights.

White outfits dress up the skins showing how dark during the day they've become.

She catches a few smiles being sent out her way trying not to be distracted.

"CAMPANINA!" This is it!

She crossed the street on the first green light.

At the entrance, a line is waiting, and it's much longer than she predicted it would be…

That is not a problem; once she gets inside, the therapy will begin. Dancing always does to it her- uplifts the spirit, brings relief.

Inside the club, she has made it… the music is pulsating, yet it's still a bit too early to step onto this huge dance floor; this is the perfect time to grab a drink. And to cruise around to check who has decided to show up tonight…

It seems that everyone is here: pretty, ugly, poor, rich…

Diversity… that's good… we are all equal under the disco's lights…

DJ appears behind the console table and puts his head phones on. After a minute, a grey-white smoke takes over the entire dance floor.

This is the time for her to merge into the music and blend with the very first song.

This one is for her feet, the second one, for her arms, the third one for her body to spin around, the fifth one to lose a sense of time and go with the flow…

The sounds completely take over her senses. She keeps going on and on and on… letting go of every concern… every worrisome thought… and while doing it getting so lost in the process she doesn't realize that a young, good looking guy is dancing right in front of her.

He's tall, lean, and quite handsome, and he's trying to get her attention.

Finally, she sees his blue eyes and his bouncing blond hair.

How she could miss so much hair? His head is full of light blond angelic curls…

The brightest blue suspenders stand out from his white shirt and hold onto loose jeans rolled up at their bottoms.

A big smile is stuck on his boyish face, exclusively for her.

"Hello, bella! Que fantastica ballerina tu sei!!"

"Excuse me?? It's too loud! What did you just say?!"

"Oh, English? Where are you from?!"

"Sono Pollacca!" she shouts out into his curls.

"You speak Italian, que bene!"

"Oh… no… no… I just happen to know a few words!"

"That's nice! What is your name, bella?!"

"Ania!"

"Maurizio!" His hand reaches out through the grey-white smoke.

"I like your suspenders… they're very cool!"

"They're nice, right?!" He pulls on one of them.

"I love that color of blue!"

His hand points at the terrace.

"Would you like to get some fresh air?"

"Yes, great idea!"

She touches her forehead, and with one swoop, a cascading droplet of sweat is wiped off.

"Here... oh, God, this is a comfortable chair!" His laughter makes her smile. Her legs are saying "thank you" for getting a well-deserved rest.

"So, where are your friends, Ania?"

"I came here by myself."

"What? Are you serious?! You are a brave girl."

"Brave? Why do you think so?"

"The nightclubs are not the safest place. What made you do that, if you don't mind me asking?"

Maybe later I'll explain to him... not now...

"It's a long story..."

"I have plenty of time."

"So do you work or study Maurizio?"

She knows how to change the subject.

"I study philosophy."

"Then I guess you must be a very wise man."

"I hope so." His lips lift in the corners and she likes the dimples they make.

"And where is your school?"

"Two glasses of water, please!" He waves to a waiter and turns right back to look at her.

"In Florence."

She holds onto her breath.

"I love living there. God, I am thirsty..." With one sip, he empties his glass.

Meanwhile, she keeps scanning his blond hair... his heavenly blue eyes...

There's something about him, something she knows she can trust...

"Today, the girl who has invited me to Italy has kicked me out of her house."

The words by themselves are flying out from her mouth.

"She told me that her schoolmates are coming and they need to study for a huge exam... And, there is not enough room for everyone..."

"Excuse me...?"He looks at her like the world just came to an end.

"How awful... That is horrible..." His curls are shaking to the right and left.

"What kind of person would do such a thing…?"

"Tell me about it. Imagine being in my shoes. She told me that by Monday I have to leave."

His eyes gaze at an empty glass as if all the answers are in there, and then as soon as they lift, get glued to hers.

"Don't worry. I know what we can do."

"We"… What is he talking about…?

"My friends live in a big house in Tuscany, and Florence is half hour drive. There's plenty of room. Tomorrow morning I'll arrange it with them. I'm sure they will not mind. Don't worry. Everything will be all right."

EVERYTHING WILL BE ALL RIGHT…

The Voice rings back in her head…

"Are you sure? I am a stranger-someone they've never met…"

"Trust me, I know them, they are good people. That's why they are my best friends. But what I'm concerned about is how you get back home. To Poland, I mean?"

"By the bus; I already have a ticket on August 24th…"

"Oh, that's great! One week is nothing! I'm sure they will be okay with that. Now, the only thing you have to figure out how to get to Florence by yourself… You see, I would take you with me, but tonight I came here with a bunch of other guys… I know!" He jumps up from his comfy chair.

"You can take a train! And I'll pick you up! Now what? What's wrong now…? No… no more crying, I'm happy to be helping you out! I'm sure if you were me you would do the same. How could she kick you out…? I have no words…

"Here, please, take my number and call me once you get to town. Now let's go dancing, for God's sake, we came here to have fun!"

"How was last night? Did you have fun?" Petra's sarcastic voice and the sound of a zipper come at the same time. Finally, she has finished packing her carry-on bag.

"It was great. Don't worry, tomorrow I'm gone. I'll be taking a train."

Without any last word, Petra walks out of the room. She throws the bag on the upper bed, thinking if a week ago she only knew what she knows now, she would not have been so respectful about walking around so quietly above Italian head to avoid waking them up.

"Coffee… this is what I need…"she says out loud to herself.

"Grazie, Donna Francesca." She grabs an espresso and finds herself on the same metal chair, under the same oak's branch and the bright sun and the fresh breeze above her head…

Pink roses to the left… yellow lemons to the right…

I'M GLAD THAT YOU WENT...

The Voice returns from inside.

I did... thank you for the advice...

TONIGHT, GO THERE AGAIN...

Again... to the same club...?

YES... THERE IS A REASON FOR IT... SOON YOU WILL UNDERSTAND WHY...

As if the time has been reversed, she repeats last night's steps: the make-up, the dress, the Mother's shoes, and the lipstick, in a bright red.

The same club, though different people, yet the same songs. Like living in a deja-vu, after the fifth one, all of her concerns are gone.

Maybe Maurizio is still here... that's why the Voice told me to come...

Her waist twists to the left… and then she sees him… the most handsome man in the club…

He stands behind the ramp, looking like a Greek God…

His dark brown eyes are hypnotizing.

His fitted grey T-shirt shows how nicely his pecs are build up…

His black hair is quite long, but it stays motionless thanks to an extra-hold gel shining from a distance…

"Hello…!" She hears from behind and wonders how has he managed to be next?

"You're not from here, are you?" His eyes hypnotize from up close as much as his Aqua di Gio smell.

"You are a great dancer. I've enjoyed watching you."

"Thank you very much, I think so too."

"And, you are funny! What a great combo! My name is Augusto."

"Oh, just like this month?"

"Yes! Exactly! May I get you a drink? My table is there, behind the ramp."

His gladiator's arm points at the spot.

In less than five minutes two cosmopolitan martinis appear at the front of them. Soon there is the second round… followed by the third…

"Let's go outside to look at the stars."

His hand takes her to the beach where the sky delivers more magic than it had last night.

"How long will you be staying in Viareggio, Ania?"

"Tomorrow morning I have to catch a train."

"To where?"

"To Florence."

"That's where I live!"

She freezes, but *not* from the cold wind the sea has just sent.

"Come with me, I drove here by myself."

But I don't know him at all…

She looks up at the stars.

His arm goes around her without any pressure to say "yes."

"What do you for work, Augusto?"

She feels suddenly inspired to ask.

"I'm not sure if I should say it…"

"Why?"

"I don't know how you will take it…"

"What is it?"

"Well… I am a police officer."

She remains silent with his hand placed over her arm.

It takes two minutes to explain her situation and half an hour before she is again climbing above Petra's head. Without making a sound, she grabs her carry-on bag…

Then, very slowly, as if her life depends on it, she steps down over the wooden stairs…

How strange they don't make any noise as they always do?

The gate is the last step of her journey and… the bag lands in Augusto's hand.

His face shows pure satisfaction, his watch 5 am.

In the car, she exhales.

"How did it go?" he asks.

"All good. She was sleeping." And as he steps on the gas, she looks out the window at this narrow street where, two nights in a row, she walked to find help wearing Mother's heels…

An old Citroen is shaking from the randomly placed stones that keep on throwing it in every direction over a sandy, dusty road.

She ignores the notion and continues to gaze ahead, trying to capture a view that could hang in any frame.

Here, from the top of the Tuscan hills, Florence takes her breath away… with these allies of cypress trees… with these old fences with missing bricks… with these unexpected turns…

Oh… another one…

She gets a glimpse of the "Vinci" sign… while Maurizio points at the lonely house.

"Allora, here we are. That is my friends' place, three hundred years old. You'll enjoy staying there.

"Look, Stefano is waiting outside!"

The car pulls up at the front of the narrow stairs, and Maurizio's blond curls jump out to take a short flight.

Then it's her turn to be embraced by the long and skinny arms.

"Welcome to Tuscany, Ania. I'm glad you made it safe."

"Thank you, Stefano, for helping me out…"

"Oh. My pleasure. It's not that big of a deal. Trust me, we have enough rooms in this house. Carla, come over here! They have arrived!" Stefano screams into depths of the house.

And while they are waiting for whoever Carla is, she cannot stop thinking how much he reminds her of a young Karl Marx. These intellectual frames show someone who reads a lot. That laidback linen outfit is the evidence that fashion to him, does not mean a diddly squat.

"Ania, let me introduce you to Carla, my lovely fiancé."

The most genuine smile greets her from a porcelain face.

"Nice to meet you, Ania, we are so happy to be able to help. You see, when you do good, only good can come back."

The couple blends together, and as she watches their bodies, she can tell, there is the kind of love between them that will never see an end.

"Maurizio told me the same thing in the car; no wonder you two are so close."

"Indeed, we are. We share the same values. And, with that being said, I think it's the time to show you around our place. It is quite special; soon you will understand… follow me, please."

She follows his wrinkled shirt, first through a modest small kitchen that smells like freshly baked bread… then through the living room with mosaic tiles… and through a big door that leads outside into a vast yard.

Her arm is grabbed and together they take a few more steps ahead.

"Can you see that hill over there, Ania?"

Her eyes are directed by his hand.

"That one… which is the closest to us…?" she asks.

"Yes, that one, can you see that house standing on its top?"

She narrows her focus and sets it on those ancient bricks.

"Yes, I do see it… what about that house?"

"That's where Leonardo da Vinci was born."

"Vinci"… she recalls a sign they passed…

"Enjoy the view. I will leave you alone."

The silence takes over and her own breath is all she hears.

Here, under the Tuscan sun, she begins to understand why everything wasn't unfolding according to the plan… why she was kicked out of Petra's house… why she was guided to meet these men who have helped her out…

THERE IS A REASON FOR IT... SOON YOU WILL UNDERSTAND WHY...

The Voice rings in her ears as she looks through wet eyes ahead at Leonardo da Vinci house…

CHAPTER 8

Babcia

What a summer... she thinks as she passes through the hallway… so much turmoil in her life already and now Grandma… in this hospital…

Will she be able to overcome that...?

The white doors are lined up as if they were post-communist guards watching over each room and their powerless occupants.

This place is old; not much has changed from the time she was born in here. The till, bare impoverished look with the same faded posters randomly hanging everywhere. They were inherited from a different age, that era before "Solidarity" fought for the end of the Soviet's curse.

The Spartan chairs occasionally block her way. She hits one of them, noticing its leg, a battleship-gray paint that almost covers the rust.

Other visitors hear a cheap creaking sound and turn all their attention to look at her now.

Instinctively, she straightens the chair and stretches out her arms; somehow, the sensation of the soft fabric on her skin calms her down.

She's thought about how her outfit for this visit means a lot. It's all matching, in a white linen, a long-sleeved V-neck blouse, and a wide-leg pants falling over flat Greek sandals that are crisscrossed around her ankles and the most comfortable shoes she's got.

She sees a dead-eyed nurse through the thick glass.

The information room is small… an old wooden table… one scarred chair and… a frameless mirror hanging from a rusty nail…

The fluorescent light buzzes over a nurse's bonnet, which has been attached by a countless number of pins to her dry brown hair. These pins are doing nothing to control this mess. The starched uniform is nameless and without any shape. The cheap-looking buttons are fastened, and her angry face flushes with blood running over swollen cheeks with each breath the nurse tries to take into her massive chest.

She looks at this dehumanized woman and hears them again:, spit out and careless, directing her to Grandma's dying words:

"The second floor, half-way down the corridor, room 56, that's where you'll find her, that's where she is!"

"Thank you so much. You're very kind." she murmurs to the aggravated face.

"And the visits end at five!"

"Yes, I am aware of it." She remains undisturbed and quickly turns her face toward the post-German stairs. There, right above them, a round clock continuously counts the time:

"Two o'clock"... I will make it...

Silver hands keep moving, oblivious to her pain.

The second floor... somewhere here...

Her climb stops by a metal tag.

The patients are everywhere...

This place is packed...

Their sick bodies are either quietly entombed in the beat-up beds or walking along the corridors in a zombie-like state. Clothed in uniforms of a near death and medicated to their very last cell, they remain either hopeful or numb with whatever days they have left.

The unmerciful walls, painted in a cheap chalk white, and the floor's black and white ceramic tiles echo their cries for a bit more of an extended life... for mercy... for help...

She tries to breathe, but the humidity is stuck and now hangs high in the air, clinging to everyone. That's what summer in Szczecin has always been like: airless, suffocating, and incredibly hot.

The darkest thoughts come back to haunt her mind again...

She can't pretend any longer that Their Family's anger will end somehow...

It seems as if even Babcia's death is not going to make Them change... still, there are Their screaming voices... still, there is Their pointless blaming...

And, those cursing words, and those quiet days... her entire childhood has been built upon that...

Grandma's room was the only place where she was able to escape... It was there, at the end of the corridor, where she found refuge from Them...

Just one knock away was the door of that room, which always welcomed her inside.

And there was her Babcia holding onto a little bible, remaining still in the midst of all of that.

"Babciu, can I come in, please?" She was asking for escape... and as soon as Grandma heard her little voice, the white door opened for her.

That smell of intense valerian emerged from those leaves that Babcia boiled in the kitchen in an old beat-up green pot, never missing a day, for that tea was a secret ritual behind her vitality and clear mind.

And she always wore grayish brown skirts… and blouses with flower prints… and during summer, her stockings were dark nude… and in the winter they were green…

"Come on over, Wnusiu! We will read my cards and see what the future holds for you. I'm sure it will be wonderful."

And with a wrinkled smile, she would make her feel so safe…

Then, once she was seated on the top of the big bed, Babcia would walk toward that shiny mahogany cabinet. The smell of Lily of the Valley was bursting out as the deck of cards was pulled out to be shuffled—always three times. Then, she was asked to spread those cards into three piles and lay them out exactly in four straight lines.

The gray frames covering her focused eyes were slowly moving over those symbols that Grandma knew by heart. The long old fingers pinpointed at the torn kings, queens, and jacks… and as soon as she cleared her dry throat ending an anticipated wait, the reading would begin:

"I can see a dark-haired man in the evening hour coming your way… and… that you will live abroad… in another country… somewhere far… far away.

"Hmm, it looks to me like it will be across big water… Oh, my dear… you will be so happy there… You will build a family… and do great things in life…"

The old finger touched several cards. "Look, Wnusiu, can you see it? It's in all of them! Don't ever give up on your dreams! My cards are telling me that!"

Right… those dreams…

Suddenly, she awakens into forgotten heat, back into the awareness that soon all she will have left will be those memories…

How short life is… if I could only turn back the time… I would have been so much nicer to her… more gracious… more polite…

All of a sudden, the noisy sounds cut through her thoughts like a surgeon's knife.

Disturbed and dragged back into the present, she stops and turns around. Behind her, the wheels of the metal carts are harshly being rolled by the nurses over the floor's stone tiles.

It looks as if doctor's' inspections are over, and so now the smells of alcohol and disinfectant bottles are being stirred up. Her peace is taken away, that noise has affected her, for she has always been sensitive to it from the time she was a little girl.

These squeaking wheels with no consideration for quiet and peace of mind make her want more than anything to leave this place behind.

I have to find her!

With desperation, she reads twin numbers, to the left and right…

Fifty-three, fifty-four, fifty-five... there... room "fifty-six"...

She exhales deeply and stops.

Her hand moves closer to the door… and pushes it through the already slightly opened crack…

Still not quite ready for what will unfold…

The sterilized white room appears…

Every bed is occupied…

All eyes stare at her with this last hunger for another chance to live…

There she is… so full of vibrancy, fresh and young, which those in the beds would do anything to get it back into their mortal lives.

A soft smile shows up on her face for this modest place, so far away from elegant is deeply humbling to her.

She puts cockiness aside and looks around this bedazzled space.

And then… there… straight ahead in a deep right corner on a metal bed… under June's sun, lays her quiet friend… her teacher of life…

Ninety-four years lived through dramas, sorrows, and two world wars' pains are ending so unfairly hard…

And then it hits her again…

So this is it? This is the end of such a great life?

Something no one has power over… is there… she's looking at it now…

Her throat starts choking… the tears are ready to burst out…

How is it going to be at the house when she's gone...? No... I cannot cry...

She forces her feet to the side of the bed where the old body rests in peace, the fragile head with thin soft hair is placed on two starched pillows in some kind of divine way.

It seems that Grandma is fully accepting the transition with dignity and grace.

She looks at this blissful sleep, which now her visit is going to disturb.

"Hi… Babciu…" she says very softly. The invisible eyes open up. The pale skin turns toward her.

"Oh, Anusia… you came… I am so glad…"

Grandma whispers trough a wrinkled smile.

Just one spark of joy, that's all it took for this old heart to lighten up again…

"Yes, Babciu, I'm here. How are you feeling today?"

She swallows the sadness and gently grabs a veiny white hand.

"I'm good, Kochanie… I'm good… I'm ready for God to take me away…"

Grandma's eyes turn from blue to gray. Their color says it all. The suffering can no longer hide inside of them.

She pulls an old metal stool closer to the bed. The wave of hopelessness flows all over her face.

She takes a deep breath in… and another one…

"Oh… Babciu, please don't say it. This is nothing for you… you've survived much worse than this. You'll be fine…"

But the words cannot make up for what they both know very well…

A brief moment of silence enters their realm. And she hears the Voice saying from inside of her:

YOU STILL HAVE SOME TIME… BE GOOD… AND KIND…

She looks out the window at the sunny light that bursts in so unaware of those who are suffering on those beds.

And as she holds onto the bony fingers with yellow nails, her eyes move around Grandma's aura that is hardly visible to her… It's almost as if Babcia is disappearing… slowly going back into being a child… a universal sign of transition of a full circle of life.

"I have something important to tell you, Kochanie."

The dry voice breaks their silence up.

"Please… listen to me carefully."

"Yes, Babciu, I'm listening. Tell me, what is that…?"

"I want you to be happy… I know it wasn't easy for you to grow up at our house… but, you are just like me when I was young… so brave… so strong."

"Oh… Babciu…"

"Please. Just hear me out…"Grandma's voice is shaking…

"I know it was difficult to live with Their fights… They were so hard on you… it was just too much… But you don't have to repeat Their misery, you can have a different life. You have power over your happiness… I've prayed for you every night… Please remember it when I am gone…"

She sits there quiet, blown away. The river of emotions showers every memory she has.

Time doesn't move… neither does the world…

She didn't expect this… not to hear these words…

"When she was praying it was… for me…?"

Her brown eyes swim with two streams of overwhelming tears. They no longer can be prevented from falling down… She wipes them off with her blouse's long sleeve.

Just being there is enough. Talking became unnecessary. Everything shifted… Now she knows why she had to come.

"I love you, Babciu…"

The Grandma smiles softly with that wisdom gained from a well-lived life. Now released and freed, she can leave the pain of human existence far behind…

Those trees outside the window somehow became greener… the Sun somehow got brighter… and the clouds softer… or maybe they were like this before… it's just she couldn't see it through a closed-off heart…?

On the early morning, of December 24th Grandma said: "Goodbye," and in a deep sleep returned to God.

By Christmas Eve's table, prepared for supper, she looks down. There, under a beautiful tree, is a gift in a perfectly wrapped box. Its shiny blue paper with a golden bow on the top would forever remain untouched by those old hands that used to shuffle the torn deck of cards.

Father's wet eyes stare into hers. A death that was so hard to be accepted has become a fact; an empty chair is the evidence.

"She told me to be happy..." She recalls that day when she was seated by the metal bed and holding onto tears she listened to Babcia's words…

CHAPTER 9

Ships

44

“And where is this place exactly?” She pulls another picture from a big pile.

These palm trees, these crystal clear waters, these golden beaches and the faces with the happiest smiles completely take her attention away from a plate of pizza. Her good friend is back in town, so they can catch up on what was happened in the last year.

“Oh, this one is in St. Lucia; my boyfriend comes from there.”

“Amazing, Sylwia… truly amazing… you must have traveled around the world…”

“No, not around the world, but as far as the Caribbean Islands, I’ve seen pretty much most of them.”

Sylwia takes a sip from a huge ceramic mug and a smell of mint goes up into the air.

“It’s been over a year already since I’ve seen you last, am I right?”

“Hmm… let me think… I’ve done two contracts… had one break… yep, over a year and a half.”

“How long is one contact?”

“Usually six months, after that, you get two months of vacations.”

“That’s quite intense.”

“It is but when you’re there time truly flies. It feels kind of awkward to come back into this slow pace, almost as if everything stands still here.”

“Oh trust me, I completely understand, if I wouldn’t travel I would go crazy myself. So, tell me Sylwia, where did you go with those ships?”

“Sure. So we went to Antiqua, Jamaica, Barbados; they have the best rum over there, I’m telling you! Then we went to Mexico, Grand Cayman, Bahamas, oh, and Alaska as well.”

“Oh wow, you’ve been to Alaska? I’ve heard it’s a really beautiful place.”

“Indeed, it’s also very quiet and has the cleanest air. The cruise ships always go there around March; that’s when their itineraries change.”

“It sounds to me you like living that lifestyle?”

“I do, but to be honest, it’s not for everyone. Some people are not mentally able to handle this kind of job. It can be very tough, Ania.”

“Tough…? It’s hard to believe. To me it looks like a dream job.”

"Well, when you have a little time to go ashore and explore the places then it surely can be.

"But when you work sixteen hours at the bar, share a cabin with three other girls, including the bathroom- so imagine having zero privacy, not even mentioning not having a full day off…"

"What? How can it be… no days off at all?"

Sylwia swallows the last bite. Her pizza still chills on a plate.

"Yep, you heard me, no days off at all. Starting the late shift the next day is what is called "a day off." Trust me, ships are physically exhausting, you don't get too much rest while you're there."

"But you're managing it somehow?"

"Of course I do, and that's because I choose to focus on the good aspects like meeting different nationalities, seeing the most beautiful places in the world, practicing English, learning how to efficiently manage time, and, last but not least, also falling in love."

"Falling in love? Excuse me? What do you mean?"

"Having boyfriends, Ania, having boyfriends. It's good to have them when you're there so you don't get lonely or even worse, depressed. Girl, you're the last one to worry about finding a nice guy."

Sylwia's face leaves no room for any confusion.

"You should do it. Don't even think twice."

"Well… I don't know, Sylwia… I do love to travel… but my parents… I still live with them…"

"So…? What's the problem?"

"So I would have to explain why I want to leave Poland again… Remember when I went to Sweden it didn't turn out too well…"

She looks out the window where an old tramway has just splashed the color of bright red. The people walk down the street carrying sadness stamped into each of their faces without a bit of hope about how to meet their lives' ends…

What a contrast to these pictures… as if "that" world does not exist…

She pulls another image from the pile.

But it does, and I could enter it too… just like she had…

"Yes, I remember what happened, but this is completely something else. There you have a guaranteed job and make money, by the way, the passengers tip very well.

"Besides, you gain great life experience, something no one can ever take away from you, my friend. Tell me, when else are you going to do it? If not now when you're still young and have the energy for that?"

"You're right, Sylwia... you're right... maybe I should leave everything behind...

How do I even go about it...? How do I apply?"

"Just call the company, I'll give you the number, their office is in Puck, it's a small town."

"My family lives not too far away in Rumia... how strange..."

"You see, it's meant to be! Call Mrs. Lucyna; she takes care of everything. The first interview you'll have with David, he's the boss. For the second one you will go to Warsaw, but no worries, you'll be accepted right away, especially with your experience from the Radisson hotel."

"Does it help that I've worked there, Sylwia?"

"Of course it does! The cruise ships are like five-star hotels. After you get approved, the next step will be getting a crewman visa at the American Embassy, and after the first contract is done, I would suggest you apply for a tourist one. It allows you to visit the US without any invite and lasts ten years."

John would never believe that I went to the States without his help...

"Girl, you will have so much fun! Let me know how everything goes, and let's stay in touch because we may meet again on the other side of the world!"

"Who knows, maybe in Alaska... It was so good to catch up."

All pictures disappear in the vastness of Sylvia's tote.

"Best of luck!"

Her friend is gone.

She grabs the fork and digs it into cold pizza- the taste of which is already gone.

Or perhaps it's her hunger that has been changed for something very different from food on a plate...

The door opens up. The heat hits her face. Miami welcomes her to the United States.

She steps outside under the bright sun, diving straight into a humid air that blows as if just got exhaled from an invisible monster's mouth.

"It's so hot for January…"she says out loud to herself as she throws a black winter jacket over her left arm and tucks a light cotton top into an A-line skirt. Now, these patent leather boots are the only reminders of the Polish cold that she left far behind about twelve hours ago.

The yellow cab pulls to the front of the curb; as soon as she jumps inside, a small paper slip lands in the driver's hand.

"Oh, Collins Avenue, miss? I know that hotel very well. Mostly crewmembers stay over there. I am assuming you are one of them?"

"Yes, sir, I am." She settles down in the back. "This is my first time here."

"You mean on the ships?"

"Both, on the ships and, in the United States"

"Oh wow! Benvenuto to Miami! Well, I must honestly say it's much more Cuba in here than it is the USA."

"Oh, is it? I didn't know that. Are you from here, sir?"

"No, miss, I am not. I also have moved from Havana a long time ago… so long that I'm sure you were not even born yet." His chocolate eyes turn around and the sweetest smile showers her face.

"How old are you if you don't mind me asking?"

"Not at all, I'm twenty-five, just had my birthday on the fifth of this month."

"Twenty-five… what a beautiful age… A whole life ahead of you; it has barely begun…"

"I think so, especially with this trip."

The line of palm trees stays behind as they approach the bridge.

She turns left, noticing where several yacht boats are docked by the piers.

"What a beautiful island…"

"Star Island…? Oh, yes… it is. It's very, very expensive; only the richest people can afford to live there. That one…" His hand points at one of the mansions, "…is Gloria Estefan's estate."

"Wow… so stunning… I like her a lot."

"Me too, miss, you see, here, in Miami, everyone likes The Estefans. They do help people. Not just talk like those celebrities with big, empty mouths."

"I kind of got that impression listening to her interviews. You know, sir, she just came out of that serious car accident? Have you seen that great performance she gave in Atlanta at the Olympic Games?"

"Yes, miss, I enjoyed it very much. Good idea, why don't we listen to some music now?"

His hand reaches toward a switch.

"If I could reach higher… Just for one moment touch the sky…"

Oh my God... this is "the" song she sang at the Olympic Games! ... How strange that we were just talking about it...

The lyrics take over her thoughts…

"…I'm gonna be stronger, knowing I've tried my very best, I've put my spirit to test…"

"Look at you miss, very nice voice. I think you're going to have lots of fun working on those ships…"

"Thank you, sir. I will. I'm sure. So, please, tell me who else lives over there, you must know everything, have you driven any of them? Any famous people sat in this back seat?"

"Well, there's some truth to that, indeed taxi drivers do know a lot of things, miss.

"As a matter of fact, I've driven Madonna, Will Smith, and Sly… Oh, also Gianni Versace, by the way, his house is very close to your hotel, right on the corner of eleventh street and Ocean Drive.

"It's a huge villa in a Mediterranean style, has a gold Medusa on the fence; it's very easy to find.

"Although you may have to pull some leaves aside; the bush is very thick… privacy… that kind of stuff…"

They come to a soft turn by the sign: "Miami Beach."

She catches a glimpse of half-naked men that are flashing their shining torsos while speeding by on rollerblades.

"Washington Avenue" she reads the name of a street and pulls down the window.

"Can't wait to see it, sir… Is this place always so crazy hot?"

"Yes, miss, it is. Especially after the rain, it always comes unexpectedly, but it doesn't last long… ten, fifteen minutes, then it's gone."

"That's not too bad."

"Not bad at all. Here you can go every day to the beach if you wish. How long will you be staying?"

"They've said about a week. It depends on how fast the paperwork is done."

"Do they pay for it, miss?"

"They do. Thank God!"

"Oh, good, then enjoy it, I've heard working on the ships is not an easy job, but somehow I also have a feeling that you will be just fine."

They stops at the front of the building

It looks like a sick flamingo has vomited on it… she thinks while acknowledging a bottle-less bar accompanied by several young men without any drinks.

Probably the crewmembers…

She feels their eyes touching her skirt.

"It was a true pleasure to be driving you, miss."

"Likewise, sir."

A fresh ten-dollar bill arrives into his hand.

"Oh, thank you very much, miss, I appreciate…"

"No, thank you, sir, maybe next time I can give you a much bigger tip."

"It's not the amount that matters but the intent. May God bless you, miss, and always keep you safe on those ships…"

What a kind man…

Ignoring some "hellos," she puts a suitcase into a motion, but then, just for a moment stops and dives her hand inside the purse…

Still there… very good…

"Good Morning! " A door-bell rings with the Hispanic voice.

"You are Ania from Poland to join the "Galaxy", correct?"

"That's right, ma'am, how did you know?"

"Here," A twin of Salma Hayek pushes some documents toward her.

"Please, sign it on the bottom. This is your key to room 105, on the same floor, first door to the left. If you have any questions, don't hesitate to ask; we are here to help."

"I will. Thank you very much."

The suitcase moves five more steps ahead.

She unlocks the door and walks into a space that looks like the refugees have just left their camp… Three sets of metal double beds are pushed to the walls, which in some parts of them have old imprints of shoes' dirty soles. On the floor are no rugs. Outside the window is no view, but a reflection of the opposite camp…

Temporary…

Undiscouraged, she parks the luggage by the closest bed and quickly walks out of the room.

"Excuse me, ma'am, I have a question: Where is the nearest phone?"

"Just turn around, my dear. Behind that glass door, mi amor."

Ones again she dives into her pocket. The time for a coin has come.

"Hello?" a stranger answers.

"Good morning, can I please talk to John?"

"One moment, please. John… you have a phone call…!" the same stranger shouts out.

"Who is it?" She hears the voice that used to stir up butterflies in her gut…

"Some girl, like why do you ask me, do I ever know their names?!"

"Hello… this is John."

"Hi, John, it's Ania, how you've been?"

Deathly silence dominates the space.

"Ania…? Oh… hi… what a surprise…?"

"I know it must be for you after such a long time. Anyway, John, guess where I am?"

The silence comes back.

"Are you in… the US…?"

"Bingo! I am in Miami, twenty-nine degrees Celsius in January? Can you believe it's this hot?"

"How did you do that…?"

"You mean how did I come here without your invite? Well, to work on the ships; I just signed the contract, will join in about a week. Listen, I've got to get going there is so much to see. Just wanted to say "hello" and check if you're all right."

"Yes… yes… I am… thank you for asking. Can you call me again?"

"We'll see how things go… Take care, John. Goodbye!"

She hangs up the phone with a satisfied smile, now ready to find that golden Medusa over Versace's fence on Ocean Drive.

"Next!"

she hears, and the line moves a little. Surrounding walls keep bouncing off the sounds of the crewmembers' feet passing her by at the speed of the light.

"Ha! You see, they don't want to be late! The evening shifts start at five."

The girl standing at the front of her unexpectedly turns around.

Her olive skin, black hair, and dark brown eyes introduce some Asian vibes.

"Marry Ann, Philippines, Manilla, how about you, girl?"

"Ania, Poland, my first contract."

"Your first contract? No way, I could never tell! You look very confident, dear, try to stay this way. For me this will be the third one."

"Wow, you've done so many of them…"

"Yes, now I'm a bartender, but I was a cocktail waitress first. Which department will you be in?"

"At the bar, at least that's what they've said."

"Fantastic! We will work together! It's important to have good people around, so they won't screw you like banana. I hate those sapos, bumbaclot!"

"Excuse me?"

"Don't worry, it's a ship's language. Soon you will learn."

More people keep rushing by their side wearing every possible color of skin a human can have.

"It's like the United Colors of Benetton in here."

"Girl, you are funny. To be exact is ninety-eight."

"Are there ninety-eight nationalities on board?"

"Yeah, there are nine hundred crew-members and over two thousand passengers. It is a small town. Don't worry you will find your way."

"Did you ever get lost in those corridors? I've heard there are thirteen decks…"

"Of course I did! Everyone does! But only in the beginning, after two weeks, you become a pro. That's the last thing you should be concerned about."

"Next!"

Another call gives a glimpse of an office door.

"Ha! You see how fast it is moving? No wonder; it's a brand new ship, you're lucky to have such a good start. Those old ones are a piece of crap, but there is much less stress. Do you know why?"

"No."

"Because they don't freak out about the three-buckets systems; those stupid inspections from USPH."

Three-buckets system…? USPH…?

She's ready to investigate on that… but all of a sudden a loud laughter twists their heads to the left. There is cause of the distraction: those three European-looking men.

One of them, paled-skinned, who's wearing Lenin's style frames, freezes his eyes on her dress. Then, very slowly moves them up and sets into hers.

We can play this game forever.

She remembers how good she was at it at school. He starts approaching… perhaps he's figured it out too.

"Mary Ann, you're back! The last time we saw each other you said: "I'm done with this shit!"

"I know, Damir, I know… well, here I am once again. Those last two months of freedom had flown in a blink of an eye… How much do you have left, dear?"

"I'm right in the middle of it, three and a half. New friend of yours?"

His eyes return into the game.

"Well, we've just met, but I'm sure that with time we will become great friends.

"Let me introduce you to Ania. Ania, this is Damir. We've known each other for years."

"Ania… Eastern European?"

"From Poland. Correct."

His hand has a surprisingly soft touch in comparison to his eyes.

"Damir from Croatia. Nice to meet you."

"I don't think you want to be late."

"Good point. Then, I guess… see you around?"

"Well, where else could I go?"

His smile is softer than his touch.

She catches his wink sent to Mary Ann.

"Ho! Ho! He likes you! Good for you, he's really a great guy.

"Very respected here, no one dares to mess around with him. Very loyal, incredibly smart."

"Not my type. What does he do, by way?"

"He is a waiter. One of the best, very close to the maître d."

One of the best…? Let me decide on that…

The ice melts down, breaks into pieces to then vanish into a silver space.

She heard about it over and over that what's visible is only twenty percent, the other eighty of the glacier remains underneath the crystal sphere, undiscovered, unseen to the eye, yet still captivating to any passenger.

Somewhere there lives a mystery, those quiet secrets of planet Earth, and from now on, there will be hers too, since it was here, in Alaska, where her heart was broken again…

The cleanest air goes into her lungs as she recalls Sylwia's words:

"When you're there, the time flies…"

In less than a week, she'll be gone from "Horizon," the second ship she has joined.

But before she says "goodbye"… those images keep playing in her mind… four eyes appear from behind the curtain as soon as she has just pulled it aside…

"How could you…? I have transferred here for you…" She put the key to his cabin down on his desk… turned around without a breath… but also without a single tear shed…

"The ships toughen you." The crewmembers had said. Now she knows they were right.

"Time is the best doctor, Wnusiu…" Grandma used to say…

Somehow she knows that with that time those images will fade away…

Ahead of her the most glorious nature plays music on instruments made of ice.

Perhaps Damir has served his purpose... we were from different worlds anyway…

She recalls how many cruises it took before she gave him a chance… but it was his persistence that won him to be her date…

She recalls what the people were saying… that he had problems with the Serbian mafia, borrowed some money and had to run away to stay alive…

"Come on, girl, that's why he's on the ships!" The words were flying around.

"They're jealous because they want what we've got." That was his response to it.

Indeed he had proven himself. He was caring, loving, protecting her from any harm… and became her best friend and the wisest teacher who explained what powers governed the crew- members' lives.

"What counts here, Ania, are connections, ranks, and sex. It's who you sleep with, who in power likes you, and if you are part of the crew or the staff. Always remember that."

She did remember and didn't have to learn it the hard way. Luckily, unlike many other girls was always accepted by the high-ranking officers. Luckily had a great boyfriend who, as she found out for a fact, was one of the best waiters a dining room has ever had.

The time was flew when they were together… week after week, month after month, the same itinerary was repeated, the same ports were seen, the same beaches were laid on and the same Ocean was dived.

She served those drinks. She cleaned those bars for the visits from USPH.

She showed up on time and got those great tips, just as Sylwia has said…

Another blow of cold wind brings her awareness back to deck ten and hits her with a realization to go down to the cabin and to warm herself up.

The bed brings simple comfort, the TV's remote control a chance to distract from the shroud of Damir's guilty face stamped inside her mind…

She will do anything to find a relief, even watch CNN with a red endless stripe that keeps cutting through a screen.

And as the words unfold she forgets about her pain as she reads them:

"Paris… Ritz… Princess Diana… a tunnel… a car accident…"

CHAPTER 10

Klaus

44

The apartment has 46 square meters. The living room and the kitchen are one. Her decision to have no walls in between them was based on having more access to light.

And so, this light comes in through the big windows, which both face the West, and then spreads out freely around an open space.

It reaches the entrance hall that has a floor covered with terracotta tiles.

It touches salmon paint on the walls and a mirror in a golden frame hangs on the left side.

It flies over the doors to the bathroom and moves onto those to the walk-in closet that she intended to have, for here she can finally organize all of her shoes and clothing; this is her flat that has been visualized for 26 years.

It has come to fruition. It has turned into a tangible fact.

The only thing during the moving-in process, which was disturbing the joy she was feeling in her heart, was that invisible critic constantly talking inside her head:

"It was Father's money that bought it, not yours, which after two contracts on the ships you should already have saved. Where did it all go?" The critic kept asking, reminding her of the problem…

Yes... I know... I am spending the money as soon as it touches my hand...

Maybe this new job at Sephora will help to solve it for good... the salary they've offered me is great...

She gazes around her new space, realizing that everything came to her at once…

Why do I feel like still, something is missing...?

WHAT YOU ARE MISSING IS... LOVE...

The Voice says from inside.

"May I please speak to Ania?" an unfamiliar voice asks.

"This is she…"

A quick scan through her memory, still she no idea who's on the other side…

His voice sounds deep… could it be his age? And rusty… could it be his addiction to cigarettes?

"I'm glad you're the right person! For a moment I thought that agency was a scam. And, as for the first impression, that would be a real shame."

"Agency…?" Once more she digs into her memory file.

"Do you recall, Mrs. Helena, International Matrimonial Agency? Does it ring any bells?"

"Oh… yes! "That" agency…!" Suddenly her memory gets a flash.

It was a few months ago when impulsively, she responded to a newspaper ad and sent her precise description of what she was looking for in a man:

"Tall, handsome, intelligent, can be older, no problem with that, travels a lot, has a great sense of humor, open-minded, genuine, well-educated, kind, and if he's got some sense of fashion that would be great. He's honest, supportive, has an interest in art, also financially successful because it says a lot about a man."

"So, you do remember? I'm not calling the wrong girl?"

"No, you are not. That was me. Sorry for confusing you in the first place."

"Oh… what a relief… my name is Klaus Zoltz. I've read your profile about a hundred times."

"A hundred times, maybe a bit too many?"

"Perhaps, but considering that I got very impressed?"

"Impressed, by what?"

"Well, obviously by your looks, but even more so about your absolute clarity of what you're looking for in a man."

"True, I do know exactly, although, I'm still clarifying it."

"Of course, you will until you find your perfect match. So you currently live in Poland, is that information correct?"

"Yes, how about you, Klaus?"

"In Istanbul."

Hmm, that's quite far away…

"Turkish, are you, really? I can hear some German accent in your voice?"

"Good ear, I'm originally from Dusseldorf. My company transferred me here in 1994."

"I see. Do you like living there?"

"Very much, I love the culture and the energy of this town… the recent earthquake has really affected us…"

"I saw it on the news… so many victims… it was horrible to watch…"

"Seventeen thousand, I've joined the rescue team."

Wow… that's a noble act…

"…I had to do something, could not just look at their pain from the comfort of my home…"

"I admire it…"

"Thank you… I felt an urge to be a human… to react… to help… in any way I can…"

I wish I could be more like him… sometimes I feel that all I care about is myself…

"I have no access to your profile."

"Right, the agency provides full information only to the men… Well, let me tell you a bit about me. I'm divorced, have no children; last month I turned forty-five…"

Seventeen years of age difference…? How is this is going to work for us…?

"I'm the CEO of a German company that designs water pumps. No-too-sexy field." His voice softens a bit from the way he laughs.

"But you, Ania, seem to have a much more colorful job, at Sephora, I've read?"

"Yes, just got the offer, it hasn't started yet. First, there's training in Warsaw, after that the opening of a new store. They're part of the LVMH group."

"Their president is Bernard Arnault."

"You know it? Now I am impressed…"

"Of course I do. I collect fragrances. I love beautiful bottles and smells."

Interesting…

"So, which one is your favorite?

"Well, there are many… but if I have to pick up only one, then I would probably have to say Dior's Fahrenheit."

"Hmm… really?"

"Is there something wrong with my choice?"

"Not at all, it just says a lot about personality traits."

"Oh, does it? You're much more intriguing than I've already thought…"

You bet!

"Anyway, Klaus, not to be rude, but I am supposed to meet with a friend."

"Yes, of course… Is it okay to call you tomorrow? What time would be best?"

Hmm... the guy is on fire... and actually, I don't mind...

Taking a minute to think it over is a great tactic that works on any guy, almost as if when they're uncertain their interest always goes up.

"Tomorrow… I can't."

"How about Friday?"

"Friday… I guess that should be fine…"

"All right, I will try you on Friday, maybe then you will expand my consciousness."

His voice sounds like he has just hit the jackpot and is ready to celebrate with a glass of champagne.

"Your consciousness, excuse me?"

"Explain my personality traits."

"Oh, those… right… right…"

That's amazing... he's paid attention to every word I've said...

A headphone is detached from her ear, no wonder it has gotten hot.

Two hours and fifteen minutes...? Not bad for the first-time chat!

Swiss chocolates, supposedly the best ones in the world, next to a glass of French champagne and a bestselling book that she has recently bought are placed on a tray table at the front of her.

If excitement could have wings, then hers would be now flying faster than this plane.

Maybe it could even catch up with speeding events taking place in the last two weeks.

Like getting a new cell phone, like falling in love, like being on the way to meet with "Mr. Right" because there is a big chance that's who Klaus is.

Logically thinking, what kind of a guy calls a woman three times per day and flies her to meet him first class? Only serious men go through such afford. If they have zero interest they don't waste their time.

Heart-shaped chocolate melts in her mouth in a cliché velvet way, proving that indeed Swiss ones are the best.

As soon as its rich flavor disappears from her sense of taste, her sense of smell takes over.

Lily mixed with violet... definitely-rose... jasmine in heart's note... sandalwood in the base...

She breaks down the ingredients ready to confirm the name.

"Pleasures" by Estee Lauder, is that what you're wearing ma'am?"

Grace Kelly's haircut turns an ageless face toward her.

"What a great nose, miss. Yes, that is correct."

"I thought so; it suits you well. Where are you traveling to?"

"Zurich then to Geneva; that's where I live. How about you, miss?"

"To Istanbul."

The details I will spare.

"I've heard that Switzerland is a very beautiful place. Hopefully, I'll be able to visit it one day."

"I'm sure you will. Indeed it's beautiful. So let me ask you..." The woman's eyes move to the cover of the book.

"...was it a passion for alchemy that has attracted you to this read? Because that's not quite what it is about."

"Oh... I haven't started it yet..."

"Very good, so now having a new awareness you can approach it with the right mind."

"What do you mean?"

"Well, all I can say that although it's written in simple words the truth it delivers is incredibly profound."

A woman smiles, and with an unquestionable class, brings an ageless face to the previous spot.

She reaches for the novel and, as if her future depends on it, opens up to a random page,

"WHEN YOU WANT SOMETHING THE WHOLE UNIVERSE CONSPIRES IN HELPING YOU TO ACHIEVE IT…"

The words jump out at her face…

The carousel's been set into motion, its red light flashes above the belt, aligning with a disturbing sound of a siren that is so loud it could wake up a dead man in his grave.

Luckily, the suitcase has made the journey. It slowly approaches from afar, and as her hand is getting ready to pull it, she exhales with relief.

It's here, thank God...

There's only one chance to make a first impression, therefore it has to be great. The looks have been selected by the theme "sexy-modern-confident." The knowledge of how to put things together is quite useful when dealing with men since they are all visual creatures-this lesson she has already learned.

The cell phone buzzes with a brand new message: "Can't wait to see you, waiting outside."

She brushed her hair, applies lip-gloss, and now her spine can straighten up.

Time to put these heels into work and give her confidence an extra boost, although currently, it's not lacking anything, but it might be very soon… To be exact, less than five minutes is how long it should take to reach the exit door… Then, once it opens up, she will enter a reality zone…

Face to face could kill this dream so beautifully built over the phone, and after it dies, the importance it held for her no one will ever know…

But for now, when it's still alive, it means everything; it's love, it's romance, it's relationship with a successful man, it's a chance to build a family, it's a future without needing to work, it's that closet filled with designer stuff, it's those trips to take around the world...

There is so much we both have in common... I wouldn't be here otherwise...

I'm sure we will like each other... nothing to worry about...

Two more steps forward, two more clicks of the heels for the door to react...

It reads her presence and with one swoop slides to both sides.

Like a Polaroid's snapshot of the moment, a picture of the crowd jumps out of the people gathered in anticipation behind barricade's silver bars.

These bars force her feet to turn left... she obeys a direction... goes along and there... sees his eyes hitting her figure like an x-ray scan...

I think he likes me...

Her walk continues toward his face that seems to have much softer expression than in the pictures he'd mailed to her.

His hair reminds her of Thomas Gottschalk's, the same color, almost the same cut, maybe just not as long as that German TV host's got...

He mentioned he was done with work for today yet strangely his body seems stressed...

Tense but quite handsome...

Her smile grows bigger, seeing him looking younger than his age.

"Hello, Schatz. You made it." His hand comes out of his pocket to wrap around her waist.

"And you are beautiful," he whispers, "But I was expecting that."

This means "approved." She comes to a quick conclusion allowing his hug to naturally end.

"Thank you, Klaus. Well, I guess no more phone conversations... here we are... face to face..."

Even with a straight look into his eyes, still she can't decide if the phone-call-only-relationship was a better place to stay.

"And so? How is it? Do you like me?"

Oh wow, he is direct...

Her instinct chooses the right answer.

"I think you already know."

"Wunderbar Schatz, I like hearing that. If that's the case then let's go!"

His hand makes a rapid move toward hers. She's just released it from pulling on the bag to now let it be completely dominated by his bossy strength.

"How was the flight? Did you enjoy it?"

He keeps on walking as if they are running out of time.

"Yes, thank you for flying me the first class. I read an amazing book…"

It may not be his topic...

"Fantastic, Schatz, luxury is a necessity in my life."

And, I was right...

"Beautiful weather…" She catches some breath, already regretting not wearing flats.

"Yes, Istanbul has this kind of weather throughout most of the year."

His lips do the talking while his eyes zoom down her legs.

"Nice. Slim and long. They were the first thing I noticed when you came out of the plane."

"Oh really, my legs were first?"

"Yes, Schatz, I was watching them. That's what turns me on."

His voice gets deeper, his grasp tighter. His walk changes its pace.

Hmm... maybe it's good that he's so straightforward... it will make it easier for us to communicate...?

The walk ends next to the silver "Pajero." A Jeep was not the car she would expect him to have.

He throws the luggage in the back and heavy-handedly shuts the door.

Inside, she can finally slow down and take a look around his space.

The car is immaculately clean; no signs of rubbish; only a few organized documents.

In the air, hangs the smell left by two companions he must enjoy the most; an extra-strong cigarette and his dog.

He turns on the engine and, as if being chased, steps on the gas.

Wow... very aggressive...

44

Her thoughts are kept silent, too early to comment on his driving style.

"We will take a few roads through the city so you can get a sneak-peak. Then, I'll check you in The Ciragan Kempinsky; my assistant has just confirmed."

"Thank you, Klaus, that's very generous. I would be just as happy with a regular hotel."

Without asking for her permission, his hand reaches out for a cigarette.

"Of course, I know that you would, Mein Hertz."

Why I don't say that I hate smoking...?

The inner battle begins in her.

"Are you familiar with Kempinsky?"

"No, I'm not. But I do trust your judgment, one hundred percent."

Clearly, she should use compliments more often; they seem to be taking his tension away.

"Oh, Schatz... you're so polite. So, please tell me, where do you see yourself in the next five years?"

She ponders for a second.

"Where I don't know yet but with whom I think I can already tell."

Why am I doing it...? I don't even know him... people can say anything over the phone... but... maybe I'm overreacting...? He seems like a good man...

"Oh dear, you are so sweet."

The cigarette is put aside.

The traffic is steadily growing, a sign they must be entering the town.

Indeed, as if they've driven into a different dimension, everything shows up all at once: cars, bicycles, people, even some ponies that have riders on their little backs.

The past blends present with the future into one Istanbul world. She's read about this city and how it stood the test of time...

So much history here... what a unique mix...

Outside the window, the noise intensifies... The crowd is getting bigger...

She's never seen anything like it before...

How people can even co-exist without killing each other or completely losing it? There must be some kind of rhythm that controls this mess...

"What the fuck?" All of a sudden she bashes the horn with his furious hand.

She lands on her seat from a jump.

"Did you see that fucking bastard?! He just cut me off!"

Oh wow, what an attitude... is this the kind of man that I want?

Without a word of reaction, she moves her attention away, thinking that a strong man can be sexy, but about an aggressive one? For that she could not care less.

Good thing this city is filled with things to distract her, and so the subject to clean the air is found very fast.

"That's an area affected by the earthquake, isn't it Klaus?" She points at the hills where the ruins lay flat like the decks of cards.

The steam carries out his answer.

"Yes. It was there. Correct."

She looks closer at those bricks which put thousands of lives to an unnecessary end...

A few months ago, they used to be homes and then, within barely a few minutes, people lost everything...

"That what as true tragedy... We should really appreciate what we have... Look..." She points at the hill, "...if this doesn't change one's perspective then what else would? I don't know... Don't you agree with me, Klaus?"

Another cigarette is on its way.

Whatever nicotine does to his nerves it's something good.

He turns to her with a smile as soon as it's inhaled.

"What I do know is that I'm incredibly lucky to find a woman like you, especially through a Matrimonial Agency I considered to be a scam."

"Well, sometimes life writes a story that could make a great screenplay one day."

"So true, dear, so true..." he says, leaning on the steering wheel, preparing to take a turn. The road falls down like a ribbon, leaving no choice but to go with its flow.

The closer they get to the end of it, the more of the view gets revealed and the more she comes to understand how he defines "luxury"…

There… that Moorish style building… it absolutely delights… it must be it…

"Schatz, this is Kempinsky, it used to be Ottoman's Palace."

Palace… that would explain its beauty… its breathtaking magnificence…

"Bosphorus River is right behind it. Later on, we will take a walk."

Her mind tries to wrap around scenery unlike anything she had ever seen.

Maybe except those travel channels, but TV doesn't count, this is in full 3-D.

The valet boy appears from nowhere.

"Welcome back, Mr. Zoltz."

Welcome back…? Hmm… I'm not sure this is a good sign…

Concerns need to be put on pause because of another man who pops up in a red uniform with a golden tag…

"Butler-Evren." She reads it quickly.

"Mr. Zoltz, as usual, room 205?"

As "usual"?

"Yes, Evren, that would be great!"

"Wonderful, sir."

"When we have business visits in town my company always books this hotel."

She didn't ask for an explanation; he must have read her mind because she put on her poker face. Men hate insecure women; hopefully, she won't be perceived as one.

They step into a hallway, straight onto a marble floor that's been polished to such a degree that it has become the longest mirror of all. And now, this mirror reflects everything that hangs above their heads. Including those massive chandeliers that a gentle wind has just caressed and created a sound of the purest crystal to drift by passing guests…

How strange… but none of them are walking…? They all seem to be floating in the air…?

"Schatz, are you okay?" His voice pulls her back.

"Yes… yes… I am… I just adore this hotel…"

"Glad to hear it, Mein Heartz."

The butler points at the lift.

"Only two floors, Mademoiselle."

But of course 205! That's common sense.

"I'll take it from here. Apres Vu."

The door is pushed by the bossy hand.

The canopy bed appears, on the right.

Not a single king would refuse to spend here several nights in it.

Across from the bed, stands the mahogany desk that, any writer would appreciate because, he could to start that one book that would later on sell all around the world.

And, there, in that massive armchair placed under the lamp, an exhausted businessman could finally stop his hustle, exhale, and slow down.

Her eyes move to the round table placed near the balcony…

Is this set up for real…? Or am I dreaming it…?

One-touch confirms that the silver ice bucket is as cold as the pink bottle of champagne chilling inside of it.

"Crystal…" She reads the name and touches the tall roses waiting in the vase… They have the softest petals her fingers have ever felt… There's got to be at least two dozen… all in her favorite color of light tea…

He remembered it…

"Klaus… you are so thoughtful… thank you so much for doing this…"

His eyes must have been anticipating her response, for they meet hers as soon as she turns around.

"Oh, Schatz… it's my pleasure, I am the luckiest man. Somehow we were able to meet in this crazy world. Do you like this room?" he asks while scanning the walls.

"Of course I do. You don't?"

"Not so much. Evren!"

"Yes, sir?" The butler didn't make it too far.

"We would like to exchange this room for 805!"

"Not a problem, sir. Let me confirm with the front desk."

"There is a much better view, Mein Hertz."

A reminder to self: "Do not question his actions, even when they don't make sense."

"And this, too; take care of that."

The bossy hand points at the flowers and champagne.

"Absolutely, Mr. Zoltz"

There's no point to object his will, only to return to the previous spot, which elevates them once again.

There couldn't be a better moment for wearing her poker face than now.

"Schatz, let's have a toast on the balcony."

Champagne is divied out. He pops up the cork as if he just won the Formula 1 Championship.

The bubbles start buzzing. The lace curtains slowly fall over their backs.

His hand lifts the glass.

"For our meeting, I'm glad that you came."

A formal kiss seals her lips before her heart has a chance to be expressed.

For our love... she thinks her toast and, promises herself, she-will not complain. Instead, she will take a seat on his lap, so united they can contemplate the view ahead.

The first one of those thousand nights to come...

Has Scheherazade asked all the stars to appear and wished the best of luck to them?

Or have they shown up to highlight the bridge that brings together two continents?

Or was it the restaurant that put a request for their light to shine over the tables while dinner is being served?

"Excuse me. Let me get up." All of a sudden her body is pushed away, and his face turns into a stranger, who walks back into the room and sits down under the lamp.

In a complete shock, she's unable to move...

Over the phone, he seemed too cool to lose control of himself...

Long-distance is enough of a challenge for their relationship...

The curtain falls in the opposite way as she settles on the floor by his legs.

"Klaus, talk to me, what's going on…? Why are you upset?"

His eyes stare at the Persian rug without a single blink.

"This is not going to work."

"What do you mean?"

"The two of us, you're not the woman I thought you would be."

She hears it and wishes to be deaf so these words wouldn't hurt her ears…

"Klaus, I just arrived… you must give us some time to get to know each other…"

"There is nothing "I MUST"! Nothing! Do you hear me, girl?!"

She has underestimated the potential his anger has…

As if a fire alarm went on, he rises up from the chair.

BREATHE… DON'T REACT… DO NOT SAY A WORD…

the Voice says inside of her.

"First thing in the morning, I'm changing your flight. The butler will give you the details. A taxi will pick you up."

His back does the talking.

"Good that you came. Now we have zero regrets."

The door gets shut. Her eyes freeze on the "Do not disturb!" sign that dingles on a little gold chain. After a few seconds, it stops and just hangs over a small silver hook. The silence is almost complete, if not for this fizzing champagne that has not been consumed…

And it won't be since there's nothing to celebrate besides spending a night in a five-star hotel.

Her knees hit the floor… Is there anyone who can explain any of that…?

Is there anyone who can tell her what went wrong… and why men always leave her with a broken heart?

Why is it so difficult for her to have a relationship?

Perhaps her crying is too loud for the divine answer to come…

"Are you kidding me, Ania?!"

"No, Aga, I'm not... That's what has happened last night... it was crazy..."

"I can't believe this! And he seemed so classy...?! What a jerk! Listen, you're in big trouble; I'm catching the first plane."

What a great friend who calls to check if she's all right, and is even willing to fly over to pull her out of this Turkish mess.

"No, Aga... please don't... I'll be fine."

"Did he call you today? "

"Nope, he did not..."

She checks the time; 11 am.

"The butler has mentioned that my flight leaves at six pm."

"Seriously, when he does, tell him to go fuck himself!"

"You know I won't, I never speak to people this way."

"Well, you should. He needs to hear these words!"

Suddenly a front door echos two heavy knocks.

"What was that?"

"Room service... I guess...?"

A strange feeling goes through her skin, telling her she may be wrong...

"Did you order anything?"

"Breakfast, a while ago... Let me get it, Aga, please, don't hang up..."

"No worries, I won't."

Again, two more knocks, much louder this time.

She presses on the handle... opens the door and... stops.

A "nothing has happened" smile appears in front of her.

"Good morning, Schatz, did you sleep well?"

She has no moves, breath or words; for what's there to say when the pain is still fresh?

It's better to remain numb.

"Can I come in, please...? I know that you're upset..."

Upset?! He must be joking...! It wasn't me who exploded last night!

"Go ahead. I'm on the phone." Her hand makes a gesture. He has paid for this luxurious experience, she almost forgot.

"Of course, Mein Hertz..."

Can he at least save me that insincere sweet crap?!

“Aga, it’s him.”

“What? He’s there? Put that jerk on the phone! I want to talk to him!”

“No, Aga, no… I can handle it myself I’ll call you later… during the day, all right?”

As if a vulture has landed right behind her back, she feels his ears absorbing every spoken word.

“If you need help, call me right away. Promise me, Ania, I don’t trust this man…”

“I promise. Thank you for being such a good friend.”

“Be careful. Love you!”

“Love you too!” The headphone is put down.

“It sounds so sexy when you speak Polish, Mein Hertz.”

It’s time to face it and be done with it.

“Why are you here, Klaus? What do you want from me?”

From numbness to strength, her face shows everything.

“I came to apologize for what happened last night. You didn’t deserve any of it… I tend to lose control… and then… after…” His eyes drop down, “I deeply regret…”

Well, sometimes for those regrets it’s already too late.

Stillness is always the best choice when one’s uncertain what action to take.

“Sincerely, I’m sorry, give me another chance to make it up…”

JUST WATCH AND LISTEN… DO NOTHING ELSE…

the Voice says from inside.

“There’s chemistry between us and that’s hard to find…”

For sure, talking from lots of experience with those girls who had stayed at 205.

“Today, if you allow me, I would love to show you around. You have not even seen the city and you’ve come from so far…”

Oh, how concerned he sounds; it almost makes me believe that he cares?

“And, I’d love you to visit my house and meet my family. My parents can’t wait to be introduced to that special Polish girl…”

Introduce me to his parents? What the heck? Today I'm special, but yesterday it was not going to work?

"Besides, you can meet Sebastian too!"

And now this... he even uses his dog as an argument!

Of course, he does! He knows that watching *"Lassie Come Home"* was one of her favorite things when she was a little girl.

Sebastian being the same breed as Lassie had added more excitement to this trip. She was never allowed to have a dog since The Parents decided it would be too much work. Work or no work, no human loves like a dog does, and that's what she should do, get one a soon as she returns home...

"So what will you say, Mein Hertz?"

No bending, I've got to be firm.

"I'll say that in eight hours I have to catch a plane."

"You don't have to go... I apologize..." His begging eyes keep staring at hers.

"Come on, Schatz. It was our first fight; we'll get over it."

But how about the first impression, that's been forever engraved?

She has to sit down to process it... look at each angle... consider every fact...

Last night, in her prayer, she asked God to bring him back...

And here he is; isn't it strange...? Could it be a sign they can work it out? Shall she put pride aside... forgive... and forget? Still... there's something about him that she cannot resist... not sure if it's his charisma, his money, or his confidence.

Besides, nobody is perfect; people make mistakes.

But what if... in the middle of town... he goes crazy again?

Well, then she can call Aga, and together they will figure it out... At least she could see Istanbul, that's worth the sacrifice...

"Okay, Klaus, I will stay as we originally planned."

Hopefully, I won't be the one who deeply regrets that...

"Oh, Schatz, we've made peace! I'm so glad! We're going to have the most amazing day! I promise you. Have you already had breakfast?"

"Not yet."

"Great, neither have I. Let's have it in the restaurant downstairs. It's next to The Palace."

"But I've ordered room service."

"I will cancel it, Mein Hertz!"

Again her hand is pulled. Although today his touch seems less intense.

They fly outside the building where the sun requires shades.

"Let's go inside The Palace. Oh, you will love the design."

Why not? She would rather explore an area than sit down and eat. Food has never been on the top of her priority list, not like shoes, clothes, and, trips. That's what holds the most value to her: experiencing things and looking damn good while doing it.

Therefore, her lip gloss matches her hot pink top and her eyeshadow matches her khaki pants. The entire outfit fits her like a glove because in showing off her great shape she finds confidence.

His confidence must be found in his purposeful walk that takes them toward the massive doors on the top of the marble stairs…

Not a tiny bit of dirt appears underneath their feet.

"Truly impressive, Klaus…"

"Oh yes! But wait till you see what's inside."

And soon as he says it, they step into the white space the white marble covers every inch of the floor… and every inch of the ceiling… and every inch of the walls …

Those Ottomans were not cheap… she thinks, experiencing his hand pulling hers higher and higher until they reach the first floor.

Suddenly, his body pushes hers to the nearest wall…

Pressed by his chest, she can hardly breathe… His strong hands hold her face between them…

Her lips are forced to a kiss, unable to escape his dry mustache…

She gives up the struggle and waits until he's done…

"No," is not an acceptable answer, more evidence of it.

"All right, let's eat! Are you hungry, Schatz?"

She brings herself back together to respond,

"Very much."

After this experience, food may go up on her priority list.

They find an empty table; a young waiter lands by their side.

"Good morning, sir. Good morning, miss. My name is Kaim."

The boy receives her friendliest smile, for she still remembers how much it meant to her when those passengers on the ships were kind to her.

"Three scrambled eggs, no bacon, two extra croissants, and a large bottle of Perrier. That's it for now. Oh, and coffee! Hot and fast! Hurry up!"

He speaks to him like the boy is his slave...?

"Yes, sir... of course..."

"The boss" reaches out for his nicotine.

Shall I even mention that smoking on an empty stomach is one of the worst things?

Two minutes pass by, and he starts to move as if being attacked by millions of invisible ants.

"Where the heck is my coffee?!"

"You've just ordered it, Klaus, relax."

Maybe because they're in public he doesn't bark back.

A silver pot appears in front of them.

"And why has it taken forever?!" His eyes are full of hate.

"Sir... I truly apologize..." If the boy could, he would already run away.

She takes on the mission to rescue an innocent.

"Thank you, Kaim, it was very fast. What a great service, we appreciate it."

"Please enjoy, miss, and let me know if I can be of any more help..." The boy bows down, connecting with her eyes.

Absolutely pathetic!

She turns to him, disgusted.

"So, Klaus, what's your plan for today?"

Let's talk in his language and see how he likes that.

"Right, Schatz. Here's the list: The Hagia Sophia, Turkish Market, and after it, my place."

He says in one breath, on the second coffee cup and, already the third cigarette.

"Sounds good, are you ready?!"

How about for a change she'll be in charge?

Perhaps a woman who dares to be brave takes him by surprise. He leans over to try to kiss her.

"Schatz, you're a very special woman…"

Instinctively, she backs up. His words are irrelevant for they are not the precursors of what will come.

"Thanks! How long does it take to get over there?"

Can't she be in a rush too? *Oh, this can be fun! Let's play his game!*

"To the Hagia Sophia about half an hour; on Sunday, traffic isn't too bad."

"Wonderful. What are we waiting for?!"

"Hmm… you're excited… I like it a lot…" His body moves closer but people's eyes make it stop. There it is; she found the way to deal with this man.

Mirroring his attitude is the approach she will take, and that means setting the radio's volume higher than she ever would for herself… And then patiently holding to the noise, all the way, until he parks the car, takes her by the hand, and says:

"This is her, the Hagia Sophia, a one-thousand-four-hundred-year-old mosque; used to be the largest church in the world."

She looks up at the four towers shooting high into the sky. In the middle of them, a huge dome humbles any believe, either one of Allah or God.

Regardless of one's faith, the sun equally shines on every entering neck.

Her eyes circulate the walls, which are covered with white-blue mosaic tiles and touched by some golden Arabic words.

The main hall is guarded by columns wrapped up with those tiles. The ceiling is painted with saints and Christ. They are holding onto their holy books with skinny long-fingered hands.

Small windows permit daylight to come in and blend with hundreds of candles placed over huge stands.

And then she hears a man's cry… it comes from the side… repeating the same words…

"It's time for prayer." He leans toward her.

"What is he saying?"

"Allah is great…"

She looks to the right where a group of men keep bowing down their backs.

"Follow me, Schatz." His voice pulls her out of the bliss. His hand guides the way.

The darkness gets darker the lower they find themselves.

The smell of dampness goes into her nose.

The water starts to drop.

He whispers into her ear, "It's Basilica cistern... a Hidden Underground World..."

A statue of Medusa appears from an orange scene... The highlighted pillars show the only path... above the canals... underneath the ball-shaped lamps...

She grabs the camera and, preparing to take a shot, feels that after this trip is done those pictures will be the only things that will remain.

And so she presses on the button, several times, just in case...

CHAPTER 11

A Year

An indecisive rain hangs in the clouds. She looks down and counts the steps.

July's streets are empty and missing life. The air prepares for the news to break.

Time moves slowly and wants to be reversed to an hour ago when she still had the job…

It took a few minutes for the garment of her life to be turned inside out…

It took a few words for her joy to be destroyed… and one decision for her stability to be gone…

The manager's voice is stuck in her head and keeps validating her corporate worth: "We're not extending the contract with you. Take your stuff. You're allowed to go."

She reaches the corner and stops on the top of the hill. Down there a short distance away is where her mind will find some hope.

The Parents will comfort her in her pain, will shine light over the loss, and from Their experience, will help to understand why in spite of commitment, great product knowledge, and high sales, Sephora's manager had let her go…?

"Your monthly reports are full of mistakes; something the company cannot accept. As you know, our standards are very high."

Yes, but I could have corrected my mistakes if I was informed in advance...

Also, if they would give me given another chance, I could improve my skills...

So was it a true reason or do they already have a replacement for me?

"Unemployment rate has reached twenty-two percent." *the news recently says on TV...*

Favoritism! Of course! I should call the CEO!

An idea crosses her mind, but as brilliant as it seems, it quickly goes away, because how could she work for someone who has already fired her once…?

With each step she begins to realize that nothing is ever going to be the same… no income means "no- to buying clothes, "no- to taking trips and, "no"-to going out to dance…

From this moment on, every day will be deprived of those things her life has been defined by…

She looks at the green door, exhales a heavy breath, and slowly drags herself inside.

As usual, the water runs in the sink. Mother's eyes move away from the wet pots.

"Oh, Ania, aren't you supposed to be at work?"

Somehow a mother can always tell when something is wrong with her child.

The words hesitate to give a response as if they don't want the reality to be verbalized.

"What's going on? I can see it on your face." Mother investigates.

Sooner or later, They need to know anyhow…

"I just got fired." Her mouth spits out the news.

Father steps out of his room.

Their bodies turn into wax. Their eyes stop blinking. Their pupils do not move.

A minute in time to her it feels like a century.

"Fired…? Oh… no… my God…"

Mother leans on the wall.

Father stands still. And then, as always when he disapproves of things, his head starts to shake to the sides.

"How could it happen…? I don't understand…" The Megaphone of Mother's voice keeps coming even while her back is turned.

"Mom… I don't know… that place meant everything to me…" Her voice is breaking down. "It was my passion… I enjoyed working there…"

She tastes the first tear, salty and wet, and as the second one is about to come down, Mother bounces of the wall, straightens her posture, and says:

"You must have said something rude to the boss! I told you to be nice and never criticize those above you. That's why they have fired you!"

Her veins suddenly become cold… as if the blood stopped running inside of them…

Her eyes lose the sight, for the contrast is fading away…

"How… can you say it, Mom? Don't you see that I am in pain…?"

"Have you at least saved any money?! Of course, you have not! I'm sure you have spent everything on stuff! But what did I tell you? To save! And now what are you going to do? Do you know how high the unemployment rate is?"

Suddenly, Father gets his voice back.

"It's twenty-two percent."

Now it's his gun that's fired up with bullets made of words.

"But that's how you raised her, she cannot hold onto anything, an absolutely hopeless case. Will never achieve anything in life."

She stands there wondering, if there is God… could he now come down from heaven to rescue her from this hell…?

An overwhelming sadness floods over her heart…

"You know what…?" She looks at Them like it's a tennis match.

"I really thought that you would show some compassion, some understanding, but of course, you have to criticize me again. Well, that's what you have always done, so why am I still surprised…?"

"Don't you dare to speak to your Parents like that!" Father's voice goes up another notch.

"Like what? Like telling the truth about how I feel? But you can criticize me as much as you want? Where there is logic in this?"

"Look at her, if she's so smart, then why she has lost her job?!"

Through tears, she watches his back return to his cave. The door gets shut in front of her eyes.

The Mother returns to wet pots, indeed the most important things, for in this household, it's what stands for luxury and success.

An indecisive rain still hangs in the clouds. She looks down, no longer counting the steps… but instead the number of breaths that she must take in before reaching her flat.

Bundled up on the floor, she holds on to her knees, and in this self-created shell, wants to disappear.

The front door behind is locked and knowing it brings her sense of peace that there's nobody who could enter and disturb her tears.

Paper box seats nearby with no tissue left inside… but that's all right since a three-hour-long cry is almost over anyway…

She lifts up her head and looks straight ahead; there, at the end of a corridor, rests her companion, his soft belly moves under his dog's REM. His furry legs are running through some happy dreamlands.

When she saw him at first, he was still a blind pup, the smallest Collie from the pack of nine. Then barely five weeks old, he moved in here and started to measure her unemployed time…

She named him "Nori," which in Assyrian means "Light."

That light is something a depressed mind cannot find…

For this the place where she recently started living… where sadness… sorrows… despair… is what wakes her u… and where the self-judgment… loneliness… and regrets are what put her to sleep…

Unrecognizable to herself almost, she wonders, if she got possessed by some estranged energy…?

Because this body that she used to dress up, pamper, and move in passionate dance, is now at risk of being overmedicated or cut. What will the end be? She has not decided yet…

It can be anything as long as it helps to exit this state… because in it nothing is worth living, or excites, or makes sense…

How ironic…

She gazes around her apartment… there is the newest TV set… there is the closet full of trendy clothes, but none of it counts… Unmerciful depression has washed all the joys away…

As it did with most of her friends who had abandoned the ship of her social life as soon as it started to sink under poverty's wave.

"Hard times will show you who your real friends are."

What used to be only a quote has turned into a tangible experience in her life.

What we will do, Nori…? How are we going to survive…?

And that visit that has happened two hours ago… just from thinking about it… she feels worse and worse…

Psychiatrists, she never believed in them since they live on people who are addicted to the stories they tell… and repeat them over and over again…

As Einstein had said:

"One will never find a solution to the problem with the same mind that has created that."

She couldn't agree more; there's no point to dwell on any pain, especially with a doctor whom she's never met.

But the Parents forced her to go since They were getting concerned.

And she went. Sat in front of the blank face and compassionless eyes that, per protocol, looked at her, for about two minutes, or perhaps even less.

Then, of course, came *the* question, many must have heard in that chair:

"Please tell me why are you feeling depressed?"

Standard permission was given to puke all the problems out of the chest. After, as often follows, "a happy drug" was prescribed as a universal fixer to anyone's broken life.

Father charmingly shook the psychiatrist's hand, completely unable to read what her true intent.

It's all about money..., she thought on their way out, and then overheard that:

"Her condition is really bad. Try to keep an eye on her and do not leave her alone since she can be unpredictable in her acts."

How thoughtful for a doctor to say that when the patient hasn't left, went through her mind just about when Father said back:

"Yes, doctor, of course, my wife and I will do our best."

Then, once they got into his car, everything turned to hell...

If she only knew that sharing her thoughts about how unprofessional and inconsiderate of her pain that psychiatrist was, would make him so furious... she would not have said a word...

But she did... and afterward, it was already too late to take it back...

Trapped in the passenger seat, she was bombarded by what he thinks of her.

His mouth was shooting out saliva, and his eyes were popping out of his face, that was turning burgundy.

In the meantime, her heart was pounding, her throat was getting dry, she couldn't catch her breath, and her knees were shaking from panic, and then he reached her limit.

"Stop it! Enough! Have you forgotten that you've taken me to the doctor because I am sick?!"

Indeed, he stopped.

Thank God they were at Their Place.

He parked the car… she got out… and then looked at him…

Those eyes of his… she will never forget… they were so full of hate.

"You whore! What did you just say to me?!"

She froze right where she stood, couldn't believe what came out of his mouth…

What had she done to deserve to be called such a name?

Her entire childhood flashed through her mind …

Those times when she was trying to be the best… it was for him… all those high grades, all those awards for the best student in class… all those sports disciplines she had attended just so he could impress his friends…

She never did drugs, never smoked cigarettes, never ran away from home, or got pregnant like other girls…

He had never valued me… to him, I was never good enough…

The realization hit her like a lightning bolt.

From a distance that was big enough, she saw him for who he truly was; a stranger, a cruel man… never an emotional support…

No more…

She ran upstairs, grabbed the leash, and pulled Nori out Their place.

Mother's voice was chasing after her… and calling her name.

The tears went on the street and continued until they reached her flat.

In silence, abandoned, terrified of the unknown… she sits on the floor, looking at Nori's peaceful sleeping, furry body…

Why did I get you when I cannot even take care of myself?

The Voice from within says softly:

HE HELPS YOU TO STAY ALIVE… DON'T GIVE UP… SOON THINGS WILL CHANGE…

44

The walls are splashed with golden light. The sun seems to be very generous today. There's something different about it. What exactly it is… she cannot tell…

Her back leans on the kitchen's counter. Her hand holds tight to the list with 48 names of companies that have already received her well-written CV.

Forty-eight, a rather significant number, yet not efficient enough if she is still unemployed… three weeks ago, on July 1st, the calendar has made a full-year mark.

To Nori, it meant his first birthday, to her an anniversary of the hardest times… without Mother's support, the bills wouldn't be paid… and very likely, she would have starved…

An unknown caller puts her cellphone into vibration.

"Hello? Yes?"

"Ania? This is Darek. How are you doing today?"

"Hi Darek. Well… what can I tell you…? I'm still alive…"

When cousin Hania got married to him, everyone was so glad that the newest edition to the family would be a man gifted in business skills, intelligent, humble, and polite.

"Oh, come on, Ania! Of course you are! Are you standing right now?"

"Yes… why are you asking? "

"I want you to sit down."

"Sit down…? Why? What's wrong?"

"Don't worry, it's nothing bad. I have great news. I found you a job!"

"A job…?" She almost faints.

"Yes, Ania, a job. Would you like to know what it is?"

"Yes… yes… of course…" Her voice blends with an avalanche of tears.

"It's on Danish ferry lines. Two weeks on-board and two weeks on land; they sail between Amsterdam and New Castle. The salary is great. Oh, one more thing… I'm sure you're going to like hearing this."

"Yes…?"

"You'll be working at the gift shops selling fragrances and make-up. Exciting, isn't it?! You like doing that, don't you?"

“Yes… I do… very much…”

“But first you must go through the training. It will be here in Gdynia, at the end of this month.”

“Darek,I don’t know what to say…”

“You don’t need to say anything. I know it’s been a challenging year. But listen, it’s over, so don’t look back anymore, okay?”

She stares ahead at the golden light still covering the wall. Was it why the sun seemed so generous today? Because it was preparing the atmosphere for this call?

“Thank you… for helping me…”

“Of course, we’re family. No more crying, okay?”

She sets the cell phone aside.

“Nori, come over here.”

Four legs quickly obey her command. And, as her face dives into his soft fur, she whispers into his ear:

“My boy… we have survived. Thank you… for that.”

CHAPTER 12

Face

44

He looks at her… She's terrified… Cold sweat comes over her skin… The space that surrounds her has no walls but a gray smoke that prevents her from being able to escape from him… Him… He who is in charge… one who only harms and never saves…

Under his eyes, shivering from fear, she's witnessing the devil himself…

His evil face hangs like a shroud… with black curly hair… untrimmed beard… and short mustache…

His vicious smile comes closer… gets darker… intensifies… and as he's about to tell her something… she wakes up…

Straightened up on her bed she can still feel his presence lingering inside…

An instinct moves her hand toward the curtain so the darkness can be dissolved by the bright sun.

Outside the porthole, the view of Dutch Port confirms that she has not overslept. The ferry is docked and the duty-free stores will open at 5 pm.

Although it's enough time for her to get ready, she jumps up on both feet like a soldier committed to a daily ritual, and on her way to the shower, turns on the radio, from which a German voice shouts out:

"Achtung! Achtung! Vereinigte Staaten!"

No music… hmm… very strange…

She carries her thought under hot water allowing it to wash a stigmatized image away from her head.

On the way out, she grabs a nametag and begins to proceed to deck three, for there in the crew- mess is where everyone gathers before starting the second shift.

The smell of food calls from a distance; so does a silence… unlike one she's ever heard…

Why is it so quiet…?

Curiosity pulls her inside. She steps in… and sees the ocean of heads…

All of those heads are turned toward a TV, captivated by the images it projects of the world-known skyscrapers that are recognized even by those who had never been there.

Hmm... maybe a trailer of the newest action movie...? she thinks while settling down.

"Oh my God, it's going to be a war…"

A neighbor's voice twists her neck to the right.

"What war? Are you crazy?"

The guy must not get enough rest... she thinks. His chin points up at the image.

"You don't know what's going on? They have attacked the United States…"

"They…? Who…?"

"The terrorists."

"Watch it, girl, this transmission is live…"

Her eyes join the ones already glued to the screen.

A plane hits the tower… A gray smoke comes out from the buildings… Hundreds of people are running away from an unmerciful plague of dust…

Oh my God... those are civilians...

She's hit with a realization that Hollywood has nothing to do with it…

"I… was… just there… three… years… ago…" her whisper is more to herself than to him.

"Lucky you, I may never be able to see it… this is the end of the world… "The towers falling"; Nostrodamus had prophesied it…"

As their eyes meet one another's they are not strangers anymore.

"We may not leave the harbor tonight. They've said that all airports have been closed…

Jesus Christ…!" His chair lands on the floor.

"PENTAGON, ANOTHER BUILDING GETS HIT BY A PLANE!"

Every breath goes on hold.

The megaphone burps out the coming message:

"Attention, crewmembers! This is the bridge, your captain speaking. We are sailing away as planned. Please… pray for New York…"

"Have you finished restocking?"

"Yes, sir, I have already."

"Great job, before you go, could you please do one more quick check?"

Danish officers, as she has learned, are always appreciative of others' hard work. On the ships, that appreciation is important because, those who don't grow a thick skin can be affected by stress and in some cases even jump overboard because of it.

She made herself a promise that it would never be her... One year of depression was enough to experience the pain... When the body stays busy the mind has no time to drift into the dark place...

"Of course, sir, I'm doing it right now."

Her eyes bounce from wall to wall. As usual, those New Castles' passengers have emptied the shelves of the store.

Perhaps they do so because of the high prices they find ashore. That England is expansive, everyone knows.

Beauty and fragrance-off the list...

... clothing... liquor and cigarettes...

... done!

She repeats the agenda in her mind.

Oh... books and newspapers... I almost forgot...

Lately, this section is the hardest to keep organized. One book is what causes such a mess; it keeps selling like hot bread.

She heard about its author who, while writing it, was clinically depressed, also as poor as a beetle, and now, is a multi-millionaire.

"Children book... and so successful... who would have ever thought..."

A few copies go back into the designated spots.

Suddenly, something pulls her focus away from a boy with a wizard's wand...

Some kind of strange energy draws her sight to the left...

Her heart starts beating faster... as she is getting closer to the local newspaper's front page... and huge capital letters...

Her hair rises up... Her skin feels chills... Her hand begins to shake...

"The terrorists who have kidnaped the planes..."

Her hand begins to shake…

His evil face hangs like a shroud… with an untrimmed beard… short mustache… and black curly hair…

This… is… him…

She stares at the picture, feeling a cold sweat on her neck…

Her mind starts to spin in circles that are made of questions to which answers she doesn't have…

CHAPTER 13

Armand

"It's got to be him; he's never late." Julia says while swallowing the last bite. Soon, an empty plate lands on the floor. "Please, tell your mom that was the best cheesecake I've ever had."

The friend gets up; she does as well except not from the sofa, but from the floor. When guests are here, the rug becomes her seat. Finding those perfect chairs takes much longer than she would have thought.

"I'm sure he will teach you, the internet is not that hard."

"Okay, Julia, I trust your word."

Another ring reminds her of the awaiting guest.

"Coming…!" she shouts toward the front door.

It's been five years since she's seen Armand the last time, then the company wasn't bankrupt yet, he was still married, just had a child, and she was getting ready to sail away.

So much has changed… now he's divorced and, as Julia has mentioned, sells used cars.

The lock clicks twice, preparing the door.

The round handle has all of her fingers wrapped around it.

They are about to twist it, but suddenly some invisible force pulls her back…

BE CAREFUL BEFORE YOU JUMP INTO THIS...

the Voice says from inside of her.

What jump…? It's not a date.

BE CAREFUL...

the Voice repeats.

Her fingers decide to move ahead.

The door opens up to how he has stayed in her memory.

He's bolder and fitter, although the same height as before but no one grows taller at age 38.

"Hi Ania, wow, is it you? You look great."

His blue boyish eyes give an extra compliment.

Bermuda shorts dress him up as well as an off-white polo shirt with a collar untouched by a woman's ironing hand.

His tennis shoes look quite worn out. His calves are more muscular than an average man's.

These muscles must come from bicycle rides because in between them stands the evidence.

"Hello Armand, you can leave it in the niche. Nobody will take it. It's a safe place."

"Okay, if you say so. How have you been?" His question keeps following her back.

"Very good, thank you." Her automatic response is synchronized with another discomfort hitting her gut once again.

"You've changed a lot. I see now you are blonde? Honestly, I would not recognize you on the street."

"Hope for the better?"

No need to ask, his eyes have already answered it.

She saw how they went down on her low-cut jeans, and then quickly moved up over her denim bustier.

"Oh, Julia is here? What a surprise!"

"Just about to leave. Ask for the cheesecake; it's the best one I've ever had."

One guest is gone. Another one is to be served.

"Armand, would you like anything to drink?"

"Yes, water would be great…"

Cutting a slice, with a side-eye she notices his head turning as he looked around the flat.

"Very nice place; did you hire an interior designer?"

"No, I've designed it myself."

"Nice… very nice… you have a gift."

His focus goes to the picture frames.

"Where are these from?"

"From Sicily; I've just come back from a trip. Here you go… enjoy it… sorry I still have no chairs."

"Floor is okay. I'm a simple man."

A simple man…? What a shift…

She remembers quite well how he showed off behind the Mercedes-Benz's steering wheels.

"You seem more relaxed?"

"Yes… I am in a much better place…"

"I've heard. Julia has kept me informed of what was going on…"

Good thing I left… she thinks to herself. Where would her life be now if she had stayed behind that desk, who knows… The legal problems the company was dealing with, has made the front pages of local magazines.

"So, how about you, how's everything? I've heard that you work on the ships?"

She takes a moment before giving a response, he doesn't need to know that the ferry line has put her "on a temporary hold"…

"I do. Love to travel." She denies the truth.

"Me too, actually considering a move to Australia, maybe next year."

"So, Armand, what's the plan?" Time to remind him that this meeting about learning the Internet.

"Right… that's why I'm here. Do you have a computer?"

"Unfortunately I don't."

"No problem, we can work on mine, the office is not too far away.

I can give you a ride on the back if you want?"

Bicycles are the last form of transportation she would choose to take.

"No, thank you, I much prefer walking."

While he holds onto his vehicle, she observes his moves, for they can say a lot about a man…

His are steady, on purpose, confident, and anxious, similar to his voice that reminds her of a radio station without commercial breaks. He talks nonstop. At least whatever he's saying makes lots of sense… somehow she has never noticed that intelligent side at work…

It takes half an hour for the internet to be figured out.

"You see, it wasn't so hard. Soon it will take over the world."

"You think so?"

"Absolutely, it's just a matter of time. Now, let's open an email address for you, pick up any name."

"Okay… can it be mine…?"

"Of course, it can be anything as long as it's not already taken by someone else."

She ponders… but nothing is coming up…

"How about AniaK?" he suggests.

"I like it. It's easy to remember."

His fingers do the work.

"All right, AniaK, you're officially in the Internet world!"

"Thank you."

"My pleasure, I can walk you back if you want?"

Where is this going...? Maybe I should say "no"? But is there anything wrong with making a new friend from an old boss...?

"Sure... why not, unless you have any other plans?"

"Absolutely none, I'm free as a bird."

There they are again, with his overextended stories carrying them back to her flat.

His question he pops by the front door doesn't surprise.

"Would you like to see a movie one day?"

"Maybe, we'll see... you have my number... anyway, thank you for helping me with the Internet."

Finally, the sofa belongs just to her. But peaceful rest doesn't last long... the cell phone starts to vibrate.

"The movie is called *"Signs"*. Mel Gibson plays the main role. This Friday, at 7 pm, I'll pick you up?"

She reads his text once more.

Who knows when I'm back on the ships... It may help me to kill some time...

"Ok, Armand. See you then," her fingers decide to type.

On paper, they've become lines, and those lines have turned into nets, and those nets have created strange codes that only Mr. Edward can understand.

The best astrologer in town is now seated across from his desk and ready to read her chart.

"Here is what the planets have to say:

Definitely, there's a strong connection between both your dates of birth... he's Scorpio, incredibly active, very bright and intelligent... Are there any trust issues with him, miss?"

"We've been dating barely for a month."

"I see it's still too early for this... but clearly there's someone who disturbs you, am I right?

"Well..." She exhales the answer,

"...he has an ex-wife, sir..."

"And one child from that marriage..."

"Wow… how can you tell?"

Astrologer's pen points at a sign while his focused eyes move along the nets.

"It's over here, miss. Don't worry about that woman, they won't be together again."

The page is moved aside. Another one is ready to be analyzed.

"Now, after Mercury's retrograde, things will be speeding up.

"There may be some tension caused by the conjunction of Uranus with Venus and Mars. Saturn, which is your ruling planet, represents strength and also brings rapid change, which can overwhelm if one is not prepared for that."

"How can I prepare for it, sir?"

"By following your gut, trust your intuition; it is very powerful, are you aware of that?"

"I am, in fact."

This guy... he's right on point... she thinks.

"Also, try to listen more than you speak."

"And that's where the problem lies, sir… I do talk a lot."

"Clearly, I can see it in your chart miss. Although I must say these communication skills will become a great asset later on in your life… Now going back to Armand… he could be "the one", but it's up to you."

His eyes lift with a smile.

"Anyway, you won't end up alone… it's obvious to me when I look at the exact moment of your birth and how then the planets were aligned."

The same pen points at the lines and makes a circle in the air.

At least there is some hope after all of those relationships…

"Hmm… very interesting… Are you with me?"

"Yes, Mr. Edward, please carry on, sir."

"So besides living abroad… about Poland not being your country, you probably already know?" Heavy eyebrows rise with the question.

"Without a doubt. For sure."

"Good… good… going back to where I was… Oh, right here… yes… in a few years from now, you will go through a major transformation… a very powerful change…

It will be almost as if you will become someone else…"

“Someone else, sir…? What do you mean?”

“Time will answer that. What I see is that it’s going to be a long process that may take many years, but absolutely necessary. For you to live the life of purpose, you must die first.”

“Die? What kind of death?”

She backs up from his desk.

“Spiritual, not physical. It will initiate when there are lots of shoes around… so many… to the point that you will get sick of them…”

“Sick of shoes…? Oh no, that will never happen.” Her head disagrees, shaking to the sides.

Mr. Edward’s face gives an expression that what he knows is much deeper than her current state of mind.

“Trust me, you will. But you’ll be very happy, and that’s what matters the most. As far as this man, I would suggest to simply go with a flow. Obviously, there is a reason why he has shown up.

“By the way, it’s not the first life the two of you share. In one of the previous ones, I believe he was your son.

Any more questions, miss? If not, our time is up.”

This could be a great chance to clarify it…

“Yes, sir… there is something I want to ask you about.”

“Certainly, I’m all ears.”

Forgotten goosebumps return on her skin.

“It happened a while ago when I was working on the ship. During my afternoon nap, I had a horrible dream. It was the worst nightmare I’ve ever had… so horrifying that I’ve woken up with cold sweat from it…

In that dream, I saw the face of a man who hijacked one of those planes…”

“You mean 9/11, that terrorist attack on the World Trade Center?”

“Yes, I saw one of them right before he crashed the plane.

Then, the next day, early in the morning, when they delivered fresh newspapers on board, I saw his face on the cover… sir… I was in complete shock…”

Edward’s face gives an impression he’s heard enough.

“Well, there it is clear evidence of how intuitive you are; you’ve tapped into the energy field and received his very strong intent. You see, there is no resistance in a state of dream. We have all been given this skill, which not many choose to exercise, but eventually, you will. Your awareness of it and your practice will help you to master it, and then it will become more natural. Anything else, miss?"

"No sir, at least not for now."

Few bills silently land on top of the charts; one should never say: "thank you" after the reading is done.

"If you need any more clarification you know where to find me."

"Yes, sir."

By the front door Mr. Edward turns around.

"Goodbye, miss. Remember, do not rush things because to discover your life purpose, it must take many years.

But you will get there and all your dreams will unfold in perfect time.

Keep me posted and let's stay in touch."

He could be the one... he could be the one...

A mantra carries her back to the flat. All she can think of is the new light that Mr. Edward has shined over her relationship with Armand.

So far, when her friends were saying what a nice couple the two of them make, still something deep inside her gut didn't feel right... some kind of a feeling, that was hard to explain...

I'm overthinking... it must be the stress caused by this stupid debt...

Nobody had forced her to land that money to buy unnecessary stuff to impress a few successful friends...

And now, without having an income, how she will pay it back...? The company that has borrowed the money is a complete rip-off... it takes an interest of 30 percent...

The more she ponders her situation the more disgusted with herself she becomes...

"Go with the flow... listen to your gut..."

Astrologer's words return into her mind.

It's good to spend time with Armand... it helps me to reduce the stress... He should be here in an hour... Or, is he already...?

The doorbell rings behind her back.

"Hey, I know I'm too early but I could not wait."

A bottle of white wine appears at the front of her face.

"Your favorite one, Pinot Grigio, I think you've mentioned it?"

"How nice of you to pay attention to what I say, considering how much I talk... *"*

"Guess what? Not more than me!"

"Some cheese… some grapes… and of course, some bread…

I'd like to take care of this wine… Where do you keep the bottle opener?"

How refreshing to finally meet a self-sufficient man...

Her hand directs his toward the drawer and soon the smell of wine takes over the space.

"Let's sit on the floor, actually, I don't mind that you still have no chairs.

In this way, we can be much closer…" The cotton of his shirt connects with the silk of her top.

For the last two months, she was wondering when he would attempt to cross the fine line.

It must be now...

"Excuse me…"

The bathroom is always a good place to step outside… and to think everything over before experiencing another abuse of her heart…

Because, if this takes them where this seems to be going, he will end up staying for the night…

What if the Voice was right about him...?

Her mind searches for the evidence of his genuine acts…

No... he is different... he cares about me... his actions speak louder than words...

Besides if I don't give him a chance... how would I ever know...?

She takes a deep breath but worrisome thoughts don't want to go away…

This debt... if I mention it to him... I will lose all of his respect...

YOU WON'T... TELL HIM ABOUT IT... BE HONEST... HE WILL OFFER YOU HIS HELP...

the Voice says inside her.

Help... no... no... that's humiliating... I can't do it... it's not okay...

She looks straight into a mirror, and there sees the reflection of decisions made in the past.

Why do I always put myself into a financial hole...?

It's time to grow up!

She finds herself back on the floor.

"I see something is troubling your mind."

She thought that some makeup would cover up the truth... but clearly, it did not...

"Would you like to tell me? Two heads are better than one."

"I'm not sure how you will take it..."

"Not sure? What is it? Did you commit a crime?"

She finds his laughter inappropriate; he must have sensed it because his voice softens up.

"Listen, I'm the guy who was chased by ZUS. But even that, things could be worse.

Trust me, nothing surprises me anymore. So what is it?"

"Well... I did something... that I truly regret..."

"Nobody is perfect. We all make mistakes."

"I guess... you are right..."

Uncertainty is exhaled and that brings her a bit of relief.

"What is it, just tell me."

And then all of a sudden the words come out by themselves.

"I've put myself into an unnecessary debt... it was a ridiculous decision... and now it's already too late.

I got stuck with those payments... which I cannot afford... since the ferry line has placed me on "temporary hold." To be honest, I'm not even sure if they will ever call me back...

I have been asking around, but none of my friends are willing to help..."

His eyes stare at her without blinking... she tries to find a judgment in them, but she can't...

"Of course, usually, in this kind of situation, you learn who your true friends are.

How much do you owe?"

His calmness is like the yin to her stressed-out yang.

"Oh, no I'm not telling you this."

"I'm serious, how much?"

"Two thousand zlotych."

"Two thousand, that's not too bad."

"Maybe for you… for me it's a lot…"

His kind smile does nothing to her overwhelming feeling of shame.

"I'm going to help you. Tomorrow I'll go to the bank."

"No… you can't do this. It doesn't feel right… besides, I don't even know when I can pay you back…"

"I want to help you. It's not that big of a deal. You'll give it back when you can.

Now, can we enjoy this evening? Pretty good wine, isn't it?"

The cotton of his shirt moves closer, and as it blends with the silk of her top, all she can think of are Mr. Edward's words:

"He could be the one, but it's up to you, miss…"

Those naked trees outside the window seem more miserable than they were last March or perhaps they're just reflecting her current state of mind.

Looking at them, she keeps asking the same question of God:

Why did the first pregnancy have to find me in such an uncertain time…?

Unemployed… insecure… dependent on the man… The reality of becoming a mother is so far away from how she used to envision it then…

Then, in those happy dreams, when such a moment arrived, it was filled with joy and bliss, it was soaked in pure love… it was built on excitement about carrying a new life… not fear of the unknown or resentment toward Armand…

"Positive", says a description in regard to two blue parallel stripes. The third pregnancy test she has run cannot possibly lie.

Another hour of reading it won't change the result.

While trees are expecting the spring, she is expecting, a child.

Do I want this baby…? Do I want it with him…?

If she could only turn back time to a year before, she never would have started their financial dependency… And then, none of this would have happened… and she wouldn't lose her self-confidence… which has become a mere shadow of what it used to be…

But when one is under someone's mercy, then one starts to question the abilities one used to possess…

"Are you ready, Nori?" She gazes at the dog. To him, life is very simple; all he cares about is his walk.

"You have no idea how much I've messed up my life… and you still love me, regardless…"

His wet nose gets a kiss before a leash is attached.

The rain drops coming down on her jacket still carry bits of late snow.

Pulling a hood over her head, she can't stop thinking that where Armand currently resides, there is no need for a winter coat. Supposedly, in Las Vegas, the weather is great all year long. At least that's what he's told her before he was gone.

It was ten days earlier when he decided to take a trip to the U.S. and join a group of five like-minded friends. And off they went to a city where nobody goes to resurrect, but to overdo gambling, drinking, or having sex.

Of course, she had to stay. "It's just for the boys."

"You don't bring wood to the forest…" She recalled an old proverb when she heard his response to why she couldn't join.

Are we still together…? Or have we already broken up…?

The longer these thoughts are dwelled on the more they handicap.

But what about this child… how will I be able to survive without his help…?

The trees with leafless branches, somehow protect her from the rain…

She looks down at her boots and at the mud that has completely overtaken them…

The noise of speeding cars brings no relief to her mind, as it comes from both sides of the street… from the right… and from the left…

The agony of existence… the awareness it is all her fault…

I am the only one responsible for my mistakes…

All of a sudden, Nori's fur goes up on his back. She looks at his nose.

It's moving in big circles in the air surrounding them… and goes on… and on… and on, sniffing as if he's aware of something invisible to her…

She turns around, but there's nobody… yet the energy field feels more intense… more tangible… almost as if someone is standing right next to her…

Then suddenly she feels the massive wings coming from behind, and as they wrap up her body entirely, the Presence says:

REST... BE AT PEACE... THIS TOO SHALL PASS...

Her head is gently forced to lean over one wing.

As soon as she allows this to happen the Presence goes on:

DO NOT WORRY... YOU'RE NOT ALONE IN THIS...

The tears fill up her eyes, for she had never felt so loved…

I AM WITH YOU... TRUST... EVERYTHING WILL BE ALL RIGHT...

Holding onto the leash, she feels this is a true Home…

The mind relaxes… all the tension is gone…

Slowly, the wings release their hold… the Presence drifts away…

She stands in awe, touched by the Unseen Divine.

The rain finally stops.

And Nori shakes off his fur.

In this church, she was baptized and had her first communion at 10 but never knew that in a silent back room, in a golden box, was a white cross with Jesus holy heart that answers every lost man's prayer.

She has also heard, that when one prays inside this niche and gives their soul to God, then one always receives, that help is provided, all heavy burdens are taken away, and even the most crooked paths get straightened for one's life to move ahead.

And now she's on her knees with her head bowing down, knowing that this prayer is her last chance to decide what to do with the unborn child.

God... I'm so afraid...

Her palms tighten their grasp.

You've sent me an Angel who told me that I'm not alone... and that everything will be all right...

Her eyes focus on the cross.

And so I came to ask for your help to make the right decision that I won't regret...

"You cannot keep this baby. It could be dangerous."

A skinny man in a white kilt directs these words at her.

"Let me explain why, in your case, an abortion is an absolute must."

An office chair under his back is making a squeaking sound.

"At first I thought you should give birth, because when if not now? How old are you, thirty-two?"

"Yes."

"Exactly, this would be the time. The longer the wait the bigger the risk but then, after doing the last test, I've noticed an irregular activity in your pregnancy that has made me very concerned."

He throws the recent scan on top of his desk.

"Here, these pictures clearly show that pregnancy isn't correct. Can you see an empty spot?"

Her eyes move on a white zone, which has hardly any shape.

"Yes, I see it."

"And "this" shouldn't be there. How to explain it..." Under his weight, the chair squeaks some more, perhaps in his busy practice, he already got used to its noise.

"The baby is not growing properly because the egg is not complete, although, this part still evolves..." He pulls another scan and points at something gray and big.

"This part is what's dangerous. Some women have died in similar cases."

The chair is redirected, and a white kilt faces her again.

"We must do abortion as fast as we can. You know it will cost you?"

"Yes. I am aware."

"Good. Is that man who came here with you going to pay? If you don't mind my opinion, but he didn't seem too excited about being a dad."

"Of that, I am also aware…"

Her attention moves toward the trees… they have become so beautiful, wearing first spring's leaves… Suddenly, as she is looking at them, she realizes that this must be the answer from God…

"What's your first available date?" She turns back to face a white kilt.

"Thirtieth of March. I'm glad we agree. Just to be up front, we don't use anesthesia, so try not to scream."

But she did scream a lot…

Now, already in the comfort of her bed, she's resting on a soft pillow, still recalling when she was back there…

… in that dark room where she was trying to verbalize an unbearable pain that was followed by the doctor's senseless response:

"Be quiet! You're too loud! It will scare my patients away!"

How dare he…? How cruel… but taking money from me was okay…? she was thinking while experiencing those cold, metal tools pulling from inside the parts of a never-to-be-born flesh…

"It was a girl," he mentioned before she almost faded away.

"I'll see you in a week. For two months, no sex."

Her beat up body was barely able to sit straight on a chair.

All the strangers' eyes were on her, staring with either hate or compassion… her awareness wasn't clear enough to tell…

And then she waited… and waited… an hour later, Armand arrived:

"Sorry, I had a great sale."

A car deal is more important than my aborting your child…?

That was her last thought before, like a leaf, she felt into his arms…

They carried her first to his car and then inside her flat… where, as if she was the biggest burden, they placed her on the top of her bed.

Left alone in complete silence to increasing pain, she kept asking God the same question:

Why am I still with him… why don't I respect myself?

44

YOU WILL LET HIM GO WHEN THE TIME IS RIGHT... NOW REST... THE BODY MUST HEAL the Voice answered from inside.

CHAPTER 14

Goodbye

"Why does it have to be the States? Can't you move to the UK, since they've recently opened the borders for us? You'd be able to legally work there?"

The same wrinkle appears, as it always does when things don't go Armand's way, right above his nose, uneven and deeply engraved.

She looks behind his back and there, in a dark window, sees reflection of her face.

Those snowflakes falling over it are softening the tough decision that she's already made.

DON'T GO TO ENGLAND... GO TO THE UNITED STATES...

the Voice again confirms from inside of her.

"From now, on I will no longer support you, and this is the last money I'm spending on you."

She can feel the blood pulsing faster from hearing his words, for if he only knew how much she wants to be independent… and accomplish something on her own.

"Thank you for all you have done. I will do everything to give it back…"

A brief silence confirms his disbelief in her ability to survive without his support.

"Okay, then I will call Arthur tomorrow. Let's see what he says. At least for a week or two you will have a place to stay."

"Does he now live in Las Vegas?"

"He does."

EVERYTHING IS GOING TO CHANGE...

she hears the Voice as she watches Armand turns around.

A fluorescent light disturbs their eyes, exposing each imperfection of their faces. Under its influence, whatever was able to hide is brought up to the surface and forced to be confessed. Here they are, in a soon-to-be-leaving train, in a cabin unusually empty for early Monday's Express, almost as if some divine power had arranged such a setup for Father and her to meet face to face.

Her relaxed posture and steady calm breath are quite a contrast to his bowed head.

Crocodile tears...

she thinks, watching his old eyes tearing up.

A little too late for that...

He always does it when she's about to leave; suddenly shows that he cares a lot.

Her heart used to feel compassion when seeing it, but that was a long time ago; at 32 she does not buy into it.

"I'm truly sorry we have not given you a loving home…"

His powerful statement shocks her to the very core.

But to smooth the rough past would take more than just a few words…

"I know it was difficult for you to grow up in the middle of our fights… but I was really trying to do my best…"

The confession continues and she looks straight into his eyes.

Shall she feel sorry? Or maybe pretend that suddenly everything is all right? But it's not, and it never will be, that's one of the reasons to move far away.

"What time is your flight?" he asks for probably the third time.

"Tomorrow at 5:45 am."

"And after you land in Miami, are you going to the hotel?"

"No, I'm going straight to the ship."

Of course, she had to lie. They could never handle the truth, and so even this trip can't be officially about her big move to the United States. Something that, in a normal household, would be a great reason to celebrate, sadly, with her Parents, she has to keep only to herself.

"All right, Dad, let's say goodbye. I promised to text Armand."

As soon as she gets up, she is suddenly embraced by an awkward feeling of love coming from his hug.

"I'll call you as soon as I arrive."

"Please do and… take care of yourself…"

Trust me, I will, much better than you have ever done.

His face shows up on the other side of the train.

"Remember… you can always come back…!" she sees a steam of a warm air coming from his mouth.

"INTERCITY TO WARSAW LEAVING FROM PLATFORM ONE!" the megaphone shouts, and soon his crying eyes stay behind…

The fluorescent light loses its grasp against the brightness of the rising sun.

She sits down and deeply exhales, for the day has finally come.

"Don't worry, I will be okay…"

Her palm disappears inside Armand's. His eyes, she has noticed, have changed color from a sky blue into a muddy gray.

"You will come to me once I settle down, yes…?" As her head rests on his shoulder, she realizes that this shoulder was always there for her, in spite of all the ups and downs of the last three years…

"Of course, I will. If anything goes wrong you must call me right away."

"But before you have said you will no longer support me…"

"It doesn't matter what I have said before…"

She's glad that he also wants to remember only good times… for indeed, there have been many, and that is why her heart still cares so much.

"Arthur has promised to give you shelter at least for the first two weeks. Honestly, I would do much more if I were him…"

His eyes become muddier and move away from hers. Some topics, she has learned, need to be left untouched.

"His mom is also there, helping him with the kids. She's going to like you. You will get along."

"How come you are so certain about this?"

"I have a feeling. She's a decent lady, just talks a lot."

"And that shouldn't be a problem with me." Her laugh softens the air around.

"Much more than you think, soon you will see."

He smiles, and she savors it to recall on for all those months or years ahead she will have to spend without him.

"Flight to Chicago: Gate 8," appears on the board of departures above their heads.

"Well, this is it… I gotta go…"

His arms wrap around her, adding another layer of warmth to her shearling coat.

EVERYTHING WILL BE GREAT...

the Voice says from inside.

She walks toward the gate, but before she enters it, she turns around to whisper:

"Goodbye…"

CHAPTER 15

Las Vegas

44

As if it's an illusion made of thousands of lights, an image of a neon city appears in front of her wide-open eyes. Whichever direction she turns her curious head, there is another casino flashing off its colorful name.

The car stops at the red light, and, at the corner where the two green walls unite, sits the one who unquestionably rules the animals' world, perhaps also the kingdom of MGM, as those two huge billboards placed next to him show.

Across from the majestic golden lion, a white statue lifts the famous torch in front of several buildings pretending to be New York.

But such a fake skyline cannot fool those who have ever stepped on Manhattan's land.

"This is kurwa Las Vegas, the best city in the world!"

Arthur curses a lot. She's noticed it right away, at the airport, when he picked her up.

Now, watching him up close, she wonders how hard it must be for a man whose charisma was opening every door in their town to become a mere shadow of the boss she once had?

What an irony that his American dream has already been lived outside the United States…

Because it was there, in Europe, where he was rich, it was there where he drove the most expensive cars or flew to Milan, to buy Versace's silk. Here, a red hot Viper got replaced by a silver Nissan van.

"It's a family car." He seems to read her mind.

"Sure, with three kids you need lots of space."

I shouldn't be critical… he's providing me a place to stay…

"That's right. I do." For a split second his eyes penetrate hers but do not stay there long. His heavy foot pushes on the gas, putting the green walls of MGM one block behind.

"Are you happy to be in the U.S.?"

"Yes, very much."

Uncertainty or excitement-she cannot decide which emotion dominates her newly relocated mind. Although the surrounding neon lights are tempting her to go out and have fun, the Voice from within her whispers:

FOCUS ON FINDING A JOB…

The pink façade pulls her attention to the left, making her realize that a pink massive bird is what inspired the name of the street they're driving on.

"To be honest with you, Poland has never felt like my place."

"The same with me, kurwa, that's why I have three citizenships." Arthur says. And with each statement he makes, his head seems to expand. Good thing his neck is thick enough to handle a new weight.

"So, I've heard from Armand that you are thinking about opening a fashion boutique here?"

She pauses for a second on what she is supposed to say back…

For sure, it cannot be the truth… it must be Armand's lie created to convince his longtime friend to provide her shelter for the first few nights…

"Arthur only cares about cash." She recalls Armand's words spoken into her ears over twelve hours ago.

If he only knew that all I have is a thousand bucks...

"We'll see…," she finally responds. "First, I must check the market… and then I will decide…"

"In my opinion, it sounds brilliant. Seriously, look at them. They all could be your potential clients!" His masculine hand points at the crowd, which reminds her of restless ants.

Hmm... is this Rolex fake...? No... it cannot be... it's getting dark... and I cannot see...

"How many people live in Las Vegas?" she asks, trying to distract herself from the inevitable fact that no darkness will hide that his watch is fake.

"Around six hundred thousand but four million visits the city each month."

"Wow… that is impressive…"

"I'm telling you, kurwa! Las Vegas is the best!"

He keeps promoting it like he is Donald Trump...

"Right there are the Forum Shops." The fake watch moves to the left.

"The best shopping experience in the entire world."

Her eyes follow the motion toward the ancient walls, which are a far cry from those found in real Rome.

Suddenly, an erosive explosion throws the towers of water into the air.

"This is Bellagio. *"Ocean's Eleven"* was shot inside that hotel."

Mesmerized by the fountain and its smooth dance, she can't stop staring at it.

"Have you seen it?" he asks.

"Yes, Arthur, I have."

"Do you remember that moment when Andy Garcia looked at the mirror and said: "I was born ready!" That moment, kurwa, was the best!"

Arthur's body strikes a pose that she remembers very well, except then, when he was in charge it represented power, not pathetic awkwardness.

The fountain makes a splash, must be the last. The music ends.

"We have twenty more minutes to go. My house is in Summerlin, the best area of town."

The shops stay behind; so do all the flashing neon lights.

She looks ahead at the unknown highway, thinking,

I will be fine... One day at the time...

There is a smell to a desert that arises with the morning sun; it's a blend of dirty sand with the dried plants that have been carried by a wild wind over hundreds of miles.

Later on, around 8 am, the smell gets enriched with an odor of gasoline, for it's at that time when the soccer moms on their way to school are getting into their massive SUVs.

The bigger the car- the smaller the driver; she has already discovered one of the American truths. Anything bigger seems to be better here: houses, TV sets, portions of food.

As well as those dreams one should always have... Therefore she keeps reminding herself to dream big, even when the circumstances aren't that great... Even when finding a job takes much longer that she thought it would...

But then, sometimes come mornings like today when no thought can rise above her hopelessness...

"Mrs. Tessa... I'm considering going back..."

A black-haired head pops out from the kitchen.

"No, Ania! You can't give up! How long have you been here? Only fourteen days?"

There will be a speech, she can sense it. Indeed her instinct is right.

"Listen to me…"

The monumental body of Arthur's mother is approaching and soon puts both of them onto a couch in a wave. And as they briefly float together onto that couch which at night turns into her bed, she recalls the very first time when they shook hands.

In that instant, she knew they would get along because what she saw in those mature eyes were the qualities she admires a lot: dignity, confidence, strength, and a "no bullshit" approach to life.

This woman is no joke… she thought.

"Listen…" Mrs. Tessa's speech starts.

"You've moved to a foreign country completely alone, and that is courage, my dear. To do something like that takes balls. There aren't many men who would ever attempt doing something as brave, and therefore you should be proud of yourself. But more importantly, you should be patient because nothing good in life comes fast. You will learn this lesson when you reach my age." A serious face welcomes a smile and big chest expands to catch some breath, just enough of it to carry on without allowing a bit of space for her to throw in a few words.

"Your English is fluent. You're attractive and smart. With all of the above, it is just a matter of time before you find a job. Arthur is helping you in the best way he can, in spite of his situation, which is not great…"

"Yes, I know, Mrs. Tessa, taking care of three kids is a lot of work. And I have to admit he does an amazing job." Somehow she was able to throw in a few words.

"In my opinion, he doesn't. He should be much stricter with them, and teach them discipline, and, respect. Have you seen how they throw dirty clothes on the floor and wait for me to pick it up? I didn't come here to be their maid. You see, Ania, this is my America, not quite a dreamland."

She's right…

"But back to you; Armand also supports you."

From hearing his name, her eyes drop down. In the back of her mind replays his voice yelling at her over Skype:

"I can't be there to walk you everywhere by hand! It's not Arthur's responsibility to find you a job! Go and take a fucking bus; you will not lose your crown!"

Maybe that's his way to motivate…? she thought while he carried on with his rant:

"I got you the ticket, gave you pocket money, so what else do you want me to do?! Go take the fucking bus! Move your ass!"

"What happen? Did you fight?"

"Yes, Mrs. Tessa… we had…"

An unexpected feeling of love comes from Mrs. Tessa's hand.

"That's okay, my dear, there are no perfect relationships-another lesson you will learn when you reach my age."

Mature eyes transmute some strength, and as she connects with them, she realizes that is what was needed to wake her up inside.

"And where are you going, if I may ask you?" Mrs. Tessa asks from the couch.

"To take the bus to Las Vegas and look for a job."

It stands on a corner and tempts her like a chocolate bar with the bright four-letter name that doesn't apologize for screaming loud from its very top. That highlighted name, she has heard, is very well-known in this town because of Steve Wynn who has already put several other ones on the strip. Except, this particular casino, he named after himself. And after naming it, he had climbed on the rooftop to give it an advertisement like no hotel has ever had before.

"Officially the highest privately owned resort in the country." The local news constantly reports the facts.

"Two point seven billion dollars have been spent. Grand opening: April 2005."

In less than two months…

She confirms the date, reading it from a distance on a glamourous construction fence.

It wasn't that long ago when projects of such a scale were only visible to her on a TV screen inside her flat.

And now she is here, hassling, working her butt off and rediscovering over and over again that in Las Vegas, city transportation sucks. What normally would take any car 25 minutes or less requires two changes of busses, and comes to two hours if they aren't late.

She tightens her grasp with her left hand that holds onto the envelope with her resumes. Today five of them went out… the same number as yesterday… and the day before… and the day before that…

The sun throws the golden rays freely over her tired face. But a blissful state doesn't last. The loud sound of a motor wakes her up to the bus she needs to take.

Here we go; round number one…

Her back leans on a seat. The envelope finds rest on her lap.

The hassle is over, at least for today.

*How much longer will it take me to find a job…?*she asks herself.

IT WILL HAPPEN… JUST KEEP GOING… EVERYTHING COMES AT THE RIGHT TIME… the Voice says from inside.

She exhales and for a moment closes her eyes.

The only sound in between them comes from a newspaper swished by Armand's hand. Lost in his reading, he doesn't realize that all of her attention is exclusively on his face.

The last five months have flown by in a blink of an eye, almost as if they were never apart.

Now, watching him from across the library's table, she wonders if this reunion will enhance their relationship or not?

The walls made of books surround them; what lies ahead of them is a field of the unknown. Behind them, is the past- walked, done, and to her very obvious. Somehow she was able to manage an early immigrant's life on her own.

She steps toward the window to ponder the recent events… wondering if there has been some invisible higher power that put everything into place…?

Otherwise, how could she explain that, out of the blue, she has met that man who directed her to the Polish Deli, and then, from there, she was guided to her first job. Even though that job came with the lowest pay, it has still allowed her to move out of Arthur's house and into a tiny room rented out by an old lady whom she found in a newspaper ad.

One month has passed, and the same boss who hired her recommended her to another Polish entrepreneur.

With that new employment came more freedom and access to the company's phone, but there were also disadvantages like being back on the buses and dragging incredibly heavy catalogues. That catalog had images of Polish blown glass, which she was supposed to sell to the flower shops all across town.

Since those shops weren't placing orders she ended up in a retail store that was run by the same owner…

A four-year lease…

A silver metallic color changes the pattern of her thoughts…

How am I going to make those payments with my low salary…?

There stands the tangible evidence of what Armand has accomplished since he has arrived-got his friend Arthur to sign the lease for a brand new car…

"Very nice," she responded while thinking:

It could be preowned… it would be much cheaper…

"I told you not to overanalyze. You must take it day by day."

She hears him from behind.

Easy for him to say… when I pay all the bills… I must find a better paying job…

A wrinkled newspaper swishes in his hand, and as soon as he releases it, her eyes are pulled toward one ad.

It stands out from all the others as if it is meant only for her.

"Personal assistant needed. Contact marina @sephora.com… for more details."

CHAPTER 16

Chanel

In-person, the aura around her feels larger than life itself. Her long, diamond-clad fingers keep playing with Louis Vuitton monogram bag.

The traffic at the store has slowed down, as usual on Wednesdays by nine, and so with no one around them, they can have their exclusive one-on-one.

It's been a month since she was hired, but it's taken her two weeks to become sure that LV won't last long as her employer, from behind the curtain, the brand is not as glamorous as she had once thought.

Back then, when living in Poland, she would have done anything to own an authentic bag from Louis Vuitton, but now, even the most attractive discount cannot convince her to purchase three layers of canvas coated with PVC, a fact that many clients don't know…

"It's quite a sophisticated water container. Rene will love it. He can use it on our trip to Disneyland."

Angel's voice pulls her out of her funk. In a split of a second, all disappointments evaporate: the midnight shifts, the low salary; none of it matters. For if she weren't here, this encounter would not be taking place.

"I'll take it, miss, please, wrap it up. Thank you for showing this thing to me, it's great."

"My absolute pleasure, Mrs. Dion, it's been an honor to be of help. Is there anything else I can assist you with, madame?"

"No, for now we're all set."

"Of course." She bows down and professionally places just sold item inside a yellowish pouch.

As soon as the strings of a dust bag are pulled, she lifts her eyes to looks into eyes that remind her of her own because they also have a full almond shape, also splashed with light green over dark brown.

If only she had an idea how many memories I've built of her songs.

"May I ask you a question, madame?"

The famous neck curiously twists to the side, reminding her of a beautiful swan.

"Of course, go ahead."

"Who does your make-up, ma'am?"

"My make-up? Well, I do it myself."

"Oh, you do? It looks incredible. I thought you always have a makeup artist on hand?"

"No, I do it every night before the show. Have you seen it already?"

"Unfortunately, I haven't yet…"

Would I ever be able to on this ridiculous salary?

"I hope that soon you will and that you will enjoy it."

"I'm sure I will."

How humble... how polite... considering how much international fame...

"I will do everything to make it happened, madame. Your music has been uplifting to me in the hardest times…"

"We all go through those, don't we?"

Returning a smile, she handles the shopping bag with both hands. This new beautiful gesture she has learned from a Japanese co-worker friend.

"We truly appreciate your visit, madame. I'm sure your husband will be very pleased with the choice you've made."

"You're an excellent salesperson. They should give you a raise."

Long fingers take full charge of the brown handles.

"How long have you been working here?"

"Last Tuesday was exactly one month."

"One month? Oh dear, you're heading for success!"

"If it comes from your mouth, Mrs. Dion…"

She turns around, pulled back to the counter by the reality of her job.

Success... it certainly won't happen where I currently am.

Her eyes freeze at a spot where the star has shined its light over her cheap-looking, dark gray uniform. There her future has been prophesied, but not a direction she supposed to take.

Where can I go to make a great living...?

The story is empty, but not in her mind that is so busy looking for an answer. And the answer comes.

"There is only one place, and that is Chanel!" She says it out loud.

Anticipation fuels her steps as she continues a steady walk. Its length is measured by a wall on the left that goes on… and on… and on…

The transparency of it allows her to see what's going on inside the boutique; that breathtaking glamour would be on a full display if not the mannequins.

They stand in the window in the most awkward poses, confident in conquering the fashion world. The tweed jackets have turned into their armor, the golden chains on their handbags into their weapons, and there, in their red-lipsticked mouths, are bullets made of silent words.

Those bullets shoot toward whoever happens to pass by, saying:

"Please do not enter if you cannot afford what we sell!"

She receives their uninviting message and, in the very moment, decides that any form of discouragement must be ignored.

Everyone starts somewhere... let's remember that...

The inner talk fuels her steps.

Those who now work here and act like they are Coco Chanel were hired as well.

She crosses the doorstep and, as soon as her feet are inside, all clerks' eyes move over her crossbody bag. A few days ago, she found it on sale, thrilled with the way it looked, and now, she's no longer sure since it seems that these x-raying eyes don't agree with her. To them, it must hold zero value without a designer's name.

Perhaps that is why nobody says "Hello"... or approaches... or asks if she needs any help...

It doesn't matter how they perceive me...

She straightens her disgraced strap with her intimidated hand.

STAY FOCUSED...

the Voice from within her whispers, and helps to realign with the inner core again.

Those judgmental eyes can remain at the front on their hunt for filthy rich.

Anyway, what lies ahead of her is something she would much rather be surrounded with... the shoes... the shelves full of shoes... and right behind them a view of a waterfall...

She's heard that Steve Wynn is also into the ancient art of Feng-Shui.

Great chi here... Her nose reads the air that is suddenly enriched by an intense rosy smell.

Number 5… must be it…

“Good morning, miss.” A friendly voice makes her twist.

“Welcome to Chanel.”

If there were a contest of this woman’s beauty against nature, the waterfall would not have a chance.

“Are you looking for anything in particular?”

She pauses while faced with the most stunning hair.

It shines like those fine diamonds Elizabeth Taylor has collected throughout the years and falls so gracefully like that brilliant hair cut owned by Catherine Deneuve. It frames with perfection a flawless face covered with makeup that even Sophia Loren wouldn’t refuse to present.

“My name is Boriana. Please let me know if I can be of help.”

B… o… r… i… a… n… a

Her eyes scroll down to a black and white tag.

“Isn’t it an Eastern European name?”

“Yes, it is. I’m from Bulgaria.” The purest smile gets even brighter exposed next to a contrasting it red pomade.

“I was there a long time ago…”

“Were you? How cool! What year was that?”

“It was the summer of 1989. I remember exactly because communism had ended in Poland that year.”

“Are you Polish?”

The rosy fragrance intensifies as a well-moisturized hand reaches out toward hers.

“Yes. I am. My name is Ania.”

“Oh, in Bulgaria, we have the same name! Anyway, we’re kind of neighbors, so I shouldn’t be surprised!”

“You’re right, considering the distance, we are neighbors.”

How friendly, compared to those who have scanned my bag.

“This store is amazing. Have you been working here for a long time?”

“Five years.”

“Five years…? Means you must love it, Boriana?”

“Of course, I do! I love Chanel! I love my job!”

Brown hair waves to the side as its owner has suddenly decided to add another layer to already very thick red pomade. Then, as if out of habit, the moist fingers swipe through pure silken hair.

"And you? Where do you work, if you don't mind my asking?"

"At Louis Vuitton, a few doors away."

"I see..."

A change in the tone of her voice makes her conscious of anything she will say.

I must be careful... The world of Wynn is a small place...

"Please, tell me, is it true, Ania, that they don't pay their employees well?"

SPEAK THE TRUTH... YOU CAN TRUST HER...

the Voice reinforces from inside.

"Yes. The salary there is a joke; that's why I am here, to apply for a job."

Brown hair bounces up from excitement. It seems the Bulgarian one is hard to sustain.

"How great; that's what you should do! We've moved here to have better lives. Not to work for nothing like slaves!"

Oh, wow, she understands.

"Don't worry, I get it. I am also an immigrant. It's good that you came here, Ania, because in the United States, you won't find a better retail job. Chanel is... The. Best. Period!"

"I hope so, because those at the front weren't too nice ..."

"I know... I know... that's how some of them are. They judge a book by its cover and then get very surprised when someone who looks like a bum spends twenty thousand like that."

Delicate fingers click in the air, showing off bright ruby shade.

"Gorgeous nail polish, Boriana."

"Isn't it lovely? From a pre-fall of 2006. It's a limited edition, by the way."

"You know your product; very impressive..."

"Thank you. We have lots of training, plus I always strive to do my best."

"No, chto? No, chto is the best?!"

A rough Russian accent cuts through between them.

"Who are you talking to, Boriana? Some Polish girl, I've overheard?"

"Oh! Perfect timing, Lana! Yes, Ania is from Poland and came to apply for a job."

Does she have to share it with everyone else…?

DON'T STRESS… EVERYTHING IS FINE…

the Voice from inside her calms her down.

"Hmm, is she?" The platinum blonde steps closer, introducing a pale face and blue, almost transparent eyes. These eyes give her an aristocrat's look and scroll down over her crossbody bag.

Oh, not again, haven't we been there already…?

Instinctively, she backs up, but the blue eyes don't let go; they keep moving to her pants.

"So…"All of a sudden, a pale hand pulls hers aside.

"…did I hear it correctly that you want to apply for a job?"

Unexpectedly, the Russian language turns into Polish inside her ear.

"Wow, you speak, Polish, Lana? How come?"

"Yes, I learned from my ex-husband. Listen, I could recommend you to the boss if you'd like?"

Why is she doing that…?

DON'T ANALYZE… TAKE IT AS IT COMES…

the Voice says from inside.

"Would you do it for me?"

"Of course, I would. All of us from Eastern Block should help each other as much as we can. Come back tomorrow, around noon, with your resume.

Our regional director will be back from Paris, and that's the only person you need to see."

"It's very kind of you, Lana…"

"Of course… of course… it's important that when she asks you how we know each other, you must say we've been friends for a long time."

"I will do that, certainly."

"You're very lucky because just recently, they let two people go. It's not easy to get in here, but now, with two openings, you have a big chance to get this job."

They have two openings. I can't believe it…!

"You won't regret it. The money is great. Oh, one more thing before I forget, don't get intimidated by the way she acts. She's known to be unfriendly. Ask for Jennifer, that's her name…"

A movie is put on a pause.

"Are these Chanel boots…?" still rings in her ears. Someone has told her to watch this DVD, that it is "a must" because of Anne Hathaway. Although not her first choice of an actress, the topic plus Meryl Streep became the two determining factors for her to press the play button and roll it out on a small screen.

And once it started playing, she quickly realized that fact. It is Chanel, not Prada, that runs an entire fashion world, without a doubt.

"So what do you think, Reeses, shall I give them another call?"

Pink ears arise to her question while hazelnut eyes follow her moves, getting up from the floor.

In the last few months, this pit-bull beast has become her best confidant, something that would never be the case in the presence of Armand. He and the dog were unable to separate.

Half a year apart is enough time for her to think over the future of their relationship, since lately things haven't been great, but how could they be great if she is the one who takes care of every bill?

He was helping me when I was unemployed. It's my turn to give back to him...

The same old mantra, when repeated over thousands of times, stops doing anything to her more and more confused mind.

"You're a good boy, Reeses." Her hand gently pats his strong head.

"I have nothing to lose, right, my boy?"

The dog follows her feet to the edge of the stairs. And as they settle down together, she looks straight ahead.

There, in a small window above the door to the yard, Nevada's sky presents another predictable day with no deficiency of Vitamin D, with no clouds swinging by…

"Good afternoon, Jennifer speaking, Chanel at the Wynn."

The Ice Queen's voice freezes her blood. Good thing she had set her intention on what she wanted to say before she dialed in.

"Hello, Jennifer… this is Ania… I hope you remember me… I stopped by two weeks ago with my resume…"

Her breath gets stuck inside her chest.

"I'm calling to check on the status of my application… Hello? Jennifer? Are you there?"

The same kind of silence must be found in Antarctica with no sign of living life.

"Yes, I am, haven't I told you already that Kimberly, the store manager, is the one who will decide?"

"Yes… Jennifer, you've mentioned it… I just thought since you're the regional director… you might…"

"Listen, if we are interested, we'll call you, all right?! But to be honest, we have received hundreds of applications from much more experienced candidates. Just so you know, in my opinion, your chances aren't that great."

Can a cold wind be transmitted via a phone wire? These goosebumps appearing all over her skin are evidence that indeed it can.

"Anything else, Ania? We're having here a hectic day."

DON'T REACT… STAY CALM…

She hears the Voice just in time before she loses all of her nerves.

"No… Jennifer… that's it… it was a pleasure…"

The harsh click of the phone hanging up doesn't allow her say "Have a great day."

How rude… unbelievable…

The dog knows her value. His pink nose touches her face.

"It's all right, Reeses… it's all right…"

Her arms go around his warm body, expressing how much she appreciates him being nearby.

"It doesn't matter what she thinks of me, my boy…" she says into his fur.

"Because what she doesn't know yet is that I NEVER… EVER… GIVE UP!"

The night is about to come. Her focus stays on the road. The straight highway doesn't bring any surprises, except a green sign that says: "50 miles to Henderson."

About forty minutes or less... she converts the numbers into the time that is left to release her hands from the most exhausting grasp they have ever had. For the last two hours or so, they've been glued to a steering wheel, holding onto it as intensely as if two lives entirely depended on it.

"You must get better at driving, in the U.S., without knowing this skill, you are dead. And that's why this country is so corrupted. Everyone depends on oil here. It's going to collapse anyway. The history has shown over and over that every empire eventually had to fall. America won't be an exception. Luckily, I won't be here to watch as it sinks, I hate this place!"

Then why did you come back...? she wanted to ask him but kept her comment silent, very saddened by the statement Armand has made. Especially since just a week ago, when she picked him up from the Las Vegas airport, he seemed overjoyed with a surprise trip to LA that she arranged for them.

Now, already on their way back home from California, as he fell asleep in a passenger's seat, she ponders on where those butterflies that used to be in her stomach just from hearing Armand's name are now...? Where is that physical attraction that used to magnetize their hands to one another...?

Why do we drag ourselves into something that has no future and only gives us pain...?

The brightest light appears out of nowhere, and as it cuts through her thoughts, it wakes Armand from his nap.

"Where are we...?" He turns toward her.

"The Premium Outlets. Let's stretch our legs, okay?"

"Of course... more shopping. You are addicted."

She chooses not to respond, a lesson that has taken her six years to learn.

Indeed the first store brings relief. Here she hides behind a denim pile.

The softest blue fabric melts under her fingers.

Diesel... these are my favorite ones.

Suddenly the cell phone goes off and pulls her out of a shopping mode.

"Hello? Is this Miss Ania?"

In a split of a second, she recognizes the friendly voice. In the last three months, she's heard it frequently, when it was giving her the exact same response:

"We are still interviewing, Ania. I promise we'll call you back as soon as we decide."

"Yes, Kimberly, this is she."

She looks around for the most stable pile just in case the answer is "no", and her world is crushed.

"Are you sitting down, missy?"

Oh my God... it's this bad...

"No, Kimberly, I'm standing… but I can handle it… go ahead…"

"Well, great because I would like to ask you if you would be interested in becoming a part of Chanel, and join our team at our beautiful boutique at the Wynn Promenade?"

"One can die in a second, and in a second, one can be born." Now more than ever, she understands that saying; she has just experienced it on her own.

"What… are… you… saying, Kimberly…? You mean I got the job?!"

"Yes, missy, you did. And your reaction makes me believe your answer is "yes", am I right?"

"Of course it's "yes", Kimberly! Thank you so much for giving me a chance…"

"Thank your persistence, my dear, it impressed me very much. The next question; when can you start?"

A different denim pile helps her with dizziness.

"In two weeks. First, I must resign from my current job…"

"Wonderful! Say goodbye to Vuitton, and we'll be seeing you on October sixteenth."

"That's right, Kimberly, I cannot wait!"

The phone goes back into her pocket. She lifts her eyes and faces Armand's that are staring at her from a distance, unable to hide behind a clothing rack.

44

"Armand, I have received a job offer… from Chanel… at the Wynn!"

"Oh, you did? I'm very happy for you."

"Thank you… it's so hard to get in there… it's almost like winning the lottery…"

"Great news… from now on, you won't need me. My role in your life is done."

His face turns away, and as she begins to walk behind him, she hears the Voice within says:

HE'S RIGHT ABOUT THAT…

CHAPTER 17

The Secret

"Thoughts become things. you can be, do, or have, anything you want because you create your own reality."

I swear that I've heard it somewhere before...

Her eyes are glued to the screen where the teachers keep changing, but their message does not. It profoundly resonates with her, waking something deep inside.

"Most people create their lives completely by default. This law is called the Law of Attraction. It never sleeps; it's always at work. This law states: "Like attracts like.", and, "The energy flows where the attention goes. "This is the Secret of the Universe."

The movie ends, and her eyes begin to scroll. One by one, she's reading the names of each participant:

John Assaraf...

Michael Bernard Beckwith...

Jack Canfield...

The last one brings a tingling sensation that moves through her veins.

HE IS THE ONE WHOM YOU SHOULD SEE... the Voice tells her from inside.

YOU MUST STUDY WHAT HE KNOWS... GO TO HIS SEMINAR...

The blanket is smoothened without a single crease. The pillows are in perfect order. The bed is empty. Armand is gone. And she is okay with it.

That this day was a long time coming, both of them have already known.

Not at a little bit of surprise. Not a glimpse of regret. Not a shadow of sadness; she is relieved because when she looks back at those seven years spent together, through all the joys and pains, what stands out the most is the latest expression of an angry face.

There it was: his response after she had pulled the trigger by saying those words:

"I want you to go back to Poland. We can't live like this anymore."

As always, that wrinkle had appeared when, according to him, things were going wrong.

And it has stayed there, unmoved, cutting through the skin in between his brows.

"I see. So now, when you no longer need me, you want me to go back? Fuck you, bitch! Fuck you!"

She stood there quiet and calm…, somehow.

And as he went on, expressing how he has felt, she appreciates the gift of confirmation, that indeed the right decision has been made.

"Without me, you're nobody! Even the dog loves me more!"

Reese's ears went up in the air, as he rapidly stood up from the floor.

She swallowed his hurtful words while reminding herself, *"do not react"*.

"You will end up alone, bitch, with those millions of dollars you'll eventually make! Fuck you!"

How sad it has to end this way... but it's my fault... I should have let him go a long time ago...

But her regret didn't last. It ended quickly by the bedroom door, where he has stopped and delivered his very last words:

"No man will ever last with you. You are a pathetic bitch! So ungrateful, so fucking difficult, you're just impossible to be with!"

The old forgotten chills came back and brought a memory of Father's talk…

"You know, Armand, I was truly hoping we could remain friends."

As soon as she said it, she realized the fact that some people come for a reason, some for a season, and some for a lifetime.

She swipes the blanket with a calm hand. Since the last two weeks, this room has not seen any fights or unnecessary argument. Instead, what this room has witnessed was a transformation of her mind, for there peace has moved in allowing a new vision to come.

"A list of attributes of an ideal man whom I want to attract into my life…:"

She grabs the pen, feeling an urge to write it down.

"He's tall… very handsome… with dark hair… He's got beautiful deep eyes…

"He is loyal… honest… with a great sense of humor… and a good faithful heart… he is my best friend…

44

"He always respects me and never lies to me…

"He values my opinion… puts our relationship first… and introduces me to his family…"

For a brief moment, her eyes look straight ahead as if, from the wall, more specifics can come about her ideal man.

"He's financially free… also generous and kind…

"He travels internationally a lot…

"He's never ashamed of me…

"He is my number one fan."

She puts the pen aside, folds the page in half, pulls the book off the shelf, and places the list inside.

Now, when the vision is safe, her quest can be released.

Let's see if this Secret really works and who the Universe will bring to me.

CHAPTER 18

Soulmate

"Sex on the beach," she hears and turns around. Her ready-for-a-cocktail fingers quickly get a hold of an ice-cold glass.

"Have fun tonight!" The bartender delivers an additional smile, making her wonder if his behavior is a result of extra ten bucks pushed toward him over the countertop.

Or it is caused by what she is wearing tonight? For indeed, next to dominating the club miniskirts, her well-fitted white pants stand out quite a lot.

It's good to be different.

Her eyes leave the bar and do the first scan of those who are gathered around.

Everyone is vibrating in some unique way. Some guests, to the music, some others to the opposite sex. Some others do it to the booze in their hands, which they've ordered to cover up the loneliness.

He has promised to stop... I should celebrate.

She reminds herself of what intention has brought her to this place tonight, and that was to release the tension that's been building up during the last two months...

Those emails from Armand were nagging... harassing... stealing her newly found peace of mind...

There he is, a million miles away, wanting to reunite...

Here she is, wanting to be alone, and to move on and forget their past...

Another sip of a drink and a quick gaze at the dance floor, to hit it and, let go of the stress, would only take her a few steps if not for that VIP lounge. It blocks her way with those hunger games going on inside of it.

There are cleavages showing off fake chests. There are skirts showing off cellulite-covered legs. There are the most expensive watches showing off their owners' enormous success.

Ten grand per bottle... that's absurd...

Her thoughts fly over the velvet seats, which are occupied by eight men.

Black, Asian, White- Caucasian, all colors of women are circulating the lounge, waiting for just that one sign, that one moment of eye contact that will win them a trophy of a night.

Amused, she looks at how their bodies are coming to attack. How their hair is flying high in the air, how their hips are twisting like the rubber bands. How their lips pumped up to the limits are trying to create the most seductive smile that silicon filler can make.

And then she sees him… he stands right in the middle of this craziness…

He's tall and beyond handsome… and has a black hair…

His business-savvy navy-striped suit has, underneath it, a white, open shirt…

He seems as if he's not quite present… as if out of his element...

Intrigued, she keeps observing his attractive persona as it's becoming the highest stake of the game. Indeed, to any gold- digger, he must be a true dream-catch.

For a second, her eyes go down.

She realizes the glass is already empty… on the contrary… to… his… eyes…

The music is gone. The time ceases to exist. He looks at her. She looks at him.

Chills go over her back, speeding up the beat of her heart.

Her focus remains on his attractive face that is undisturbed by human-bees flying around his striped pants.

Some unseen energy is screwing her feet to the ground, and as it disables her from making any move, she hears the Voice saying from inside:

KEEP YOUR EYES ON THIS MAN...

The second round of chills goes down on her back just about when the stranger's arms decide to throw themselves over his neck.

Although his body got into a prison his eyes have not. Still they are holding onto hers.

Hmm… is that who you like? Then, I wish you good luck.

An empty glass stays behind her and she begins to burst through the crowd.

The music keeps pulsating and stimulating her brain to create new stories and let go of that no longer serve in her life. Her feet touch the dance floor and move to the first beat… and, they do it again… and again they repeat.

Fear, hopelessness, despair… all those low vibes which she has felt in the last two weeks, one by one, are deliberately being released. A new sensation comes over, and as it elevates her mind, all of a sudden she feels someone touch her back…

Pulled out of her trance, she turns around to an ebony face.

"Hi! I'm Sam! Come, join us for a drink! We love the way you dance!"

A body-builder arm points at nearby spot.

"Our lounge… is over… there!"

She follows the direction of his shout.

And there are those eyes, still holding onto hers in spite of the same stranger who is sliding down on their owner's striped pants.

Was this idea his…? she wanders to herself, hearing the lyrics of a song:

" If you want it… you already got it… if you feel it… it must be real… the time is waiting… no hesitating… tick… tock… tick… tock… tick… tock… four minutes left to go…"

I guess…

Surprisingly, these velvet seats are much more comfortable than she assumed from afar.

Regardless, 10k per bottle is still absurd, so is the company of Ebony Sam.

Because it was him, plus a can of Red Bull, that occupied the last hour she spent without dancing.

"Thanks for tonight… I gotta go, working an early shift tomorrow."

She stands up while thinking,

At least the tension is gone…

The final gaze at those newly made couples that are meant to survive one night.

And then… out of nowhere… her neck is being caressed…

And then… out of nowhere… a man's voice comes from behind:

"I was watching you when you were dancing."

His breath is soft… and warm… and, as she turns around, she realizes that his eyes are darker… and deeper… than she thought when looking at them from afar…

"Good, I hope you've enjoyed the view."

He has a beautiful smile.

"I have. You are a great dancer."

"I know I am. Thanks a lot."

"Oh? You do?"

He seems entertained.

His eyes switch their look into those which puppies tend to have.

"Are you leaving, already?"

His lips lean closer, almost touching her ear.

"Do you want me to leave?"

"No…"

"Then… I… will… stay."

His hand moves closer and introduces his skin.

"Come over here, let's take a seat."

"To make your girlfriend upset?"

"You know very well that she's not."

Somehow the battleground is clear with no gold-diggers around.

"I'm Jason."

"I'm Ania."

"A… n… i… a… What a beautiful name you have."

Hmm... there must be a highway paved with hearts he has broken...

"So Jason, what do you do for a living?" Right away, she directs their chat.

"Music industry. I find new talents. How about yourself?"

"Fashion. High-end retail. Chanel boutique. Upstairs."

"Really? Do you live in Vegas? And you work here at the Wynn?"

"Yes. And where is home for you?"

"In Minnesota."

"Hmm… I've never been… Are you married?"

"Ha! You're straightforward!"

She holds onto the question as tight as to her rule number one: "No" to a married man, no matter how hot."

"I got divorced two years ago, how about yourself?"

44

His eyes get deeper, waiting for her to respond.

"Recovering from a relationship of seven years… just recently broken-up…"

His arm goes around hers as if it's destined to only be resting there.

Their bodies connect… Their energies make an exchange…

Something familiar touches her soul and teleports her mind… far… far… back…

There is a memory of their lives being shared…

I feel like I've known him forever…

Confirmation is found in his eyes, and in them she stays de-attaching from the outside world.

CHAPTER 19

Goddess

Cheesy turquoise falls over dirty windows. Lazy pink rests on the overly used velvet couch. Golden Buddha framed by cheap-looking silver, hangs on the wall next to a wooden Jesus and his pale crucified arms.

Two blocks away from the Strip, Vegas turns into a different kind of town, here staying glamorous is what matters least, here what matters most is staying alive.

Afternoon sun pushes her forward. She crosses the doorstep and slowly walks inside straight into a smell of death: flowers sticking out from the vases, which a few steps further blend with a lingering smell of mirth.

"Hello…, anyone there?" Her call goes into the vastness, and in there, it disappears like a drop of water inside a dry sponge.

The silence remains undisturbed. And so she repeats:

"Hello… anyone…?"

Suddenly, someone's feet are being dragged on the floor… and a smoky voice comes from far back:

"You're punctual! Very good, my dear! I hate when my clients are late!"

A gypsy woman emerges out of the darkness, the laser-focused eyes cut straight into hers.

Do they already know what has happened in the past? Or what's currently going on? Or what lies ahead?

Black, messed up hair, whose owner must have just been napping, makes her conclude:

The business is not doing great...

"You are Ania, right, my dear?!"

The smell of mirth coming closer is getting enriched with an odor of strong cigarettes.

"Yes, ma'am, I am."

"Call me, Kathrine. Please, let's not waste our precious time!"

A door behind them is pointed at by long, acrylic nails, which are covered by a shade of the freshest blood.

A small room has not much in it but a table, two chairs, and a single lamp with a shade that stands over an old bible, its cover once upon a time had to be black. But now, already faded, it matches very the well-aged tarot cards.

A quick look at their splitting corners makes her re-conclude:

Maybe the business is not that bad...?

"So, what brings you to me, my dear?"

"Clarification," she answers while settling down.

The least I share the bigger chance for an accurate reading...

"I see... any specific question?"

"No, I would rather hear you talk."

"Fair enough."

The bloody nails push the entire deck forward.

"Shuffle them well. Then separate into three piles."

Left hand... from the heart... She remembers that, although psychics may change the notion they require, never do.

Three piles flipped turns into three images.

"Well... oh well... where shall I begin...?"Gypsy eyes stare at the revelations.

"All right, let's start here... you're a wise, intuitive woman... you're psychic yourself... are you aware of that?"

Her head bows down in agreement.

"You are? Very well! So, are you also aware that you're not in the profession in which you're supposed to be? Although I must say, you became quite good at it, but selling handbags and shoes...? No, no, no! That is not the purpose of your life! There are much bigger things ahead...!"

Dark eyes go up to the ceiling and there they stay, circulating for a while.

"You see, you're meant to fly with the eagles, not to walk among those turkeys whose wings will never soar...! Do you understand me?!"

"Yes, Katherine, I do, but to be honest, I really love my job."

"Hmm... that means... you aren't ready, but you will be, it's just a matter of time."

Heavy brows come together to screen the second pile.

"Oh... poor thing... your heart has been broken... over and over... man after man...

"Hmm... just recently, someone has left your life, am I right?"

Her head bows down in agreement, again.

"But about that one, have zero regrets! He was sucking your energy like a parasite! Finally, you shook this monkey off your shoulders!"

The laser eyes penetrate hers.

"Hmm… there is a new man around you… and his name starts with "J"…"

"Jason… we met two weeks ago at the club."

"Yes! Him! He is your soulmate. The cards are telling me that."

Kathrine smiles as if the biggest secret has been exposed.

"You see, my dear, it has been clarified! My cards never lie to me! In the near future, you will move to New York City because of that man."

"But he's not from New York. He's from Minnesota."

"It does not matter where he is from, do you understand?!" Suddenly, Gypsy's voice turns into one of an angry crow that lost stability and support of his branch.

"I will repeat, to make it clear: You will move to New York City because of that guy!

And there… I see many flags around you… I see an international crowd…

"Also, there is a building… you are walking toward it…? Hmm… it must be the U.N…"

"The United Nations? I've never been there."

"But you will, when the time is right.

"This Jason guy has too many women around him… he's confused… kind of lost…

"He doesn't realize that you are "the one"…

"Eventually, he will come to you… though it may take many years. Until then it will be a real rollercoaster… up and down… up… and… down…

"There's something that's blocking him from getting closer… look! It's right here!"

A long nail points at the card with a man hanging from a tree branch. And, as it hits several times, the room fills up with a woodpecker's sound.

"Yes… *this thing*… is much more important… than that new Jason man!

Let me ask you, my dear, have you seen a doctor lately?"

"Yes, I have, in fact…"

"OBGYN, am I right?"

How in the world does she know that…?

"Yes… it was an OBGYN… for… an annual check…"

"And, what did they say to you?" Long nails keep galloping over the table top as fast as they do on her nerves.

"Nothing yet; they're still running the tests."

"Ha! Good! They should run them because you are sick!"

An impulse pushes her chair far away from the deck of cards.

Now, it seems it is her who has lost the stability and support of the branch.

"Sick…? Excuse me…?"

"Yes, sick, it's cancer… but don't worry, I will take care of it."

"Cancer…?! What kind of cancer…?"

"A tumor… in your left ovary…"

Dizziness comes over her and spins the world around.

"Not to worry, my dear, I've healed hundreds of clients with the same issue. Trust me, you'll be more than fine!"

What is she talking about…?! She's not a doctor!

She remains silent with a dry, open mouth.

"Let me investigate where this *thing* has generated… hmm… I see… it had to be over there…"

The final pile goes under scrutinizing eyes.

"…When you twenty-one years old… your heart got broken in another land…"

A card with a man gazing ahead and three sticks goes under the light of the lamp.

"It was near the sea… somewhere in Europe… on the north, am I right?"

A memory of Magic flashes through her mind, it's gotten so old that it has already turned into black and white.

"Yes… it was in Sweden, about fifteen years ago…"

"Lord Jesus…! God have mercy…!" Kathrine's voice turns back into the one of a crow.

"It was his mother who did *that*…! Oh, what an evil woman she was… and it was just innocent, puppy love…"

Magic's mother…?

Another flash brings back a memory of those eyes that had always stared as if they've wished for the worst…

"She had put a spell on you never to find true love… and, that each time you start to have feelings toward any man, he will leave you with a broken heart, and so for the rest of your life, you'll end up alone and depressed…"

Magic… John… Damir… Armand… face after face appears in her mind.

Could that be the reason why none of those relationships lasted…?

"Let me ask you, my dear. Did that boy break-up with you unexpectedly?"

Bloody nails click in the air.

"Just like that?"

"Yes… he had… over the phone… he said that he was about to propose to another girl…"

"Exactly, to someone who his mother had chosen for him!"

Oh my God… it does make sense…

Another flashback… brings her back to that afternoon when she answered his call… when she slid on a wall and dropped the phone… from her hand…

"I also see that there was very heavy vomiting on your way back home…?"

"Yes… I almost died on the ferry line…"

"Good thing your cabinmate called for the doctor… God bless her soul…"

I can't believe it… how does she know that…?

Gypsy hands stretch out toward the Bible; it's time has finally come.

"In the name of Lord Jesus, I will rebuke that evil curse! We need to act as soon as we possibly can! You must participate in the process! Listen carefully to every word I say…! Are you with me, dear?"

She pulls herself together.

"Yes, Kathrine, I am…"

"Good. Go to the best grocery store in town and get one fresh chicken egg. Make sure that nothing is wrong with it. It must be pure white, without any spots. It is crucial… VERY important…! Did you hear what I've just said?!"

"Yes."

Dark eyes almost cut through her soul. Gypsy face has no glimpse of a smile.

"Then, once you're at home, put that egg under your bed, right underneath where your ovaries are; you MUST be very careful, you CANNOT break it! Do you understand?!"

Her head nodes "yes".

"After you're done with the egg, go to take a hot shower, wash every part of your body twice. Scrub it, really, really well. Then, before you go to sleep, pray from all of your heart to Jesus Christ!"

The holy book makes its way into her hands.

"Here, take this Bible, it has healed hundreds of lives. Keep it next to your bed throughout the entire night. Did you hear everything I've just said?!"

"Yes, Kathrine, I have."

"Good. Tomorrow, first thing in the morning, I will go to buy a gold urn at my church."

"Gold urn? What is it for?"

"To bury the evil spell, it's going to cost you, but only gold gives the highest protection, and that's what you need the most in this case."

"How much for this urn?"

"Three hundred dollars."

"Three hundred…?! That is a lot!"

"Is it really, my dear, to be free from the burden you've carried for years?! Up to you, otherwise you're going to suffer for the rest of your life."

What if she's a con artist? No… it cannot be… she knew too much…

"Here…" She hands her an Amex card. "Go ahead… charge the full amount."

A terminal burps out with a receipt; “Readings by Goddess” it says on its top.

“Be here next Wednesday, May ninth, at the same time… bring the egg and the Bible…

Then, I will do my part!”

A white towel has all their attention. Somewhere there, in between its tight cotton-wrap, a fresh chicken egg stays well protected from any potential harm.

She has carried it from the car to the table as if it was the Holy Grail.

“I’m glad that you have followed my instructions. Pure white… Not a bit of a crack… Excellent job, my dear… excellent!”

Kathrine’s hand makes a sign of cross from above it and then points at the chair.

“Take a seat.”

She finds herself in a familiar spot, feeling as if she has never left.

Maybe her body was gone from the small room with a single lamp, but her mind remained here, wondering how it could be that this witch-looking woman had already known the result of those run by OB tests would be?

“Left ovary is affected… tumor… cancer… reaching the fourth stage…” Doctor’s call broke down the news two days after their reading had taken place.

“Before we begin, I need to warn you…” The dry voice brings her attention back.

“That what we are going to witness here may scare you to death. No matter what you see, be still… observe… and do not say a word. Understand?!”

Kathrine’s palms come together as if they were at mass.

“Now, put both hands on your heart.”

Laser eyes lift up high.

“Our Father, who art in heaven, hallowed be Thy name! Let Thy kingdom come, let Thy will be done, on Earth as it is in Heaven.

"Give us this day our daily bread, and forgive us our debts, as we also have forgiven our debtors. And lead us not into temptation, but deliver us from evil!

"In the name of Lord Jesus, I call upon the Holy Spirit to come down here and heal an innocent!"

Suddenly, the air is getting thicker… and the room starts to shrink in size around her…

"I am calling upon Your Power, in the name of Your Son, Jesus, and His sacred blood!"

Suddenly… the lights start flashing… by themselves… she can swear that the lamp wasn't touched…

"You said that no weapon formed against us shall ever prosper! Let us witness your miracle, Almighty God!"

Cold sweat comes over her skin… and covers every inch…

Kathrine's hand reaches toward the cross, lifts it high, and then, as if it is the finest sword, with one swoop cuts through a white shell… a yellow liquid is exposed and… a flash of black long and sticky hair…

Terrified, she backs up from the table.

"What… is… this horrible thing…?!"

Kathrine's nail points at the moving flash that reminds her of a snake shedding his skin…

"Do NOT touch! This thing was growing inside you… and making you sick…!"

Again, dizziness comes over her… the world is spinning around… she's unable to speak…

"You must forgive her for what she's done to you; otherwise, the cancer will return. And, you will never find true love."

She tries to breathe but cannot find enough air…

"Do you forgive that woman? I am asking!"

She's trying her best no to fade…

"Do you forgive the-mother of your ex?!"

"Yes… I forgive her…"

Numb, she looks at Gypsy's face.

"In the name of the Holy Spirit, I call for Archangel Michael to conquer the devil's work!"

44

Again, a white towel comes to the surface, as it quickly wraps around the chicken egg's broken form.

"Tonight, the darkness will be burned in fire and then buried deep underground.

"From now on you are free! Remember to use your power only for good and do great things in this life!"

CHAPTER 20

Jesus

44

Four hundred seats have been taken by those hungry for success. One teacher has brought them together, promising a breakthrough within the next seven days.

Had she not watched the movie *"The Secret,"* she would have never known who Jack Canfield was; and she never would have arrived in Arizona to write down the list of her long-term goals.

But this morning, it seems no list is required since Jack, who's already onstage, has no book or remote control in his hand but instead a classical guitar on his lap.

The dimmed lights complete the silence, as Canfield's calm voice grounds everyone.

"Find a comfortable position and straighten your back."

All bodies turn into a wave, reminiscent of fans watching a soccer match.

"Close your eyes… relax your muscles… and take a long, deep breath…"

Four hundred nostrils unite in soaking up the oxygen.

"Exhale it slowly, and now imagine a ball of light that's waiting by your feet. Soon its journey will begin."

Jack's hand pulls a string, creating a beautiful sound that bounces off the conference room's walls and flies above every participant's head.

"As the silver light will be moving, we'll be singing together one word: "Hallelujah!" Repeat… after me…"

The guitar's strings create another beautiful chord.

"Hallelujah…" She joins Canfield's voice, not sure what to expect, for meditation remains an unexplored zone for her.

"And now the silver light is entering your body and moving up from your feet…"

The ball is set into motion.

"Hallelujah…,"comes out from every mouth.

"Slowly, it's reaching your knees… passing your hips… it's moving up to your waist… your legs are getting lighter and lighter… and here, around your belly area, it will circulate…"

She feels the warmth inside her gut.

"All unresolved emotions are stored right there… So are all the answers from the Universe.

Now, move the ball up; bring it closer to your heart…"

"Hallelujah…," she keeps on signing.

"Allow its vibrant energy to heal old pains… this is your chance to let go of resentment… of anything that was holding you back…"

She feels the warmth around her chest almost as if something is opening it from inside out…

"Hallelujah…" United voices keep on singing.

"The ball is moving up. Now, here, on top of your head, let it stay for a while."

Unlike some throats, which are dropping their "hallelujahs," the guitar does not stop.

Chord by chord, it keeps touching the emotions stored in the depths of her heart.

And as she allows them to be liberated, something is lifting her up… some unseen force is pulling her high above surrounding neighbors' cries…

For a moment, she brings down the awareness and there, down below, sees her body sitting on a chair…

But the force doesn't let go… it is transferring her into a realm of clouds…

And there she sees HIM… HE'S coming out of it… wearing a long white gown…

Almost as if HE is waiting for her…

Even though HE doesn't say a word… she knows what HE does…

HE'S powerful, yet HE'S humble… HE'S dignified, yet not at all proud…

HIS eyes are blue like the sky on the first day of spring… not deep brown as she has always thought they would be…

HIS presence overwhelms her with love…

"Why do you worry so much?" HE asks without moving HIS lips.

Her heart begins to beat faster and faster than she ever thought it could beat.

"You exist… you do… you are there…"

"I AM." HE responds and, in an instant, she feels HE is the Best Friend.

"Thank you…," her heart whispers into HIS.

HE smiles, and in an instant, she knows that to HIM she was always enough…

"Open up your hands… you will receive…"

Her arms stretch out toward HIS light.

"Look." HE points at her left palm, where a scarlet heart is pulsating with a newborn life.

HIS eyes move hers toward the right hand… and there she sees countless dollar bills are made into a tower…

"I… don't… understand…"

Confused, she looks at HIM just when the image disappears from her neighbor's cough.

HIS hand makes a rapid move, and with one swoop, HE throws a velvet cape behind her back.

"They don't bother you. Do they?"

"No, Jesus, they don't…"

Under HIS cape she is safe.

HIS cape is peace… HIS unwavering strength… it has always been there; she just forgot…

"All is well…"

HIS white gown is dissolving in another dimension of a higher realm…

"Slowly, start to bring your awareness back into the room…" The familiar voice of Jack reaches her thoughts from below.

"Breathe, and on the count of four, you will open your eyes…

One…"

Her focus is back on the chair…

"Two…"

Her feet find the ground.

"Three…"

Another exhale slows down the beat of her heart.

"Four… Open up your eyes."

She looks straight ahead; there, on the stage, is Jack with the guitar on his lap.

CHAPTER 21

The United Nations

She's caught between the moon and New York City with the company of cold wind blowing from the east river's side. "First Avenue and forty-second." Those directions given at the hotel were very precise. Still, on the way of getting here, she got lost several times.

It must be a common thing for the Big Apple's first-time visitors,

she ponders while checking out navy shades of September sky. Up there, heavy rain hangs low as if uncertain about coming down to make everyone wet.

"I see you walking toward the building surrounded by many international flags." Goddess's words play in her mind like an old record.

Is helping others the purpose of my life?

Across the street is what she came to experience, those thirty-nine floors that stand for the humanitarian acts.

A week ago, the Voice from within her spoke and suddenly changed her vacation plans:

CANCEL YOUR TRIP TO BRAZIL... AND GO TO NEW YORK CITY INSTEAD...

Here she is holding to an umbrella, a very different one from those served with the cocktails on the golden sands. The reality of retail was left early in the morning and stayed at the Wynn over two thousand miles away.

She takes the last snapshot of the sleepless city from the reflection in the elevation's glass.

The rain has decided. So has she.

I will come back tomorrow to take a tour inside.

"Place your bag inside the bin." A serious voice contradicts a friendly smile. A security guard pushes the container forward. She follows the gray plastic bin as it passes under the scanner light.

"The tour will start in about ten minutes. Your guide will meet you on the second floor, in a foyer." The guard informs without being asked while gluing his eyes to her messenger bag.

She is used to that; wearing Chanel always gets people's attention. Today is no different at all. But what she cares about is not people's opinions, instead of how nicely it finishes her outfit, one of a New Yorker, entirely black, from head to toe.

Those who live in Manhattan, she came to discover, do not waste time thinking what to throw on their backs because to achieve success requires fast movement; otherwise, you're out of the game.

New York City, here even the sky is not the limit...

She takes the conclusion up the stairs, acknowledging a massive window that delivers a view of Manhattan already awoken to another gloomy day.

In the foyer, that's what he has mentioned...

A smile on an olive-skinned face greets from afar.

"Gloria, intern guide from Bolivia."

A badge over the girl's uniform confirms this is the right spot.

"I hope, guys, that you have enjoyed the tour. If so, please, leave your opinions in the comment box. Anyway, let's keep on moving; the next room is going to be our last stop."

Petite Latina leads them into a hallway that soon turns into a gallery of art.

"Most objects presented here were gifts from some of the ninety-three countries that are part of the U.N." Gloria's hand waves around.

"For example, Escopettara, was gifted to us by Cezar Lopez, who is Columbian activist.

Perhaps you've heard about him on television. Nobody? Really? Hmm..."

The Bolivian face shows disappointment. Gloria gives it another try.

"Escopettara was also given to Carlos Santana, Shakira, and Dalai Lama."

Famous names do not help much. Still, the group remains numb.

"It's a symbol of peace that sends out a powerful message: "What was used for violence can be turned into art," which brings me to an important issue on which the United Nations has been working on for a very long time.

“It is, The Children and the Arm conflict, an incredibly serious problem, mostly affecting African countries, although they still deny proven facts.

“Please, take a look at this photo, captured in 1993 in Rwanda right after the horrible genocide.

It presents a boy who, at age six, was kidnapped by Hutus to then be brainwashed so he could become a killing machine.”

A black-and-white image ricochets from the wall. The child’s eyes pull hers straight into their depth. From there she reads the message: “My joy is in taking prisoners’ lives.”

She looks down at those little hands that barely hold up a heavy gun.

“Thousands of kids are trained to kill their parents in cold blood,” Gloria carries on.

Maybe a tour guide can hide her emotions, but somehow, she cannot.

Something erupts her body… shakes it up from the very core.

Something takes over her mouth:

“How can I work for the U.N.? How can I get involved?”

One question wakes up the group from a long coma and in a second, everyone’s focus goes on her.

“The information desk will provide you the answers.” The Bolivian intern seems quite disturbed.

No wonder, the routine has just got broken, not according to the boring plan.

“And where is that desk, Gloria?”

“By the cafeteria, downstairs.”

“Thank you,” she says and turns around, but before walking away stops to shout:

“I will leave my comment that the tour was great.”

A short line inside a cafeteria helps her to decide,

First drink, after, the information desk.

She grabs an orange juice and her credit card. The visa is about to reach the clerk's palm when all of a sudden, a stranger's hand comes from behind. And as it cuts right in between them, she hears:

"Let me take care of this, miss."

She chooses not to respond. The intention that has brought her here was not to look for a man.

"Miss, I insist. Please, let me take care of it."

She hears and becomes aware that whoever it is it's not going to give up.

An Italian-looking face gives her the kindest smile.

"Thank you, sir, I appreciate it."

"Of course, you are our guest."

"Our guest?"

Her eyes go south to a white badge hanging on his neck:

"Ambassador to The United Nations."

She freezes but not from the cold juice she just grabbed in her hand.

"Excuse me, sir… do… you… work… here…?"

"I do. I have been working here for over twenty years." His smile is getting kinder, showing compassion for her attitude change.

"Is it your first time in New York City?"

"Yes, it is my first time, sir."

"And, so far, how do you like it?"

"I love it. I want to move here next year."

"Well, I'm not surprised. There is no other place like Manhattan in the entire world. And where is home for you, Miss?"

"It's in Las Vegas, sir. Would you mind if I ask you a few questions, would it be okay…?"

"Of course, I'm on my lunch break. Shall we?" His hand points at the empty chairs.

"I'm Shariar, by the way."

"Pleasure, sir, my name is Ania."

"Where are you originally from?"

"From Poland."

"I have been to Poland, but it was several years ago. We worked there on a project with the Polish government. Anyway, what would you like to ask me?"

Now or never; this is my chance...

"I would like to know how I can work for the U.N.?"

"And why would you like to be part of us?"

Shall, I tell him about what Goddess has told me...? No... I shouldn't. He will think I'm strange...

"A psychic has told me that I should do humanitarian work."

Again, something takes over her mouth as if she has no control over the words.

"And that's why I came here to feel this place out..."

"I'm not surprised." He jumps right in. "A similar thing happened to me when I was sixteen. I heard the Voice that told me this would be my life's path. You see, if I hadn't listened then, we would not be having this conversation right now. So what's your current occupation, Ania?"

"I work at the Chanel boutique at the Wynn."

His eyes lit up as if they just got plugged into the stars.

"Chanel? Oh, that's a wonderful brand. You must have many wealthy clients over there?"

"I do, in fact, many..."

Excitement takes over his face.

"Hmm... I have an idea, only if you have time?"

"I have all the time in the world, Shariar."

"Wonderful. Then, come with me. Let's get you a visitor's pass."

From left to right, the panorama of Manhattan stretches out.

From the floor to the ceiling, the massive windows allow noon's light to burst inside.

And as it does get in, it highlights the brown leather chairs, which all seem to be occupied by those wearing gray suits: serious men.

Her eyes scroll through the lobby in perhaps its busiest time. Then, quickly move down to her chest to read it for already the fourth time:

"VIP VISITOR PASS." Once more, her mind gets blown away, for it cannot explain how all these events are possibly taking place...?

Shariar's hand touches her shoulder in the front of a short, chubby man.

"Remigio, let me introduce you to Ania, my new Polish friend."

Facing her uniform reminds of those that parade on the Tiananmen Square.

"And where have you found such a lovely lady, Shariar?"

"In the cafeteria, downstairs."

"Nice… very nice."

A chunky hand strangely twists, as their shake is exchanged, she thinks:

Does he have Parkinson's disease?

But her interest in his medical condition quickly ends because his surname-"Maradonna" is much more intriguing to her.

"Yes, Diego is my older brother." He reads her mind.

"Your brother is a true legend. It's an honor to meet you, sir."

"Coffee, miss?"

"Yes, please…"

Her black outfit dives into the shades of gray.

"What brings you to IMMSAM?"

"IMMSAM…? I don't understand."

"Remigio, Ania just mentioned to me that she wants to be a part of us, I haven't explained anything to her yet…"

"I see, Shariar. Do you live here in New York City, miss?"

"No, sir, I don't."

"If not, how do you think this is going to work?"

His uniform would be about to explode if toughness could expand one's size.

"I'm planning to move here next summer.

"Well, if that's the case, we can talk."

The chubby face moves around.

"What is your occupation, miss?"

"I work at Chanel."

"Where?"

"At the Wynn Resort."

"Wynn in Las Vegas?"

"That's right. Have you ever been there, sir?"

"I don't like Las Vegas. It's a city built on sin."

She pulls back. But then quickly reminds herself that she is not the city in which she happens to live.

"Chanel, you are saying… that is a wonderful brand…"

"Exactly, Remigio, don't you think it could be beneficial for us?" Shariar adds his few cents.

A stiff uniform shrinks in size just a little bit.

An X-ray look makes an attempt to read her mind.

"Do you have rich clients over there?"

"I do, sir."

"Good… very good…" X-ray look continues to drill through her thoughts.

"Let me explain what IMMSAM is all about. We are an organization under the U.N.

Our mission is to fight hunger and malnutrition, using spirulina. Do you know what it is?"

"No, sir, unfortunately, I haven't heard of it before."

"Spirulina is an algae plant. It rebuilds an immune system and helps kids to grow. Our biggest project is in Kenya. We also work with the most influential leaders and celebrities in the world. Did you hear about Carolina Herrera?"

"Yes, sir, I have."

"Of course, I forgot that you work in fashion. Anyway, Mrs. Herrera is Argentinian, like me, also one of our Goodwill Ambassadors.

I would suggest if you want to work for the U.N., start with us, otherwise, you may never get in…"

"It sounds incredible, but how can I contribute to IMMSAM, sir?"

"Helping us to raise the money from those rich clients you've got at Chanel."

A sound of a bell cuts through their conversation.

One by one, gray suits are getting up from those brown leather chairs.

The twisted hand reaches inside the briefcase.

"Here, take our brochures and show us what you can do with that."

CHAPTER 22

Encore

"Ultimate Luxury" is Chanel's new favorite word, or rather it has been until two months ago. Because it was then when "recession" jumped into everyone's mouth, and the Encore Resort got empty, and the stock market crashed.

She stands behind the counter and gazes at the shopping promenade. There, on the other side of boutique windows, Las Vegas has turned into a set from *"The Planet of the Apes."*

It doesn't matter what the economy is like, I am going to sell this bag.

Her attention goes to the glass box inside the Diamond Forever is safe. It remains locked and protected from those who cannot comprehend its price, to some, $120k could buy a house, to others, educate their child.

But when millions are struggling, she remembers the one percent that thrives.

Aldara will buy it.

The most affluent client brings hope to her mind.

Since she collects exotic handbags and there were only nine internationally made.

"One for each day of the year," she says out loud to three 365 diamonds that are screaming "wealth" from cc-lock.

"What did you just say, Ania?"

"Oh, nothing Levent, I'm talking to myself."

"Do you worry about what's going to happen to us?"

Her eyes move over to her coworker's face.

"No, I don't, I try to stay focused on what I can appreciate."

"You are right; in spite of the layoffs, we still got jobs. We are so blessed."

They may transfer me to New York City if I sell this bag.

"Do you miss living in Manhattan, Levent?"

"I do, Vegas is so plastic and fake. There is no style in here, no city life."

"How long did you live there?"

"Nine years. God, it was fantastic… Those museums, that fashion, that art. New Yorkers are no bullshit, just like you and me."

"I want to move there this summer."

"In the recession? Are you nuts? Do you have any idea how expensive it is to live over there?"

"Yes, I'm aware of it, but somehow, I feel like I'll be fine, besides…"

She turns back towards the window and remaining dead promenade.

"…you never know who's going to walk through this door and, in one second, change your life."

A string of pearls swims between her fingers. She flips the attached charms, and one by one aligns them in perfect positions; the camellia, the quilted bag, the bottle with Nr 5. They used to bring luck to Mademoiselle Gabriele. Can they do it again to the House of Chanel? Now, more than ever, the brand needs some extra luck, for although the spring has arrived already, the traffic that used to come with that had not. Since the news consistently reports about homes repossessed by the banks, walking around with the luxury shopping bags became a rather shameful act.

Four thousand dollars for a costume jewelry piece…

Looking down at the pearls, she tries to stay positive, in spite of Aldara saying "no" to an alligator bag, in spite of the corporate office saying "no" to her transfer request.

No, I am not going to worry… something better will come out of it.

"Excuse me, miss, may I please take a look at this belt?"

Out of the blue, the gentleman appears in the front of the pearls. With the speed of light, she pulls out a velvet tray.

"Of course, sir, good morning. How are you doing today?"

"Very well, thank you for asking. This piece is magnificent."

"You have an excellent eye, sir."

The pearls land on a tray, presented as if they are in front of the king.

"It's a limited edition, sir."

"Limited edition…? Oh, my wife would be obsessed with it. You see, she collects unique pieces, as such."

"Oh, does she? Well, sir, then she will appreciate this particular one. It has been designed for the opening of our boutique."

His hand gets a hold of the Nr 5 charm.

"Therefore, you cannot find it anywhere else in the world."

"Seriously, you mean, no other Chanel?"

"Nowhere else, it's only available here, at Encore, sir."

"Incredible… it shouldn't take long to convince my wife. She'll be here any minute. Women always take longer…"

"Yes, I know, I am one of them. By the way, sir, where are you visiting us from?"

"From Scottsdale in Arizona."

"Oh, that is just great."

"How so?"

"You see, since Chanel doesn't own a boutique in Arizona, if we ship it, you will save on tax." Her fingers hit the calculator's keys. "Three hundred dollars to be exact."

She leans over the counter to whisper into his hear. "Also… I'll ask the manager to wave the shipping fee for you…"

His smile extends.

"You're one of the best salespeople I have ever met."

"Oh, thank you, it's so kind of you, sir."

"Don't call me, sir, I'm Larry."

"Honey, what are you doing over there?" A woman's voice twists their heads to the left.

"There she is. I found something for you. Come here, love, and take a look at this belt."

A tall, lean lady with short blond hair joins the focus of their eyes.

"Good morning, madame."

"Good morning, miss. Oh… what a gorgeous belt…"

"Isn't it, love? Ania has just told me you wouldn't be able to find it anywhere else in the world."

Without asking for permission, she lifts the pearls to place them on the lady's waist.

"Oh… it suits you perfectly, what are you doing to stay in such a great shape… ma'am?" The charms settle one by one. "Is it Yoga or Pilates?"

"It's Pilates, miss."

"Isn't she just fantastic at sales?"

"Yes, honey, she is."

"So tell me, Ania, how is Las Vegas doing these days?"

"Well, Larry, it's been a challenging time for us, but I try to stay positive and also remind myself that this too shall pass."

"I like your attitude; very wise for someone so young."

"Not so young, but thank you, I'll take it as a compliment. Are you originally from Arizona?"

"No, I am from New York."

"New York…? No way! That is where I want to move in June."

"This year, are you sure?"

"Yes, I am, one hundred percent, I want to move to Manhattan to do some humanitarian work."

The belt returns on the tray, Larry's eyes, on hers.

"Hmm… humanitarian work you're saying."

"Yes, Larry. Last month I attended the Goodwill Ambassador's nomination at the U.N."

"Did you? I am impressed. As far as the belt, we will take it."

"You mean you will ship?"

"Of course, so that I can save for another one." He laughs while his platinum Amex makes a short trip. As soon as it reaches her hand, she discovers another card.

"Here is my address, email, and phone number, in case you need help."

"Help, Larry, with what?"

"With getting a job, you see, I was Director of Saks for twenty-five years."

All of a sudden she feels like a deer that got hit by the brightest lights.

"You… mean… Saks… Fifth… Avenue… Larry?"

"The flagship store, correct."

The belt, the tray, the counter, begins to spin around her head.

"It's not easy to find great salespeople, they will be lucky to have you there, and I believe that some doors will still open to Larry Hill's name."

CHAPTER 23

Upper West

44

Unstoppable light breaks in through a small window and dominates an entire space.

She takes a step forward to stick her head outside, allowing the view from the 14th floor to take her breath away. Ahead, down below, an early summer rolls out a rug made of green trees right in between Upper West Manhattan's most sophisticated streets.

"Sixty-ninth and Central Park West is one of the best locations in town."

Somehow the doorman's comment doesn't distract her from gazing at the pigeons resting their wings on the nearest rooftops.

"It would be twenty-five hundred, including the utilities. It's an incredible deal, miss. There are only two buildings to reach the park."

One... four... zero... three... She adds the numbers. *"Eight"... it brings luck in Feng Shui.*

"One bedroom next door is at least five thousand per month."

"I don't need convincing, Miguel, the energy is great."

She turns around.

"I'll take it."

"Oh, I am so happy to hear it, miss, it will be so wonderful to have you as a tenant in our place."

And why people say that New Yorkers are mean?

"If there is anything we can help you with, please don't ever hesitate to ask."

"Thank you, I appreciate it."

Fresh air pulls her focus back to the view of Central Park.

"I don't have much. No furniture; only books, clothes, and shoes."

"Shoes, of course, just like my wife. And where will you be working if you don't mind my asking?"

"In Christian Dior boutique at Saks."

"Oh, wow, at Saks Fifth Avenue? That is a glamorous job. You're very lucky to find decent employment in such difficult times."

"Everything is possible if you believe it."

"Very true… holy words…"

"How long is the lease?"

"One year, miss."

"Then, I guess I'm officially a New Yorker."

Her smile follows the pigeons already stretching their wings above Upper West Side homes.

"You're new?" She hears a question and watches as the explosion of long, curly hair throws its chocolate-brown color against the surrounding walls painted in Christian Dior's favorite gray.

"I'm Maya. We will be neighbors. I work next to you in YSL."

A warm hand introduces self-confidence, full cleavage femininity without a bit of shame. The stunner's eyes in deep hazelnut have a spark of a five-year-old girl.

"I'm Ania. You are very beautiful, Maya, where you are originally from?"

"Oh, that is so nice of you to say." Voluptuous hips twist to the sides as if Shakira was their coach.

"I am Moroccan, but I was born in Paris, how about you?"

"Polish."

"Oh, European, no wonder they've put you in Christian Dior."

Long hair makes another move, introducing a smell of argan oil.

"How did you get the DSA position? There were so many people applying for this job."

"Well, it's a long story, but to give you a quick answer, I asked the Universe for help."

The sexy body pulls back.

"You believe in it too?"

"Believe in what, Maya?"

"In the power of the Universe?"

"Of course I do. Otherwise, I wouldn't be here."

She gets up from the quilted chair.

"Have you watched the movie *"The Secret"*?" The question shadows her steps.

"Yes, and because of it, I've attended Jack Canfield's seminars."

Her hand stretches out toward the buttons that give a spine to a long dress.

"No way, you have? I love that teacher. Tell me, what have you learned from him?"

"That everything comes to fruition when you visualize it."

"What do you mean?"

"What I mean is that your brain cannot differentiate any difference between what you are imagining or living in real life. As the athletes do, they practice their victory before they win a game. I have also visualized my move to New York; even the view from my apartment over Central Park."

"You saw it before you moved in there? Wow, that is insane. Here, people are so dumb. Nobody talks about this stuff."

Moroccan eyes lose a spark.

"Can I share something with you that happened to me yesterday?"

"Sure, go ahead."

"So I was walking from work to take a subway. It was raining, I had my umbrella up, and then… all of a sudden something dropped on it; it was heavy like a rock. That thing, whatever it was, knocked the umbrella out of my hands. I stopped, looked up… and, you will not believe it, I saw the angel wings, I swear…"

"Oh, you have encountered an Angel Maya, how beautiful is that?"

"Aren't you surprised?"

"Not at all, for I know they're always around."

The spark of a five-year-old is back.

"I am so glad that you got this job."

She sends some love to the horses, and as always, when passing them by, feels how her heart breaks a bit more from witnessing them being trapped-trapped by humans' need to be entertained, imprisoned by New York City's noise that causes their ears so much pain.

I will never take these rides… Her decision gets reinforced once again. Soon those big suffering eyes will stay far behind. Soon Columbus Circle will come to a turn. And here, near the Trump Hotel, traffic tends to slow down, as if those wealthy Central Park West residents find it unnecessary to be in a rush.

Golden leaves attach themselves to her boots while regrets attach themselves to her mind, making her reflect on the last four months, which have passed without fundraising a single dollar for IMMSAM.

What can I do when none of my clients want to get involved?

Her legs continue walking, but thoughts are drifting away into a place where new ideas are born.

What if, I bring a celebrity- someone everyone loves?

The street is almost empty except for the traffic generated by her busy mind.

He could become a Goodwill Ambassador, and that could bring attention for sure... must be someone with a spotless reputation...

An idea strokes her brain like a thunderstorm.

I know who: Hugh Jackman! Yes! He would be great!

"Of course, I will be there shortly."

A strangely familiar voice disrupts the discovery she just had. It seems that is coming down from the top of the Trump Hotel stairs. She stops, looks up, and freezes right where she stands.

Is... that... Hugh Jackman...? How could this possibly be...?

"Yes, I'm on my way, waiting for a car."

His voice confirms that, indeed, he is who she thinks he is.

A black limo appears at the front of the curb. His famous persona flies down by the stairs. As if it's a dream, she catches his smile sent to her before the chauffeur shuts the door behind his handsome back.

The car is gone. She's left with a company of a new regret.

It was my chance, and I let him go.

THERE WILL BE ANOTHER CHANCE FOR THE TWO OF YOU TO CONNECT...

the Voice says from within.

But where? But how...?

SOON YOU WILL KNOW...

The Voice drifts away.

Her feet return to the rhythm that they lost by the Trump Hotel. Like a horse that always finds a way back home, she finds herself by her apartment's door, unaware of how she even got in there. As soon as she steps inside, the Voice returns:

GO ON THE COMPUTER... AND SEARCH HIS NAME...

Her fingers restlessly type until one sentence appears on the screen.

"Hugh Jackman is currently performing on Broadway in a show called *"A Steady Rain"* "

44

NOW YOU KNOW WHERE...

the Voice confirms from within.

"One ticket for *"A Steady Rain,"* she requests.

A cute boy showers her with a smile. There's something special about him; perhaps it's his name because, for some unknown reason, she always liked the name "George" for a guy.

"Also, if possible, the best seat for the best price."

"Certainly, let me see what I can do... all right... all right... all right..."

She happens to like his southern accent as well.

"Oh, I found a great seat for you, number two in row twenty-eight." His blue pen points to the green chart. "It's by the stairs if you don't mind? And..." His neck turns as he looks around the tiny space behind.

"I gave you a little discount, ten percent off..."

"Oh, thank you so much, George."

"My pleasure, miss, anything else?"

Now it's her neck that does the privacy check.

"Yes..." Her nose touches the window of a ticket box. "Actually, you could be of a huge help... you see, George... I represent The U.N..."

"The United Nations?" His eyes double up in size.

"That's right, and I have a proposal for Mr. Jackman to become a Goodwill Ambassador for an organization called IMMSAM."

"No way; that's so exciting,"

His spine straightens as if the mission has entered it from high above.

"Yes, it's very exciting. So, would you be able to help me with that?"

Cute face lightens up.

"Of course. What can I do?"

"I need to get the proposal exclusively into Hugh Jackman's hands."

"Absolutely, no problem, I would love to help." His neck twists around the tiny room, just in case, one more time.

"Come before the show, I'd say about an hour or so, that's usually when Mr. Jackman arrives. I'll let them know to be expecting you by the back door. His bodyguard will let you in, but if you encounter any problems, come see me at the box."

"Thank you, George, it means a lot."

"No… no… I cannot take it…" He pushes back a ten-dollar tip.

"I feel totally privileged to be a part of it."

Like heavy curtains, the buildings spread to the sides of the street. All neon lights are on, so is the noise. The craziness of Time Square pulls her in. As if she's stepped into a flipper game and has turned into a silver ball, she bounces off the surrounding crowd trying her best to remain calm.

No level of madness will prevent the mission from being completed. Inside her purse is an envelope with a proposal for one of the biggest stars on a movie screen.

And, at this very moment, if anything could affect her state, it would be the realization that very soon she'll be shaking Hugh Jackman's hand.

The world belongs to those who never give up,

she affirms, checking out the time: 6:45 says the clock that welcomes New Years. The craziness is evaporating by the 45th street sign.

Her eyes search for a back door and find it behind a group of fans, who have gathered by a velvet rope, keep waiting for their idol, unaware of her intent.

Two heavy knocks… so they can hear her.

The door opens to a squeezing hinge. A giant in a black suit looks down at her.

"Yes?"

"Hello, sir. I was sent here by George."

"The ticket boy?"

"That's right."

"Okay. Come on in."

For a second, complete darkness takes over her sight, and then stonewalls missing any glamour get highlighted by a single light bulb hanging above her eyes.

"Is Mr. Jackman here?"

"Unfortunately, he is not."

"He's running late, f... traffic!" Someone's Aussie accent shouts from far back.

"Did George mention to you what I have for Mr. Jackman?"

"No, he did not. All he has said..." Giant's eyes are getting closer,

"...there will be a pretty lady stopping by."

She smiles as gracefully as she can. No compliment is going to distract her.

"I represent the United Nations and have a proposal for Mr. Jackman to become a Goodwill Ambassador for our organization, called IMMSAM."

The black suit goes through a shock. Suddenly she's more than just a pretty face.

"You're not kidding me, are you?"

"No, I am not. Here, this is the letter." She digs out an envelope from the depth of her purse.

"Could you please promise me that it will be given exclusively to Mr. Jackman's hands?"

The white folder touches the giant.

"Of course, you have my word."

"Do you understand how important it is?" Her eyes hold to his face.

"Of course I do, trust me, he gets thousands of letters every day, but I swear to God, nothing like this."

Respect transfers via a gladiator's shake.

"I'm going to take it straight into his room, like right away."

"Thank you. Below are an email address and a phone number to contact us. We would appreciate any response from Mr. Jackman, even if it's not "yes.""

"You got it. Enjoy the show, and thanks for stopping by."

The hinges behind her back say good-bye.

CHAPTER 24

Millionaire Match

The white paper board has nothing on it, contrary to her mind. The magazines make for her companions. Some images have already been cut out. The sharp scissors move in her hand with a precision of the finest Swiss watch, for when one vision dies, she has learned, a new one needs to be born.

Another month has passed, and gold leaves have been replaced by fresh snow. Waiting any longer won't change the fact that Hugh Jackman is not interested in becoming a Goodwill Ambassador.

As if his silent rejection put into motion a domino effect of dislikes, suddenly New York City brings her discomfort; suddenly Manhattan doesn't feel right. The traffic, the noise, the loneliness, the unpredictable weather, and the unnecessary rush; one reason pushes onto another, reinforcing to change her life's path.

It's time to move away.

The first image touches the board. The glue settles onto a paper. She looks down at the "silver fox." His handsome face she has found among the pages of the newest *"Forbes"*. The blue eyes and a sincere smile were what stood out about him the most.

Successful... generous... wise, someone I could build a family with.

Her intention is clear. One year is enough to be played with. Soulmate or not, no matter what the psychic had said, Jason is married and has two sons, something she would have never discovered if not for googling his name.

"What a liar," she says out loud and places a red rose below the successful man.

I want to experience real love, romantic, inspiring, with a true gentleman

A beautiful view pulls her attention to the cover of a travel magazine.

Hmm, Santa Barbara; Oprah Winfrey lives there...

Magically, Winfrey's face appears inside of it.

The scissors are back in action, and soon the most famous woman joins the unknown successful man. The glue settles into the board. She steps away from the vision.

Hmm... California... why not? It can be next.

"What are you doing to me…?" a warm voice asks over the phone.

She reads his energy.

Confident and... humble... gentle and... strong.

In spite of four thousand miles in between them, it feels as if he is standing next to her.

"Well, I guess I'm the result of a request you've put out into the Universe."

"Then I have done an excellent job because I like what has manifested." he says.

"12:12... December twelfth... full alignment..." she thinks while scrolling through his profile, for the very first time, the voice enriches his face.

"How is the weather in New York City?"

"Snowing and cold."

"You're three doors from Central Park, right?"

Wow... he remembers... and I only mentioned it ones...

"Yes I am, how about Los Angeles?"

"Sunny. In the low seventies. As usual."

"Oh. And where are you now exactly?"

"In Pasadena, sitting under a tree."

"Under a tree-excuse me?"

"I've pulled the car over to talk to you in privacy. You deserve more of my time." She almost sees his smile.

"I do? Oh, that's a good sign."

Silence connects more than voice.

His breath feels like a touch that gently wraps around her.

"From reading your profile, I've got an impression you are familiar with Napoleon Hill's work?"

"Who are you??" he asks, "Yes, I am very familiar, in fact, *"Think and Grow Rich"* is always on my desk. It was given to me by the first mentor who taught me how to use the principles from the book to create wealth."

How inspiring that he had a mentor... maybe he could become mine...?

She carries the thought to the window and the snowflakes that dominate the view of Central Park.

"So, tell me, Jonathan, what is someone like you even doing on a dating site?"

"I think I could ask you the same question?"

"Well, I wanted to give it a try. You see, I've never done it before, and New York can be a very lonely place…"

"I hear you. My assistant has advised it to me."

"Your assistant?"

"Yes, she knows me very well. We both went through our divorces at the same time. Pain can really connect people, don't you agree?"

"True. So, you're divorced?"

"Correct." Unexpectedly, his voice becomes dry.

"Any children?"

"One daughter." The warmth she is already used to is back.

"And you collect art, as I've read in your profile?"

"I do, also fine watches, how about yourself?"

"What do I collect? Hmm…," she ponders, "…I would say memories and shoes."

"Shoes, that is what I would expect from a woman like you. Believe me or not, I also love buying them."

"Oh, really? Then you're not a typical anti-fashion man."

Silence returns, and in its depth, confirmation is found that whatever is happening here is definitely mutual.

"Do you like to travel?"

"I do. Unfortunately, lately, there's not much time for that. Maybe later, when my project is finished, I can escape somewhere."

"What kind of project?"

"It's a development with one of the leading hotels in the world."

"Hmm… sounds intriguing."

"Well it's a great deal, it just takes much longer than I initially thought. But, eventually, we'll get there."

"I'm sure it will be very successful."

"Are you always like this?"

Two hours…

She checks her watch.

"Like what?"

"Positive and encouraging."

"I try to be, but it does take lots of practice, I must admit."

"Do you realize that we have been talking for over two hours?" He reads her mind telepathically.

"…and it felt to me like fifteen minutes."

Silence returns and within it agreement is found.

"You know we had done it before."

He feels the same way: as if we knew each other in our past lives…?

"I do." She smiles to a phone, imagining it's his face.

"I gotta go, but I want you to know that talking to you has made my day."

"Thank you for calling…"

Her breath holds onto his.

Though his voice disconnects, his energy still wraps around her, as if it doesn't want to leave.

The tree is talking. She's certain. To prevent herself from being embarrassed, she makes a full twist around the area; no joggers, no rich Upper East Side's wives, no businessmen rushing to work.

Now her relaxed fingers can embrace a canopy of old oak and, through lambskin gloves, connect with its veins as if it was her Avatar's horse.

This horse is ready to take a time flight and teleport her back to LA.

There she is, crossing St. Vincent Street, wearing her favorite beige suede pants. Chanel flats keep on stretching with each step she takes, no wonder they do, since "Stretch Spirit" is how they've been named.

The "Beverly Center" sign jumps out from the nearest facade… the butterflies inside her stomach let her know that Jonathan is nearby…

Stay present, don't think too much…

Uncertainty rises up. So does an escalator with another self-created doubt.

He's so incredibly successful, am I good enough for such a guy?

The thought cripples into her awareness, she reaches toward her shoulder bag, hoping that those Louis Vuitton heels inside it will help her self-esteem to go up.

"At the valet."

His text pops up on the cellphone just when she spots a free bench. Unsurprisingly, the mall is empty. February in retail is slow everywhere.

Her feet gain back their feminine touch, the confidence returns with heels.

"I'm on the second floor at the front of Christian Dior."

Butterflies double up.

Is he as excited as I am?

Her heart speeds up past its natural beat. As the elevator arrives at the second floor, overwhelming hesitation pulls her eyes down.

And then… she hears:

"Hello…"

Her eyes lift up and stay on his level, hit by the brightest blue light… This light surrounds him from every angle…

IT IS HIS AURA…

the Voice says from inside.

Her sponge-like legs take a step forward, straight into his angelic field. The balance is found in reflection of his face.

"You're beautiful." His words and his eyes have integrity. "Are you hungry?"

She's back on earth to answer,

"Yes, I am, very much."

"What would you like to have?"

"Some bread."

His smile reminds her of a cashmere blanket.

"I know a perfect place for that."

The sound of the engine makes a statement: "This vehicle is not for an average man."

Seated next to him, she feels upgraded as much by his presence as by the brown stitching done by some German hands. It's thick and perfectly even, and it cuts through the finest black leather that Italy makes. Her fingertips begin to study the texture. His foot pushes on the gas.

"My life was not always like this… I was born in Kentucky… in a shack…" His voice introduces a new tone.

From poverty to riches… how inspiring is this man…?

With eyes of imagination, she pictures a little boy with rye hair… his white shirt is open and messed up… all covered with an old dirt… his bare feet are taking him home… where newspapers are the windows' glass… and as the paper keeps moving under unmerciful blows of wind… this little boy is climbing up short stairs… his heart is so small and so fearful… and it shrinks with each step…

"My father was very abusive," he adds to his confession without looking at her.

"Is… he… still alive?" she asks very gently.

"Yes, but we don't communicate."

Compassion wants to touch his hand, but the ego does not allow.

Men like to chase women…

She reminds herself of what people say.

He points at the nearest restaurant, and Porsche turns left.

"I think you will like it."

"Bread bar," she reads the name out loud. "How accurate, Jonathan."

"Isn't it? Right? "His laughter pushes the sadness far away.

The green couch placed in a far corner discretely calls their names.

Soon, its soft velvet complements her beige suede pants.

"Patek Philippe." His watch grabs her attention.

"I like yours too. Is it J12?" Her wrist experiences his first touch.

"Yes, high-tech ceramic, we had a very good discount at Chanel."

Why do I always play small? Realization enters her mind.

"How is Manhattan treating you? Do you like living there?"

"I used to…" She dips a slice of bread into an oil-vinegar mix.

"But now after living there for eight months, I find it a bit too intense."

"I hear you. Personally, I could not live there. Just to visit New York for a few days is okay. I go there for business meetings with my bankers and lawyers."

His bankers and lawyers… that is his world…

And who am I…? Nobody… I don't even own a house…

"So, what's next for you, Ania?"

His question pulls back her eyes. She dives into deep blue, but judgment isn't there.

"I am creating a new vision."

"Does it include California?"

"Yes."

"Wonderful. I'm happy to hear that... You're a very powerful woman. You can manifest anything you want."

"Thank you for saying that."

YOU COULD MOVE MOUNTAINS TOGETHER...

she hears the Voice.

IF ONLY HE'D BE WILLING TO...

"So when do you think you will be moving to LA?"

"I think around June... we'll see..."

"Can't wait."

There is a hope for more dates to come...

"Listen, I have to go because I've promised my daughter I would spend more time with her."

"Of course, I understand... that's a father's job..."

Black leather still remembers the shape of her back. At the corner of Beverly and Robertson he steps on the breaks. For a brief moment there is a silence... from her... from him... and from this car that is not for an average man.

"I have no doubt that I will see you again." His last words substitute for a kiss.

The old oak disconnects from her hands.

CHAPTER 25

Oprah

A rusty chain bounces off the shelf. The bag that's attached to it is dragged down. She rushes forward to catch a fuchsia tote right before its crocodile leather could get an unacceptable scratch. Then, discussed by this form of presentation, she places it in a designated spot.

Princess Diana's confidant..., anyone hearing that story, would fall into this trap...

Rodeo Drive isn't deprived of foot traffic, unlike this prison created by the owner's bi-polar mind. Even those pictures of celebrities displayed on the window do not attract any walk-ins. If two months ago, she only had an idea what working here is going to be like, she would never have accepted the offer, and then yesterday, that phone call confirmed her growing fears:

"This woman is a crazy lunatic. She will mislead and lie to you. I wish someone had told me this when I was there..."A voice of a stranger verbalized what she intuitively knew to be true.

"She's going to call you every freaking hour to check on the sales, and if you don't reach the numbers, oh, get ready, she will scream at you!"

Fact: she already does that.

"LA is a big city. Trust me, you will find a much better job. There are many lawsuits placed against her from the previous employees, go on rip-off reports, and run away from this place as fast as you can."

She looks at the front door, and for a brief moment ponders that call, then makes a quick decision:

There's no point in staying open for a dead empty store.

Just some trash needs to be thrown away. Just some reports need to be faxed. Just the lights need to be turned off and then, the very last thing is to punch those four digits in the alarm box.

Her fingers reach toward the numbers that will soon set her free from the sickest job she's ever had in the retail industry.

All of a sudden, two heavy knocks come from the front. She takes a sneak-peek at the door.

Clients...? Seriously, like now?

A man in a dark suit and a woman in white are trying to get in.

Without making a move, she keeps gazing at the lady's head. It's entirely covered with braids as if the woman just came back from a

Caribbean trip. The sunglasses on her face are in Jackie O style, although oversized, cannot cover up their owner's identity.

Oh my God... is it Oprah?!

Her legs run forward with the speed of light. Her hand rushes with the key to unlock the door as fast as she possibly can.

"Ms. Winfrey, what an honor."

"Are you open?"

"Yes, we are. Please, come on in, madame."

From up close, a white outfit is made of linen and has a prosperity smell. The black suit follows right behind. It looks like it was made to measure by Armani, perhaps.

She leaves the keys inside the lock, just in case those strangers outside would recognize who is inside. Now it's only the three of them with those ugly chains that drag down the bags.

"How can I assist you, Ms. Winfrey?"

Oprah scans through the shelves.

"I'm looking for a gift… for a friend."

One on one... what a blessing... and I just put her on my vision board... how strange is that...!?

"I see, madame, would you like to tell me more about that person so I could make some suggestions for you?"

Jackie O's sunglasses come off, and as the brown eyes are exposed, she feels an electric touch that moves through her veins. It must have been a similar experience to those who were interviewed by them on a beige couch.

"She's not a very close friend, but I still need something nice."

Fuchsia tote makes it to the top of the counter.

"How about this one, Ms. Winfrey? It's made from Australian croc."

"Stunning color, how much is it?"

"It's twenty-two thousand, madame."

"Hmm… exquisite, but it's much more than I want to spend on her."

Tote's five minutes are gone.

"I understand, Ms. Winfrey. Some people deserve more… some people less… some people none."

"Very true."

She catches a smile from a man in black. White linen turns around, and as it was expected, the black suit shadows it right away.

"I appreciate your help."

The key reverses the twist. The door is open, suddenly, Oprah stops and looks at her.

"What is your name, miss?"

The goosebumps arise. One question, that's all it took to feel significant.

"My name is Ania, Ms. Winfrey."

Soft-touch lasts two seconds or less, but something deep inside of her is getting engraved.

YOU WILL MEET AGAIN MANY YEARS FROM NOW...

She stays with the Voice, watching as the couple blends with the unknown crowd of Rodeo Drive.

CHAPTER 26

Valentino

44

The footprints follow her climb. The gray dust settles down behind. The golden sun is waking up the city. She stops and looks at the Hollywood sign, highlighted by a brand new day; it brings new hope to those who want to give up on their dreams.

The only friend that she's got in this town lives inside her headphones and has a voice of Abraham-Hicks:

"YOU ARE A POWERFUL CREATOR. YOU CAN BE, DO, OR HAVE ANYTHING YOU WANT."

Nobody else speaks to her as they do. Nobody else understands her complicated thoughts.

"THE UNIVERSE RESPONDS TO YOUR VIBRATION."

Her feet return to the climb.

"A BELIEF IS JUST A THOUGHT WHICH YOU KEEP THINKING."

She hears and thinks to herself:

How is it that knowing their infinite wisdom, I'm still creating the same miserable life?

Alone, financially broken, on the brink of depression... without love or real friends...

The score of the current situation is taken and doesn't match what she's envisioned when she was moving to Los Angeles.

"THE REALITY WHICH NOW YOU ARE NOW IS A RESULT OF YOUR PREVIOUSLY PRACTICED THOUGHTS."

The hill gets steeper before the summit.

"YOU ARE AN ETERNAL BEING. YOU WILL NEVER GET IT DONE AND THEREFORE, CAN'T DO IT WRONG."

"Eternal," she repeats to herself while looking down at the already conquered path.

"FOR IF THERE IS NO CONTRAST, THERE WOULD BE NO EXPANSION."

I hope one day I will understand what they mean by that...

"You have one new message; to listen, press one."

Her finger touches the cell phone. Her eyes zoom around the Montage's yard.

Rich; why can't I be like them? Life would be so much easier... she thinks.

This yard, for some is a field to present their endless wealth. For her… to have lunch breaks.

"This is Thais," she hears.

Thirty-five centimeters of Himalayan croc parades at the front of her eyes.

My OB, of course, nobody else cares.

"I'm calling with results of your tests. As I was expecting, the tumor is growing big. We must do surgery as fast as we can."

Surgery...? Tumor...? I thought I was healed...?

"Don't worry about the expenses; your insurance will cover the costs of it."

Her thoughts fly back to Goddess's room and that white egg, and that flash that had come out of it…

The air becomes heavy and her eyes no longer see the surrounding wealth but only a nearby tree. It stands there so gracefully peaceful, so full of life, so undisturbed by what's going on around.

Was Goddess a scam...? Was it nothing but a lie?

"I also have good news. My good friend is a director of a Valentino store. She told me that they are currently looking for a new sales associate, so I've thought of you, since you've mentioned to me how much you dislike your job."

Valentino... there I could make more money...

A little bit of hope bursts through a thick layer of despair.

"Call the boutique and ask for Kathy, we will do the procedure after you talk to her."

His office could win an award in *Architectural Digest* magazine. Standing next to him, she tries not to show how intimidating it is to be faced with the vision created by his mind, the very mind she has fallen in love with.

"It's incredible, Jonathan…" comes out of her mouth.

At the front of them, a magnificent project takes over the entire pedestal; these buildings, these streets, these trees, although all in miniscule size, she recognizes them in an instant from her daily trips to work.

"I'm that glad you like it." His eyes touch hers with their warmth.

And what do I have to present him...? I don't even own a home...

"It may still take few years to break the ground."

I'm just a sales associate in a Valentino store...

"Let me show you the rest of the office."

She follows his steps, and as the steel stairs bring them up to the metal roof top, she hears it is getting hit by a steady rain. The drumroll continues and leads them into a triangular room.

Here, the silver desk owns the space, one big window gives enough light, a far back shelf inspires with the books.

Above those books, on a wall, hangs a black and white photograph.

"Is this..."

"Yes... it's the shack... where I was born..."

"Look... how far you have come..." she says and turns around just in time to witness that the past still holds the power to wet his blue eyes.

"Thank you. Please, take a seat."

Diving into a leather armchair, she wonders:

How many million-dollar contracts had been signed by those who sat on it?

The drumroll slows down. The sunlight bursts through the first cracks in the clouds.

He looks out through the window, then back at her.

"It's been raining for seven days straight and now, when you're here, it just stops?"

His smile tells her exactly what he wants to say.

"Did you put out a request for beautiful weather into the Universe?"

"Thank you for the orchid and for the book."

A white flower bends over the tons of papers between them.

"When I received it I knew that no one else could send it to me, but you..."

All I can give you are good books and... my heart...

"Have you started reading it already?"

"Not yet. I will as soon as I have more time."

"It's a great read, you'll enjoy it, simply written but very profound."

"My assistant has said to me: "Whoever this girl is, someone who gives *"The Power of Love"* definitely deserves your time."

"Your assistant is right." She looks at his happy face.

"With that being said, shall we do lunch at Four Seasons?"

"I thought you were busy?"

"I was but my plans have just changed."

The bed still remembers his smell, although it's been already a month since his warm body was wrapping hers with unconditional love. Unconditional; that's what she believed it was then but now is questioning if it was her empty bank account or her neediness that has made Jonathan disappear?

White pillow, wet from fresh tears, doesn't bring any comfort to her mind spinning from these repetitive thoughts:

I talk too much... I blow every dollar I make... I don't invest in important things... He drives a car he can easily afford... not like me showing off in a BMW and maxing out credit cards so I can put gas in it...

The other side of the pillow doesn't stay dry for too long.

No wonder he's gone, he can have any woman he wants...

YOU THINK TOO MUCH... the Voice says from inside.

She looks ahead at the cabinet and the enlightened books filling it up.

I read all this spiritual stuff and none of it helps...

BECAUSE YOU'RE LOOKING FOR LOVE IN THE WRONG PLACE...

So where shall I look ...?

INSIDE YOURSELF... THE TIME WILL COME WHEN YOU WILL UNDERSTAND...

CHAPTER 27

Unleashed

"Make a move! Say: YES!" he shouts, and six thousand heads echo back.

"Make a move! Say: YES!" he repeats, and her energized eyes can't pull away from his face.

There is the master of his body. There is the captain of his mind. If she could only tap into his power, maybe then she could awaken her own giant from inside?

In those last years filled with tribulations, that giant has fallen asleep, life became mediocre; her self-confidence has disappeared.

"And, JUMP!" he commands to the audience, and the floor bounces from thousands of landing feet.

"Whoa!! Yes!!" His massive hand makes a wave, and as soon as it comes down, so does the room's energy. The music softens its tone. The bright lights get less intense.

"Close your eyes. Put both hands on your heart and think about something in your life that you can be grateful for."

The exhales make a sound of the ocean found on a calm, sunny day.

"I want you to think about a moment from your past, when you knew that you were guided by divine love. Go back to that moment. Feel as if it is happening right now. Bring back those emotions into your heart…"

Tony's voice teleports her to Sweden… there she is, passing by a railway track… behind her is a tiny house and a man who had almost raped her the previous night…

Her heart is filled with a fear of the unknown… her mind with desperation to find a job…

The voice from within her whispers: ***GO TO THAT GRAY BUILDING ON YOUR LEFT…***

She stops and looks at the restaurant, feeling the divine protection spreading over her path.

"Now, think about another moment when you felt God's love." Robbins' voice teleports her to Poland… there she is, pregnant, unemployed, in a relationship with a man whom she doesn't trust…

Her heart is loaded with a heavy sadness… her mind with a fear of abortion that's considered a crime…

The Angel's wings come from behind her, and as she rests her head on one of them she hears:

YOU'RE NOT ALONE... EVERYTHING WILL BE FINE...

A sobbing neighbor brings back awareness to join their tears in present time.

"Hold onto that feeling and open your eyes." Tony's voice anchors to the room and burns the memories of the past. Her eyes return to the stage, and as they connect with his, she wonders if the strength in them is his giant, or is it hers already waking up inside?

The massive torso straightens his body and an inhuman size foot takes a huge step ahead. Like a phoenix that emerges from the ashes, Robbins' aura is highlighted by the burning from fire paths.

Right behind him on the largest screen an image goes viral within two seconds or less, showing as the heavy shuffles keep adding the hottest coals to darkest streets of San Jose.

"Oh, my Lord... what I am doing...?" A neighbor's comment makes her turn right. It seems that even a VIP badge cannot prevent one from being mortified.

"Soon you'll have a chance to face your biggest fears. Think about what this walk represents for you. What is it that you fear the most?"

Poverty... Her mind starts the list...

Loneliness... Her heart adds to it.

"Now, I want you to find a partner and start practicing getting into the state! You have twenty minutes before the doors will open!" Tony's order blends with a whisper coming from her left.

"Excuse me, miss, are you available?" The sweaty glasses stare at her face.

"Yes, sir, do you want to practice with me?" She allows compassion to take over her common sense.

"Aha..." the spineless body responds; the shaking knees, remind her of the leaves falling from the trees in Central Park.

Her right fist shoots high toward the ceiling. The lesson she has learned from the best:

"Make a move! Say: YES!"

A weak hand tries to follow, but it cannot without any evidence of life.

"Say YES!" she repeats undiscouraged.

If fear could shred glass, his would be already smashed.

LET HIM GO...

the Voice from inside her whispers.

HIS ENERGY IS DRAGGING YOURS DOWN...

"Are you ready?!" Robbins checks on them from the stage.

DON'T FEEL GUILTY... IF YOU STAY WITH HIM, YOU WILL GET BURNED...

She looks at a trembling man.

"I'm sorry, sir, but I don't think we are a good match." Compassion loses against common sense. The weakest flesh she has ever encountered turns around and goes back to the same old mundane ways.

"Are you ready?!"

Tony shouts.

Yes. I AM...! her blood answers back.

A heavy sound cuts through all ears. The exit doors are opened to release those gathered inside in a flash. Some run out. Some walk out. Some stay on their chairs to overanalyze.

YOU CAN DO IT!

the Voice encourages from within.

"F... g shit..." comes from her left and right.

JUST KEEP WALKING... JUST KEEP WALKING...

the steady Voice blocks the surrounding noise and takes the memory back to Manhattan, reminding her of what she used to do when she was bothered by New York City's crowds.

Then, she went deep within, finding the rhythm that carried her through and following her own map, whose directions only she understood.

The full moon greets from afar.

"Divorce your old story!" Robbins's mantra rings in her mind.

She takes off her old shoes, so worn out by the recent miserable past.

The burning light hit her eyes. The burning heat turns her toes from red into gold.

She steps forward, finding a stable ground. Her left foot slowly moves forth.

"Walk with me, please…,"she whispers into the dark sky. The angles can hear the prayer; she's certain that they can.

One deep inhale brings surrender. One deep exhale releases whatever was tense.

Her focus shifts straight ahead, and from now on, only there it will stay.

Her naked foot makes a move forth and, as soon as it proceeds farther, every sensation evaporates…

There is no heat of the fire… there are no burning coals…

She looks down at the path below her, and wonders:

Am I being walked…?

It's as if some invisible force is taking over her steps.

The fear is replaced with excitement! The future looks bright again!

A five-second long journey comes to an end in a stranger's open arms.

"You made it! You made it! You are so brave!"

She dives into them to celebrate being alive.

WHEN YOU FOCUS, YOU CAN DO ANYTHING!

The Voice from within reminds her of forgotten truth.

"Life will never be the same…!" She hears the song and, as it goes on, puts on her brand new shoes.

CHAPTER 28

Tom Ford

If a neon sign could freeze one's body, then hers would be now in a hibernation-state. As soon as the escalator lands on the first floor, she finds herself standing under the seven letters name. The aura that vibrates around it definitely does not invite; still, something is pulling her toward it and makes her left hand tighten its grasp.

Once Gucci's manager is done with his conference call, her resume will have a chance to impress him upstairs, for now, the waiting time may as well be killed in here, where the darkness sucks light like an expensive vacuum, where gray shades dominate every visual sense.

She pushes herself out of known comfort, just to hear one secured "Hello."

"Good evening…" How quiet her response is must tell the guy how uncertain she is about going on.

"Women's department is in far back." The same voice helps with deciding to carry through the stiffest men's shirts; if not for their brightness, plus splash of a white orchid, there would be no sign of light in this luxurious grave.

Another step, and all of a sudden, the space around her becomes a living room. Although it has two velvet sofas and a fire-place for their companion, a "home-feel" is not the word to describe it. Instead of a fire, a huge amethyst is trying to clean up the heavy air. It doesn't do much, and the dark vibes still hang up high, so does the Venetian mirror reflecting a tall, older man.

She follows his moves, to the left and, to the right; he keeps on walking as if in a park. The charcoal suit on his back is perfectly tailored and matches those displayed behind his path.

Their eyes share a moment. His head bows down out of a habit. She catches a deep sadness painted all over his face. It seems that he also doesn't belong here.

Soon, his mystical presence loses the battle against the cloud of overwhelming smells. Tobacco… vanilla… bergamot… leather, her nose dives into the unexpected blends while the room without edges keeps pulling her focus around a vicious cycle made of empty frames. Here she is stuck, with no sense of direction, neither a way out from this mirrored trap. And then, from behind her comes a question:

"Hello, miss. Are you doing all right?"

The face of young man reminds her of those which Modigliani used to paint. His confidence is straight from the runway; so are the oversized glasses that he wears.

"Yes... I am... I think... I just got lost..."

"Oh, that's quite common in our place. Women's is straight ahead. " His pianist-like hand points at the crack in a wall through which he must have just emerged.

"I'm Nick. You'll find me in Men's if you need any help." His sexy back turns around to get sucked up by an already-conquered dark cave.

The light pulls her forward and very soon showers from all around the space. She finds herself in another room, with two velvet sofas and another fireless-place. Although in this one, there is no crystal but instead, right above her head, a massive porcupine chandelier that cuts through the ice-cold air with its sharp arms.

A glimpse of inspiration calls her from a distance.

Shoes... there they are...

It doesn't take her long to grab a four-inch heel with black suede that wraps around.

"They look like a wedge, don't they?"

A woman's voice takes her off guard.

"Yes, they do... very unique..."

The shoe returns to its match.

"They are part of the newest collection. Would you like to try them on?"

"No, thank you, ma'am, I am just looking."

The woman doesn't give up, her age must be equal to her years spent working at the retail stores.

"What brings you to Vegas, business or pleasure?"

"I've just moved back here from Los Angeles."

"Oh, have you? That's where I've lived most of my life. By the way, my name is Suzanne."

Petite hand reaches toward hers.

"Ania. Nice to meet you." Out of politeness, she responds. A quick, standard shake may help to end this conversation.

"Are you Russian?"

"Polish."

"Oh, I'm Hungarian myself."

The shoes stay behind. Now winter coats are what dominate their space.

"But, I was raised in Canada…"

Her face almost screams: *Could you please leave me alone…?*

"I see." Again, out of politeness, she decides to respond.

"So, what made you leave California?"

More questions keep following her steps.

"I had enough of the traffic. I think there's more to life than spending it in the car waiting for a light to change."

"So true, I couldn't agree more, it's so much easier to live in Las Vegas, isn't it?

What job have you done there if you don't mind me asking?"

Her hand scrolls over the hangers.

"Exactly… this…"

Mature back leans over a small counter, perhaps looking for some support.

"You mean luxury retail?"

"That's right, Suzanne."

Dark eyes do not move at all.

"I've opened the Valentino store on Rodeo Drive."

"You mean, the one close to Tom Ford…?"

"Yes, four doors away. I've been doing *this* for a long time…"

"Have you… oh, really? Where else did you work?"

"Well, I've started here, at Wynn, with Louis Vuitton. Then I spent three years with Chanel and opened their Encore store. After that, during the recession, I moved to New York. There I worked at the Saks Fifth Avenue as the manager of Christian Dior."

If words could transform one's perception, then hers must have done an excellent job.

"Are you now working at the Crystals?"

Dark eyes remain hypnotized.

"No. I just came here to apply upstairs, but since the manager was on a conference call, I've decided to come down and kill some time, speaking of which… it's already up."

She checks with her watch.

The petite body moves closer.

"I used to work at Gucci for almost twenty years."

How in the world does she know that's where I went...?

The mature hand reaches towards hers.

"I want your resume, Ania."

The goosebumps run over her skin before it is touched.

"I don't think you understood me; I did not come here to apply for a job."

"I don't think you understood me. I want your resume."

The butterflies move inside her gut, and she hears the Voice:

GIVE IT TO HER... DON'T HESITATE.

But I don't like the vibes...

GIVE IT TO HER... DON'T HESITATE...

the Voice repeats. And then, it's as if something outside of her releases the grasp of her hand, opens up the folder, and pulls one page out of it.

Dark eyes scan through the facts briefly and turn to look straight into hers.

"I am the manager of the women's department. And you are exactly who I had in mind for a new sales associate."

In silence, she stands alone. Dark night has already come. Outside the window, bright lights of the Strip ground her back on the floor from revisiting the most recent past. Two hours left for the clock to start a brand new day, and for her to end it back home after not making any sales.

Her heart wants to know: *Why... oh why... does she keep on choosing the most unfulfilling jobs...?*

Her mind wants to know: *How many more designers' names it will take for her to finally realize it's all the same crap...?*

A thick carpet has stolen the sound of approaching steps. She gets a glimpse of her passing smile. The black bob makes a wave and, as soon as it turns around, balances itself right in front of her eyes.

The air vibrates in a familiar way... she almost forgot this frequency exists...

The moon-shaped face is now mirroring hers. These northern-sky eyes are much rounder than those of average Japanese.

"You've been through a lot..." A warm touch comes from the same hands that have altered her uniform pants.

"You know what I know. You know the Truth. You are aware of how the Universe works."

She holds on to the breath and pushes the words down, preventing herself from an impulsive response.

"You've done the best you could. You must leave the past behind."

The chills feel like sharp needles cutting through her spine.

"Don't worry, you won't be long at Tom Ford, but you're supposed to be here. They're telling me that."

"'They?'"-Who do you mean, Yoko?"

"The Spirits, I know you are also aware of them."

Her eyes do not blink but keep staring at the wrinkleless Asian face.

"And now they are asking me:"'Have you already begun?'"

"Begun... what, Yoko?'"

"Writing the book; they're telling me it's time."

"How do you know about the book...?"

"I see things of which many people are not aware. You have the same gift. You must practice it."

Something stirs up inside her gut.

"You know that retail is not what you're meant to do."

"A psychic told me that a long time ago..."

"Well. She was right. But she has also manipulated you."

"You know what she's done...?"

"Yes. There was no curse. Don't think about it anymore."

She backs up before a smile touches her face and the softest feeling showers her chest.

"You must write this book, for it will transform your life, and then, when it's done, everything you want will manifest."

CHAPTER 29

Abraham

The chair is empty and looks like a throne; it's her forth Abraham's seminar, but she could swear she's never seen it before. Those massive arms with the lions on their wooden tops remind her of Babcia's room, to which she used to escape from her Parents' fights.

A freshly brewed latte warms up her hand, soon, when the break is over, she will rise it up again.

Cuba, what a cute name...

she thinks while looking down. There, from the neighbor's feet, loving eyes keep staring straight into her heart.

This dog... That chair... Are these signs of what is about to come next...?

Esther returns to her place behind the pulpit and takes a deep, long breath.

"FURTHER BACK. YES, YOU!" goes in between stretched out arms and the energy stream is directed toward her refreshed, present mind.

An invisible force confirms that the turn is hers. A few short steps bring her shaking body to the top of the stage. Her warmed-up hand is now wrapping around the lion arms and all that ever was or will be is found in these cosmic eyes. For in there are the answers to every question her life may ever ask. Through a veil of fresh tears she receives their infinite smile.

"I know you know this… but I want to say thank you to you…"

Her first words are trembling. The microphone prevents her from any rapid movements.

"CO-CREATING IS A WONDERFUL THING, ISN'T IT?"

Their Voice echoes the one that has always been within.

"I know that you are with me all of the time…"

Her sobbing body remains in a chair, but her mind drifts away, and old images come forth into her mind… When she was lonely, brokenhearted, ready for her reality to end.

"IT IS PLEASING TO US THAT YOU ARE CONSCIOUSLY AWARE."

She wonders how much their eyes can read from the pages of her heart.

"I feel… I am so blessed with people who are coming into my life…"

"THOSE WERE THE PERFECT WORDS BUT WE WOULD SAY THEM EVEN BETTER IN RELATIONSHIP TO WHAT WE'RE TALKING ABOUT:

I AM BLESSED WITH REDEFINING THE FREQUENCY THAT I CONSTANTLY PUT OUT."

"Yes… so, Abraham…"

"AND, I ALSO APPRECIATE THOSE LESS-THAN-GOOD PEOPLE WHO FLOWED BEFORE AND OCCASIONALLY STILL DO, HERE AND THERE."

The laughter distracts her, she has almost forgotten that down below is a peanut gallery that listens to everything that comes out of her mouth.

"BECAUSE THEY'VE HELPED ME TO DIFFERENTIATE WHAT MY POINT OF ATTRACTION IS."

"Yes. Although," She cuts right through their speech "…I have used them as a weapon against myself."

"THOSE WERE VERY GOOD WORDS!"

Esther's head shakes in agreement; the only one whose agreement she truly seeks.

"ANYTHING THAT DOESN'T FEEL GOOD IS A WEAPON YOU USE AGAINST YOURSELF. YOU SEE…"

Divine eyes go deeper as if their intent is to touch her soul.

"YOU ARE NOT PUPPETS ON A STRING. YOU ARE AN EXTENSION OF ENERGY THAT CREATES WORLDS!"

Stupid laughter gets silent, allowing the infinite intelligence to carry on.

"WHEN YOU PUSH AWAY WHAT YOU DON'T LIKE, YOU'RE PRACTICING THE VERY VIBRATION THAT DISALLOWS WHAT YOU REALLY WANT. YOU GET TOO HEADY, TOO TALKY… YOU CONDEMN… YOU CRITICIZE, WITHOUT EVEN REALIZING THAT WHAT IN FACT YOU ARE DOING IS DEPRIVING YOURSELF FROM WHAT YOU DESIRE THE MOST!"

"Do you think I have allowed people to train me out of it…?"

"YES. YOU DID. SO HAS ALMOST ANYONE ELSE!"

A glimpse of childhood flashes… Was it then when she started not to feel good enough…?

Her wet checks are drying out. Deep exhale helps.

"I know the words are not necessary for saying this to you… but I want you to hear it with the sound of my voice… for a long time I have been looking for a perfect master… or a perfect coach… for the one who would guide me… or fix me… or help me to get to where I want to be… and, then… it just came to me when I was listening to you… and… you know how much I am listening to you…?"

"YES! IT IS OBSESSIVE!"

"Yes… I know… it is …"

"It's an escape sometimes and… it gives me a sense of comfort… and the feeling of righteousness… You are my best coach ever… Thank you for this."

"WE ARE APPRECIATING YOUR WORDS. YES WE ARE TEACHERS AT OUR CORE, AS ARE YOU! THE CREDIT GOES TO YOU BECAUSE WE ARE GIVING IT TO EVERYONE BUT NOT EVERYONE IS HEARING IT. SO WE WOULD SAY, THE BEST COACH IS I'VE CREATED AN ENVIRONMENT, AND IF I DON'T LIKE IT, I CHANGE IT BY PRACTICING THE VIBRATION OF WHAT I PREFER."

Applause distracts.

"WE ALSO HAVE AN ADVANTAGE OF SEEING WHERE YOU CURRENTLY ARE IN PROXIMITY TO WHERE YOU WANT TO GET."

"And… there is so much passion within me…"

"DON'T MISTAKE PASSION FOR RESENTMENT."

Their comment is not what she would expect to hear.

"YOUR LIFE IS NOT ABOUT WORKING HARD SO YOU CAN TAKE THE CLASSES AND THEN APPLY WHAT YOU HAVE LEARNED.

IT'S HAPPENING RIGHT HERE! IN THIS MOMENT! RIGHT NOW!

NOT WHEN YOU GET THE PERFECT HOUSE! OR A PERFECT MATE!

FORGET ABOUT WHAT'S COMING!

ALL THAT MATTERS IS NOW!"

Truth bursts out from their being, perhaps that's what she needed: tough love.

"YOU WERE NOT BORN TO DEPRIVE YOURSELF! OR TO PLAY SMALL! OR TO BACK UP!

YOU WERE MEANT TO BE EXCITED! FASCINATED! AND EAGER ABOUT LIFE!"

The reminder hits her gut.

"YOU WERE MEANT TO BE INSPIRED AND TO HAVE FUN! NOT TO BE BORED... BORED... BORED...! DRUNK! BORED AGAIN!"

Peanut gallery is clearly entertained.

She ignores the crowd, feeling another question as it's building up…

This book that I'm writing... shall I ask about it now...?

Something moves within her, as if they are able to answer her from inside.

"I don't think there is a point to ask any more questions… because I would be practicing what I don't have yet."

"THAT'S ABSOLUTELY RIGHT. WE WOULD AGREE."

In Their eyes she finds contentment. Esther's hand reaches toward the microphone and with one smooth move, pulls it away.

Savoring every second, she gets up from a chair.

"REST IN THE KNOWING THAT ALL IS WELL."

Their last whisper is exclusively for her.

CHAPTER 30

Seven Years

She puts the pen aside. Next chapter is done. His energy still lingers like old, reactivated dust… dust that's been accumulating for the last seven years…

Jason... how our lives would be unfolding if then you gave us a chance?

Before her hand had written these pages… and his name in every other word… it feels to her as if it was yesterday when, in his eyes, she found true home… and, when those eyes had pulled hers in from the crowd of Wynn's night club…

"Sometimes we don't end up with our soulmate but that is still all right."

Goddess's voice rings in her awareness, reminding her of the current facts: the second marriage he got himself into, while she was hoping that maybe one day he would realize that their souls in this lifetime were meant to reunite…?

"He can kiss the feet of the man you will be with! Let go of that Jason guy!"

Thank God I already did...

She leaves the desk behind, but still his energy lingers, like old reactivated dust… following her steps all the way to the kitchen's countertop… and to the cellphone that's bleeping with a new massage, which must have just arrived…

One touch… one look at the screen… and… she freezes at the very spot…

"Hey girl. How have you been? A lot has changed in my world…"

An email from him…? How could this be…?

WHEN YOU WERE WRITING ABOUT HIM YOU WERE TAPPING INTO HIS FREQUENCY...

The answer comes from the Voice.

Shall I ignore it… or shall I respond to it…?

IT'S UP TO YOU... JUST REMEMBER HOW LONG IT'S TAKEN YOU TO GET OVER HIM... AND THAT HE HAS LIED TO YOU...

The truth, which brought pain and confusion, cannot be denied…

Yes… but what if now he's ready to give us a chance…? What if this is our time…?

The Voice is silent to all of her "what ifs."

"Hi Jason, what's up…?" her fingers type on the screen…

The airport is quiet. Those who intended to go crazy here have already arrived.

"What happens in Vegas-stays in Vegas."

She reads the slogan, knowing that it's never worked in real life. Because in real life, people tend to regret adultery, overspending, and acting like wild animals let out of the cage.

Long hand moves on the clock, so do numbers on the arrivals board.

"Spirit Airlines, flight 107 from Minneapolis, Gate 4."

She looks up while anxiously straightening her skirt…

At any minute he'll be here... and everything will change...!

Soon, she will gaze into those eyes and, in their depth, again find home… soon she will be in those strong arms again, secured by them like they are fortress walls… soon her loneliness will be forever taken away… There have been some other men after… but none of them felt like he had…

Her breath… is becoming shallow… for the first passengers are being released…

And there… his six-foot-two-inch tall body stands out from the crowd… a white wrinkled shirt flows freely over too-lose blue jeans…

That outfit… it looks as if it's meant to cover his excessive weight…

He's not as lean as he used to be… but somehow… his smile is still warm… still familiar, as if it has never left…

His face, when given another look, doesn't have that businessman's charm her memory has kept…

A smell of cheap fragrance is about to touch her cheek…

And here they are… his eyes… beautiful… but somehow duller… somehow much less deep…

"Hi Jason…"

"Hi Ania! How have you been?! You look great!"

His massive arms spread around her being… and for a moment the past returns…

Releasing herself from his hug, she hears the Voice from inside:

HE'S NOT THE SAME MAN AS HE WAS WHEN YOU MET...

His soft hand takes hold of hers.

The airport is quiet.

"What happens in Vegas-stays in Vegas." She reads the slogan that never works in real life.

Orange velvet has their attention, its vibrant shade screams from afar.

"I love your sofa." he says, moving toward it to settle down.

She places a large pillow right in between them, so a healthy distance is kept… still not sure about him entering her own space…

"Thank you, I love it too. It was custom-made in LA."

His neck twists around the living room as if trying to check out her interior-design taste.

She's got this. She knows she does. There is no need for a single compliment.

"You've been moving a lot throughout those last years, Ania."

"Yes Jason. I have."

A strange feeling emerges…

Do I still want him back...?

No one would ever know how long it has taken to create comfort around her loneliness…

But it was that loneliness that has brought safety… it was that solitude that prevented another broken-heart…

"You were always on my mind… I am so glad we've stayed in touch…"

If I was, then why did you get married?

The question is swallowed down.

"My ex and I are going through the process… our divorce will be finalized in a month."

His hand reaches over the pillow. Hers backs up.

Divorce... well... he could do the same thing to me...

"You were waiting for me… you didn't get married… I am so glad…"

His breath is approaching… she can feel its warmth…

I've been visualizing his return for seven years... and now... when he's here... I am not sure if that's what I want...?

EVERYTHING IS POSSIBLE IF YOU BELIEVE IT... AND SO HE IS HERE AS THE EVIDENCE OF HOW POWERFULLY YOU CREATE...

the Voice says from deep inside.

Have I idolized him in my imagination...?

YES... FOR YOU SAW HIS POTENTIAL... NOT WHO HE REALLY IS...

His eyes leave no room for more thoughts to occupy her head.

Now all she can think of is the taste of his lips and the strength of his arms in which she disappears…

She stares at the ceiling. His snoring prevents her from falling asleep.

True love is not measured by the number of orgasms...

Maybe when she was twenty-one she believed in it. But with age comes enough wisdom and ability to differentiate what truly serves our higher purpose… and to her that's been clear: it's the writing, not having sex with a man.

The book… her newly discovered passion… her reason for waking up… has not been progressing since he has arrived… Three days of his presence have killed the creative flow…

She sneaks out of the bedroom, releasing herself from his snore.

Sometimes the fridge comes to the rescue, and food can turn out to be the best friend.

Eating ice-cream at two in the morning... while "the man of my dreams" is in my bed... how sad is that...

Another spoon of cold chocolate melts down in her mouth.

Absolutely pathetic...

Emptied-out cup lands on the bottom of a trash.

GO... CHECK HIS FACEBOOK...

Suddenly The Voice directs.

Too much sugar...? she asks herself.

GO... the Voice repeats.

She follows the advice.

CLICK ON HIS PROFILE... and the chills arise on her back…

44

"You show me what you can do on Monday:)"

She stares at the message sent to him from some random girl.

"I will… very soon… can't wait…"

Monday... that's tomorrow... when he's flying back...

Cold chills take over her body and the consumed ice-cream is not to be blamed…

NOW YOU SEE WHO HE REALLY IS, AND THAT IS WHY HE HAS RETURNED...

CHAPTER 31

Church of St. Pierre

44

Six a.m., already awake. There is no time to waste. She promised herself that before leaving this island she would light up a candle in that small chair of Saint Pierre.

The street is still empty and the crowds to mob Le Grande Rue have not yet arrived; only those local seagulls are accompanying her in this morning walk ahead. Soaring and spiraling over small chimneys sticking out from maroon rooftops, they're cutting through a gray field of clouds to disappear in the invisible realm…

The mildew smell of salty air goes deep into her nose, and as she exhales it out, hears a song from a nearby treetop.

This birds' morning melody feels so familiar to her… this sound so known yet entirely new… from the vastness of her soul she recalls this place…

So, this is the Normandy that she's seen before… five years ago during a deep meditation while she was living in New York…

Then, it was a vision that has come during an unconscious state…

Now, it's a discernible reality surrounding her from everywhere…

These timber-framed houses with mortar thick walls… these most-narrow-brick streets are what she had once called home…

That life… in the eleventh century… she saw as the person she had been when she lived in then… now being the same in spirit but different in flesh…

In those times of medieval darkness, she was a powerful man, a dignified warrior who had conquered the world… As him she was courageous, acted in fairness and had an absolute charge, was loved by his devoted serfs and feared by his enemies…

His word had integrity, his virtues were of the finest knights and chivalrous love for his wife had made him the bravest in fights…

She had felt his presence as if they were still one… and had seen his horse, which he so very deeply loved…

There was the bond… the strongest connection… almost impossible to break between him and that Friesian stallion covered with a black coat and marked with a white star over his head.

He was the best friend… the most loyal confidant… who had joined his master on the battlefields of wars when armies' armors had been crushed…

He carried his king over bloody rivers splattered from decaying corpses… and when the red flags were being lifted to proclaim the victory, they exhibited three golden lions on their tops…

She saw this vast coast lying under Norman's sky and recalled these endless sands where they were taking their morning rides…

She remembered those moments when she used to wrap her, then warrior's arms around the thick neck and leaned over on the smooth fetlocks' side.

The noble head turned, and those most soulful eyes looked straight into hers, expressing the grandest kind of love…

Love… that was so pure, so strong, as if it would have never ended… so everlasting… so eternal that she can almost feel it today…

And just like in that vision, the same morning breeze comes, and as it caresses her hand, she stops to look around.

Something has brought me here... something has shown me his tumultuous life...

A thousand years ago, this island had supported his journey... can it now help me with mine...?

Le Grande Rue comes to an end with a small narrow curve.

She turns left and faces short masonic stairs.

On their top, a red door is open… its hinges are covered with rust… the scarlet panels are finished with metal Calais, attached to it by black iron studs.

Her eyes move aside and set on a statue; the heroine, the symbol of France. Composed and noble, a young Joan stands still with a cade shield in her left hand and a sword in her right arm.

She puts combat boots into motion. They band over stone steps.

The pilgrimage ends; so does fresh dew by welcoming her most humble face.

Oriental smell of myrrh greets from a distance, the softest music calls her inside… reluctant to the already early hour… she hears the strings being pulled from dulcimers and lyres…

The Divine Hand must have painted this rainbow that goes through stained glass windows and then after have used those strings to weave them into an ancient floor rug.

A small niche seems to be hidden at the right side of the church. She moves closer and stops at the front of Archangel Michael who dominates the altar stepping over the dragon's dying flesh.

An evil head turns up with anger in the last desperate attempt, but an open-wide gullet cannot win this battle and is rebuked by the candelabras stands.

Amazed by power, she gazes at the angel and his arm glorified by these still-burning flames, left by those who prayed for his help.

Her hand reaches into the depth of a pocket to dive out a silver coin.

A chink sound of donation bounces off a metal box and spreads free around the church's walls.

This is the time to set her intention… to open up her closed heart…

Here she is safe… no need to pretend to be somebody she's not…

White candle joins hundreds of others in an empty spot. New fire takes off, and as soon it highlights her face, her knees hit the ground. This ground that had welcomed the kings and queens with their lives also filled with men's betrayals, also built on uncertainty.

A tingling sensation goes through her veins.

Her eyes do not drift away from Archangel's unwavering strength.

God, you have brought me here… you've showed me my past life… what is the purpose of this one…?

The wind carries the answer:

YOUR PURPOSE... IS... TO WRITE...

CHAPTER 32

Chateau de La Ballue

"Bazouges-la-Perouse, you said?" he asks and steps on the brakes. His guttural "r" reminds her again that they are in Northern France. His long pointy nose holds up the silver prescription frames. Behind them a set of nerdy eyes already expect some cash.

Like a magpie..., she thinks to herself and turns her head away to look out the window at this strange place.

A vast timberland has nothing but one empty road, which runs throughout a rich forest and ends by the property's green walls. These walls, made of the thickest bush, unite at the wrought-iron gates. At their front, jumps out a white flag with huge capital letters:

"'Chateau de La Ballue'"son chateau et ses jardins."

"Yes. This is it Jerome!" She slaps an extra five euros into a perching hand. Blushing happiness comes over the birdman's pale face.

"Please don't forget to pick me up the day after tomorrow. Sharp. At eleven a.m."

"Oh… I will, mademoiselle. Merci beaucoup, enjoy your stay!"

"Au Revoir. See you on Monday." Back door gets slammed as soon as she grabs her duffle bag.

This duffle bag…, getting it was the best decision she could have possibly made. In his mystical wisdom, Byron had advised her: "That's all you need to take. It's a Marry Poppins' style."

Again, as usual, her friend was absolutely right. In cognac brown leather, with one long and two short shoulder straps, during her vagabond trip, this bag has become the best confidant.

She presses on the button, turning on loud barks.

"Qui?" French woman asks from the smallest net.

"Bonjour madame… I have a reservation here for the next two nights…"

"Oh, qui… Is it Ania?"

"Yes… that's me, madame."

"Great. I'm opening the gates. Could you please step aside?"

Old hinges begin to cry for some extra oil and then, bit by bit, as these massive wrought-iron doors spread to the sides, the property's yard is revealed…

She takes a few steps ahead and stops, completely mesmerized by what she sees.

It looks like time has stopped in here somewhere around 1789 because it was during the Baroque era when two symmetrical squares mirrored one another, as did the Cyprus plants. Trimmed to perfection into scone's shapes, they now too stick out from ceramic vases, which look exactly the same.

Few groups of pansies have gathered into their small brotherhoods to splash the freshest shades of scarlet whites, violets, and blues. Sitting along a walking path, made of the smallest taupe stones, they lead like a royal rug straight to the chateau.

And there, at the end of this rug, the building arises with two spectacular wings wrapped up with large windows framed in a chalk white. Above them, the small niches try to hide underneath the steep roofs. Through the open front door bursts out a woman, shouting:

"Bonjour!"

An A-line, midi skirt wraps chocolate suede around the lady's legs, dominating an equestrian outfit that looks more British than French. From up close, a beige cashmere sweater is woven with many thick braids, which go up till the end of a heavy turtleneck. A khaki vest is thrown over, quilted and unzipped, the heavy stockings, perfect for April's weather, are made of gray-maroon knit.

"Good Morning. I'm Marie-France. Welcome to Chateau de La Ballue."

As the green rain-boots approach so does the sound of crunching beneath the taupe stones.

"Thank you, this place is incredible…"

The lady's smile exposes a net created by too many consumed cigarettes.

"Merci, my husband and I bought it in 1995. Originally, it was a fortress between Normandy and Brittany. Many artists have stayed here. Hope you too will have a wonderful time, and, that you don't mind the dogs."

A wet nose that connects with her leg is as black and soft as the rest of its owner's fur.

"We have two retrievers. This is Hades, the younger one, there's also Hispanot; he is a champion…, hmm, where is he…? Must be running somewhere around… anyway, Allan, my husband, will take you to your room. I apologize but I must go to town. Feel at home and let us know if you need anything."

"Bonjour." An extended man's hand takes a full charge of her duffle bag, and soon she finds herself in a narrow hallway, trying to catch up with his long steps.

The view from the back door reflects the gardens outside. She slows down but cannot get a glimpse of the view because the heavy stone stairs are already taking Allan up.

Then, on their right side, appear massive angel wings.

"It was already here when we bought the property. Previous owner had painted it."

"To the left, this way, please." French man says without turning around, and the wooden floor starts to quake from their feet or the history that's been soaked into the pales through hundreds of years.

Along the hall, the largest windows and white doors play a ping-pong game.

"We have two rooms available. You're welcome to choose whichever you prefer."

A skeleton key twists the lock. The door opens up.

Red color jumps at her face. It seems to be on everything… wallpapers… curtains… rugs…

"Nice… but a little bit too intense…"

"I understand."

The key reverses the twist.

"I knew you would prefer the other one."

Unoffended host takes three more steps ahead.

"This room originally belonged to the first owner's daughter, and therefore we've named it after her."

She gazes down at a keychain where the evidence of his words has been engraved.

"Welcome to "'Diane's'" room."

Frenchman hand pushes on the handle, and as soon as the door opens up, she steps into another world… In this world, princesses sleep under pastel drapes protected by cherubim flying above their heads. Beside the canopy bed, two marble nightstands balance the glamour with matching lamps.

Straight ahead, two windows give a glimpse of the gates outside.

Her eyes move along and stop at the writing desk. There is something calling her attention from its top…

“Dinner will be at five-thirty p.m… but if you’re hungry… you’ll find us in the kitchen, downstairs.”

Allan turns around.

“Oh… one more thing I almost forgot… We have beautiful gardens on the other side of the house.”

Frenchman disappears, and for a brief moment, “Diane” makes a dance.

The keychain settles down, her eyes return to the writing desk.

She picks up a brochure and starts to read what it says:

“Built in 1620, Chateau de La Ballue has welcomed many famous guests. Among them are Victor Hugo and Balzac. In fact, it was here, in a red room, where Hugo wrote the first lines of his last novel *“Quatre-Vingt-Treize”*.”

In that red room that is next to me…?

The paper falls off her hands.

Was I led here by those greatest minds…?

YES YOU WERE… NOW GO TO THE GARDENS…

the Voice says from inside.

Lean shadow points out the direction. She trusts it because it’s her own. Soft wind keeps following her footsteps while using oak trees as the instruments to play his song. This song has no end and no beginning, or lyrics a mind could understand, for its message is found in the vibration only by a soul of an artist who’s ready to create.

She listens to its gentle unfolding that is telling her to pass underneath a green arch. The leaves crowning her head were have been perfected this morning; she was watching a gardener trimming them from afar. Behind his masterpiece, the bright light disappears, and there is no shadow to guide her steps. Now it’s a sound of water that is pointing the direction, to a little pond, placed in the middle of a round square.

44

She looks down where the unrushed koi fishes keep on splashing tones of orange between a purity of drifting nenuphars.

She looks up where the peaks of trees keep on dancing under the relentless wind, conducting them to entertain the bluest sky.

I AM GLAD THAT YOU CAME...

A voice comes out of nowhere. She turns around but sees no one, except a gray sculpture of the man who owns the pond. His arms are crossed, his head is bold, his eyes are closed, but somehow she can see their endless depth.

YOU FOUND ME... BECAUSE IT'S THE TIME... REMEMBER, MY CHILD... 44 YEARS?

Her chest expands with a soft feeling, for his energy overflows with love.

Is it you... talking to me...?

YES... I AM... BELOVED...

She stumbles, for all of a sudden, she has lost her stability on the ground.

ASK ME WHAT YOU WOULD LIKE TO KNOW... YOU HAVE COME FROM SO FAR AWAY...

I... am... writing a book... will it be successful...?

YES... IT WILL AND THERE WILL BE MORE BOOKS FOR YOU TO WRITE...

YOU HAVE FOUND YOUR PASSION... JUST AS YOU HAVE INTENDED... BUT YOU MUST BELIEVE IN YOURSELF...

While she swallows first tears, a glimpse of a smile highlights his gentle stoned face.

WHAT ELSE WOULD YOU LIKE TO KNOW, MY DEAR...?

Will... I find... a true love in this life?

YOU WILL... AND WITH THAT MAN, YOU'LL COME BACK HERE... SOMETHING YOU ALREADY KNOW... YOUR INTUITION... ALWAYS TRUST WHAT IT SAYS...

You know me... you really know me... were always with me... guiding me... with the Voice...

THAT WAS YOUR FUTURE SELF, MY DEAR... YOU WERE CREATING YOURSELF ALL ALONG...

She stands in his presence, feeling her heart expanding from love.

NOW GO, WRITE YOUR STORY... AND WE SHALL MEET AGAIN... IN ANOTHER FOREST,

44 YEARS FROM NOW...

Dear Reader

Thank you for choosing my book.

I truly hope you've enjoyed reading if, and if you have, I would very much appreciate it if you leave a review after finishing.

If you have any question for me or need support on your journey, you can contact me at www.aniak44.com .

Until then, may you listen to your Inner Voice, allow yourself to be guided by it, and, may you Never Give Up On Your Dreams.

Ania K

Made in United States
North Haven, CT
11 November 2021

11028949R00154